JOHN BUCHAN
THE GAP IN THE CURTAIN

HOUSE OF
STRATUS

First published in 1932

This edition published in 2001 by House of Stratus, an imprint of Stratus Books Ltd, 21 Beeching Park, Kelly Bray, Cornwall, PL17 8QS, UK.

www.houseofstratus.com

Typeset, printed and bound by House of Stratus.

A catalogue record for this book is available from the British Library and the Library of Congress.

ISBN 1-84232-767-4

TO
SYBIL
AND
LAMBERT MIDDLETON

CONTENTS

I

WHITSUNTIDE AT FLAMBARD

"Si la conscience qui sommeille dans l'instinct se réveillait, s'il s'intériorisait en connaissance au lieu de s'extérioriser en action, si nous savions l'interroger et s'il pouvait répondre, il nous livrerait les secrets de la vie."

BERGSON, *L'Evolution Créatrice.*

"But no!" cried Mr Mantalini. "It is a demn'd horrid dream. It is not reality. No!"

Nicholas Nickleby.

I

Whitsuntide at Flambard

I

As I took my place at the dinner-table I realised that I was not the only tired mortal in Lady Flambard's Whitsuntide party. Mayot, who sat opposite me, had dark pouches under his eyes and that unwholesome high complexion which in a certain type of physique means that the arteries are working badly. I knew that he had been having a heavy time in the House of Commons over the Committee stage of his Factory Bill. Charles Ottery, who generally keeps himself fit with fives and tennis, and has still the figure of an athletic schoolboy, seemed nervous and out of sorts, and scarcely listened to his companion's chatter. Our hostess had her midseason look; her small delicate features were as sharp as a pin, and her blue eyes were drained of colour. But it was Arnold Tavanger farther down the table who held my attention. His heavy, sagacious face was a dead mask of exhaustion. He looked done to the world, and likely to fall asleep over his soup.

It was a comfort to me to see others in the same case, for I was feeling pretty near the end of my tether. Ever since Easter I had been overworked out of all reason. There was a batch of important Dominion appeals before the Judicial Committee, in every one of which I was engaged, and I had some heavy cases in the Commercial Court. Of the two juniors who did most of my "devilling" one had a big patent-law action of his own, and the other was in a nursing-home with appendicitis. To make matters worse, I was chairman of a Royal Commission which was about to issue its findings, and had had to rewrite most of the report with my own hand, and I had been sitting as a one-man Commission in a troublesome dispute in the shipbuilding trade. Also I was expected to be pretty regularly in the House of Commons to deal with the legal side of Mayot's precious Bill, and the sittings had often stretched far into the next morning.

There is something about a barrister's spells of overwork which makes them different in kind from those of other callings. His duties are specific as to time and place. He must be in court at a certain hour. He must be ready to put, or to reply to, an argument when he is called upon; he can postpone or rearrange his work only within the narrowest limits. He is a cog in an inexorable machine, and must revolve with the rest of it. For myself I usually enter upon a period of extreme busyness with a certain lift of spirit, for there is a sporting interest in not being able to see your way through your work. But presently this goes, and I get into a mood of nervous irritation. It is easy enough to be a carthorse, and it is easy enough to be a racehorse, but it is difficult to be a carthorse which is constantly being asked to take Grand National fences. One has to rise to hazards, but with each the take-off gets worse and the energy feebler. So at the close of such a spell I am in a wretched condition of soul and body – weary, but without power to rest, and with a mind so stale that it sees no light or colour in anything. Even the end of the drudgery brings no stimulus. I feel that my form has been getting steadily poorer, and that virtue has gone out of me which I may never recapture.

I had been in two minds about accepting Sally Flambard's invitation. She is my very good friend, but her parties are rather like a *table d'hôte*. Her interests are multitudinous, and all are reflected in her hospitality, so that a procession goes through her house which looks like a rehearsal for the Judgement Day.

Politics, religion, philanthropy, letters, science, art and the most brainless fashion – she takes them all to her capacious heart. She is an innocent lion-hunter, too, and any man or woman who figures for the moment in the Press will be a guest at Flambard. And she drives her team, for all are put through their paces. Sally makes her guests work for their entertainment. In her own way she is a kind of genius, and what Americans call a wonderful "mixer." Everyone has got to testify, and I have seen her make a bishop discourse on Church union, and a mathematician on hyper-space to an audience which heard of the topics for the first time. The talk is apt to be a little like a magazine page in a popular newspaper – very good fun, if you are feeling up to it, but not quite the thing for a rest-cure.

It was my memory of Flambard itself that decided me. The place is set amid the greenest and quietest country on earth. The park is immense, and in early June is filled with a glory of flowers and blossoming trees. I could borrow one of Evelyn's horses and ride all day through the relics of ancient forests, or up on to the cool, windy spaces of the Downs. There was good dry-fly fishing in the little Arm, which runs through a shallow vale to the young Thames. At Whitsuntide you can recover an earlier England. The flood of greenery hides modern blemishes which are revealed by the bareness of winter, and an upland water-meadow is today just as it met the eye of the monks when they caught their Friday's trout, or of the corsleted knights as they rode out to the King's wars. It is the kind of scene that comforts me most, for there, as some poet says, "old Leisure sits knee-deep in grass." Also the house is large enough for peace. It is mostly Restoration period, with some doubtful Georgian additions, but there is a Tudor wing, the remnant of the old house, which the great Earl of Essex once used as a hunting lodge. Sally used to give me a room at the top of the Essex wing, with a wide prospect north into the Cotswold dales. The hall and the drawing-rooms and the great terrace might be as full of "turns" as a music-hall stage, but somewhere in the house fatigue could find sanctuary.

I had arrived just in time to dress for dinner, and had spoken to none of my fellow-guests, so my inspection of the table had a speculative interest. It was a large party, and I saw a good many faces that I knew. There were the Nantleys, my best of friends, and their daughter Pamela, who was in her first season... There was old Folliot, the bore of creation, with his little grey imperial, and his smirk, and his tired eyes. He was retailing some ancient scandal to Mrs Lamington, who was listening with one ear and devoting the other to what Lady Altrincham was saying across the table. George Lamington a little farther down was arguing with his host about the Ascot entries – his puffy red face had that sudden shrewdness which it acquires when George's mind is on horses... There was a man opposite him of whom I could only catch the profile – a dark head with fine-drawn features. I heard his voice, a pleasant voice, with full deep tones like a tragic actor's, and, as he turned, I had an impression of a face full of swift, nervous strength... There was a good deal of youth in the party, four girls besides Pamela Brune, and several boys with sleek hair and fresh voices. One of them I knew, Reggie Daker, who was a friend of my nephew's.

I was on Sally's left hand, and as she was busy with Mayot, and the lady on my left was deep in a controversy with her neighbour over some book, I was free to look about me. Suddenly I got a queer impression. A dividing line seemed to zigzag in and out among us, separating the vital from the devitalised. There was a steady cackle of talk, but I felt that there were silent spaces in it. Most of the people were cheerful, eupeptic souls who were enjoying life. The Nantleys, for example, sedate country gentle-folk, whose days were an ordered routine of pleasant cares... Pamela Brune? I was not so sure of her, for a young girl's first season is a trying business, like a boy's first half at school... Old Folliot, beyond doubt – he was perfectly happy as long as he was in a great house with somebody to listen to his archaic gossip...

Evelyn Flambard and George Lamington and the boys who were talking Ascot and next winter's hunting plans… Lady Altrincham, sixty but with the air of thirty, who lives for her complexion and her famous pearls… But I realised that there were people here who were as much at odds with life as myself – Mayot and Tavanger and Charles Ottery, and perhaps the dark fellow who sat opposite George Lamington.

Sally turned to me, hiding a yawn with her small hand. Her head on its slim neck was as erect as a bird's, and her body had a darting, bird-like poise, but I could see that the poise required some effort to maintain it. She patted my sleeve in her friendly way.

"I am so glad you came," she said. "I know you want a rest." She screwed up her eyes and peered at me. "You look as if you hadn't been in bed for a month!"

"I'm nearly all out," I said. "You must let me moon about by myself, please, for I'm no sort of company for anybody."

"You shall do exactly as you like. I'm pretty tired also, and I'm giving a ball next week, and there's Ascot looming ahead. Happily we're having quite a small party – and a very quiet one."

"Is this the lot?" I asked, looking down the table. I knew her habit of letting guests appear in relays during a weekend till the result was a mob.

"Practically. You know all the people?"

"Most of them. Who's the dark fellow opposite George Lamington?"

Her face brightened into interest. "That's my new discovery. A country neighbour, no less – but a new breed altogether. His name is Goodeve – Sir Robert Goodeve. He has just succeeded to the place and title."

Of course I knew Goodeve, that wonderful moated house in the lap of the Downs, but I had never met one of the race. I had had a notion that it had died out. The Goodeves are one of those families about which genealogists write monographs, a specimen of that unennobled gentry which is the oldest stock in England.

They had been going on in their undistinguished way since Edward the Confessor.

"Tell me about him," I said.

"I can't tell you much. You can see what he looks like. Did you ever know a face so lit up from behind?... He was the son of a parson in Northumberland, poor as a church mouse, so he had to educate himself. Local grammar school, some provincial university, and then with scholarships and tutoring he fought his way to Oxford. There he was rather a swell, and made friends with young Marburg, old Isaac's son, who got him a place in his father's business. The War broke out, and he served for four years, while Marburgs kept his job open. After that they moved him a good deal about the world, and he was several years in their New York house. It is really a romance, for at thirty-five he had made money, and now at thirty-eight he has inherited Goodeve and a good deal more... Yes, he's a bachelor. Not rich as the big fortunes go, but rich enough. The thing about him is that he has got his jumping-off ground reasonably young, and is now about to leap. Quite modest, but perfectly confident, and terribly ambitious. He is taking up politics, and I back him to make you all sit up. I think he's the most impressive mortal I have ever met. Bored stiff with women – as stony-hearted as you, Ned. He's a sort of ascetic, vowed to a cause."

"His own career?" I asked.

"No. No. He's not a bit of an egotist. There's a pent-up force that's got to come out. He's a fanatic about some new kind of Empire development, and I know people who think him a second Rhodes. I want you to make friends with him and tell me what you think, for in your fish-like way you have good judgement."

Sally yawned again, and I respected more than ever the courage of women who can go on till they drop and keep smiling. She turned away in response to a question of Mayot's, and I exchanged banalities with the lady on my other side. Presently I found myself free again to look round the table. I was right: we were the oddest mixture of the fresh and the *blasé*, the care-free and the care-worn. To look at Tavanger's hollow eyes and hear in one's ear the babble of high young voices made a contrast which was almost indecent... I had a feeling as if we were all on a vast, comfortable raft in some unknown sea, and that, while some were dancing to jazz music, others were crowding silently at the edge, staring into the brume ahead. Staring anxiously, too, for in that mist there might be fearful as well as wonderful things... I found myself studying George Lamington's face, and felt a childish dislike of him. His life was so padded and cosseted and bovine. He had just inherited another quarter of a million from an uncle, and he had not the imagination of a rabbit in the use of money. Why does wealth make dull people so much duller? I had always rather liked George, but now I felt him intolerable. I must have been very tired, for I was getting as full of silly prejudices as a minor poet.

Sally was speaking again, as she collected eyes.

"Don't be afraid. This is going to be a very peaceful party."

"Will you promise me," I said, "that I won't come down tomorrow and find half a dozen new faces at breakfast?"

"Honest Injun," she replied. "They are all here except one, and he arrives tonight."

When the women had gone Evelyn Flambard brought his port to my side. Having exhausted horses during dinner, he regaled me with the Englishman's other main topic, politics. Evelyn despaired of the republic. He had grievances against the Budget, the new rating law, and the Government's agricultural policy. He was alarmed about the condition of India, where he had served in his old Hussar days, and about Egypt, where he had large investments. His views on America were calculated to make a serious breach between the two sections of the Anglo-Saxon race. But if he feared the Government he despised the Opposition, though for politeness' sake he added that his strictures did not apply to me. There was no honest Toryism left, so his plaint ran; there was not a pin to choose between the parties; they were all out to rob struggling virtue – meaning himself and other comfortable squires. He nodded down the table towards Goodeve. "Look at that chap," he whispered darkly. "I mean to say, he don't care a straw what he says or does, and he'll have Tommy Twiston's seat, which is reckoned the safest in England. He as good as told George Lamington this afternoon that he'd like to see a Soviet Government in power for a week in England under strict control, for it was the only way to deal with men like him. Hang it all, there's nothing wrong with old George except that he's a bit fussy, if you see what I mean."

I said that I rather agreed with Goodeve, and that set Evelyn pouring out his woes to the man on the other side. Reggie Daker had come up next me, his eye heavy with confidences. I had acted as a sort of father-confessor to Reggie ever since he came down from the University, but I hadn't much credit by my disciple. He was infinitely friendly, modest, and good-humoured, but as hard to hold as a knotless thread. Usually he talked to me about his career, and I had grown very tired of finding him jobs, which he either shied off or couldn't hold for a week. Now it seemed that this was not his trouble. He had found his niche at last, and it was dealing in rare books. Reggie considered that a lad like himself, with a fine taste and a large acquaintance, could make a lot of money by digging out rarities from obscure manor-houses and selling them to American collectors. He had taken up the study very seriously, he told me, and he actually managed to get a few phrases of bibliophile's jargon into his simple tale. He felt that he had found his life's work, and was quite happy about it.

The trouble was Pamela Brune. It appeared that he was deeply in love, and that she was toying with his young heart. "There's a strong lot of entries," he explained, "and Charles Ottery has been the favourite up till now. But she seems a bit off Charles, and…and…anyhow, I'm going to try my luck. I wangled an invitation here for that very purpose. I say, you know – you're her godfather, aren't you? If you could put in a kind word…"

But my unreceptive eye must have warned Reggie that I was stony soil. He had another glass of port, and sighed.

I intended to go to bed as soon as I decently could. I was not sleepy, but I was seeing things with the confusion of a drowsy man. As I followed my host across the hall, where someone had started a gramophone, I seemed more than ever to be in a phantasmal world. The drawing-room, with the delicate fluted pilasters in its panelling and the Sir Joshuas and Romneys between them, swam in a green dusk, which was partly the afterglow through the uncurtained windows and partly the shading of the electric lamps. A four at bridge had been made up, and the young people were drifting back towards the music. Lady Nantley beckoned me from a sofa. I could see her eyes appraising my face and disapproving of it, but she was too tactful to tell me that I looked ill.

"I heard that you were to be here, Ned," she said, "and I was very glad. Your god-daughter is rather a handful just now, and I wanted your advice."

"What's wrong?" I asked. "She's looking uncommonly pretty." I caught a glimpse of Pamela patting her hair as she passed a mirror, slim and swift as a dryad.

"She's uncommonly perverse. You know that she has been having an affair with Charles Ottery ever since Christmas at Wirlesdon. I love Charles, and Tom and I were delighted. Everything most suitable – the right age, enough money, chance of a career, the same friends. There's no doubt that Charles adores her, and till the other day I thought that she was coming to adore Charles. But now she has suddenly gone off at a tangent, and has taken to snubbing and neglecting him. She says that he's too good for her, and that his perfections choke her – doesn't want to play second fiddle to an Admirable Crichton – wants to shape her own life – all the rubbish that young people talk nowadays."

Mollie's charming eyes were full of real distress, and she put an appealing hand on my arm.

"She likes you, Ned, and believes in you. Couldn't you put a little sense into her head?"

I wanted to say that I was feeling like a ghost from another sphere, and that it was no good asking a tenuous spectre to meddle with the affairs of warm flesh and blood. But I was spared the trouble of answering by the appearance of Lady Flambard.

"Forgive me, Mollie dear," she said, "but I must carry him off. I'll bring him back to you presently."

She led me to a young man who was standing near the door. "Bob," she said, "this is Sir Edward Leithen. I've been longing for you two to meet."

"So have I," said the other, and we shook hands. Now that I saw Goodeve fairly, I was even more impressed than by his profile as seen at dinner. He was a finely made man, and looked younger than his thirty-eight years. He was very dark, but not in the least swarthy; there were lights in his hair which suggested that he might have been a blond child, and his skin was a clear brown, as if the blood ran strongly and cleanly under it. What I liked about him was his smile, which was at once engaging and natural, and a little shy. It took away any arrogance that might have lurked in the tight mouth and straight brows.

"I came here to meet you, sir," he said. "I'm a candidate for public life, and I wanted to see a man who interests me more than anybody else in the game. I hope you don't mind my saying that... What about going into the garden? There's a moon of sorts, and the nightingales will soon begin. If they're like the ones at Goodeve, eleven's their hour."

We went through the hall to the terrace, which lay empty and quiet in a great dazzle of moonlight. It was only about a fortnight till midsummer, a season when in fine weather in southern England it is never quite dark. Now, with a moon nearing the full, the place was bright enough to read print. The stone balustrade and urns were white as snow, and the two stairways that led to the sunk garden were a frosty green like tiny glaciers.

We threaded the maze of plots and lily-ponds and came out on a farther lawn, which ran down to the little river. That bit of the Arm is no good for fishing, for it has been trimmed into a shallow babbling stretch of ornamental water, but it is a delicious thing in the landscape. There was no sound except the lapse of the stream, and the occasional squattering flight of a moorhen. But as we reached the brink a nightingale began in the next thicket.

Goodeve had scarcely spoken a word. He was sniffing the night scents, which were a wonderful blend of early roses, new-mown hay, and dewy turf. When we reached the Arm, we turned and looked back at the house. It seemed suddenly to have gone small, set in a great alley-way of green between olive woods, an alley-way which swept from the high downs to the river meadows. Far beyond it we could see the bare top of Stobarrow. But it looked as perfect as a piece of carved ivory – and ancient, ancient as a boulder left millenniums ago by a melting ice-cap.

"Pretty good," said my companion at last. "At Flambard you can walk steadily back into the past. Every chapter is written plain to be read."

"At Goodeve, too," I said.

"At Goodeve, too. You know the place? It is the first home I have had since I was a child, for I have been knocking about for years in lodgings and tents. I'm still a little afraid of it. It's a place that wants to master you. I'm sometimes tempted to give myself up to it and spend my days listening to its stories and feeling my way back through the corridors of time. But I know that that would be ruin."

"Why?"

"Because you cannot walk backward. It is too easy, and the road leads nowhere. A man must keep his eyes to the front and resist the pull of his ancestors. They're the devil, those ancestors, always trying to get you back into their own rut."

"I wish mine would pull harder," I said. "I've been badly overworked lately, and I feel at this moment like a waif, with nothing behind me and nothing before."

He regarded me curiously. "I thought you looked a little done up. Well, that's the penalty of being a swell. You'll lie fallow for a day or two and the power will return. There can't be much looking backward in your life."

"Nor looking forward. I seem to live between high blank walls. I never get a prospect."

"Oh, but you are wrong," he said seriously. "All your time is spent in trying to guess what is going to happen – what view the Courts will take of a case, what kind of argument will hit the prospective mood of the House. It is the same in law and politics and business and everything practical. Success depends on seeing just a little more into the future than other people."

I remembered my odd feeling at dinner of the raft on the misty sea, and the anxious peering faces at the edge.

"Maybe," I said. "But just at the moment I'm inclined to envy the people who live happily in the present. Our host, for example, and the boys and girls who are now dancing." In the stillness the faint echo of music drifted to us from the house.

"I don't envy them a bit," he said. "They have no real sporting interest. Trying to see something solid in the mist is the whole fun of life, and most of its poetry."

"Anyhow, thank Heaven, we can't see very far. It would be awful to look down an avenue of time as clear as this strip of lawn, and see the future as unmistakable as Flambard."

"Perhaps. But sometimes I would give a good deal for one moment of prevision."

After that, as we strolled back, we talked about commonplace things – the prospects of a not very secure Government, common friends, the ways of our hostess, whom he loved, and the abilities of Mayot, which – along with me – he doubted. As we entered the house again we found the far end of the hall brightly lit, since the lamps had been turned on in the porch.

The butler was ushering in a guest who had just arrived, and Sally had hastened from the drawing-room to greet him.

The newcomer was one of the biggest men I have ever seen, and one of the leanest. A suit of grey flannel hung loose upon his gigantic bones. He reminded me of Nansen, except that he was dark instead of fair. His forehead rose to a peak, on which sat one solitary lock, for the rest of his head was bald. His eyes were large and almost colourless, mere pits of light beneath shaggy brows. He was bowing over Sally's hand in a foreign way, and the movement made him cough.

"May I present Sir Edward Leithen?" said Sally. "Sir Robert Goodeve… Professor Moe."

The big man gave me a big hand, which felt hot and damp. His eyes regarded me with a hungry interest. I had an impression of power – immense power, and also an immense fragility.

II

I did not have a good night; I rarely do when I have been overworking. I started a chapter of *Barchester Towers*, dropped off in the middle, and woke in two hours, restless and unrefreshed. Then I must have lain awake till the little chill before dawn which generally sends me to sleep. The window was wide open, and all the minute sounds of a summer night floated through it, but they did not soothe me. I had one of those fits of dissatisfaction which often assail the sleepless. I felt that I was making very little of my life. I earned a large income, and had a considerable position in the public eye, but I was living, so to speak, from hand to mouth. I had long lost any ordinary ambitions, and had ceased to plan out my career ahead, as I used to do when I was a young man. There were many things in public life on which I was keen, but it was only an intellectual keenness; I had no ardour in their pursuit. I felt as if my existence were utterly shapeless.

It was borne in on me that Goodeve was right. What were his words? – "Trying to see something solid in the mist is the whole fun of life, and most of its poetry." Success, he had argued, depended upon looking a little farther into the future than other people. No doubt; but then I didn't want success – not in the ordinary way. He had still his spurs to win, whereas I had won mine, and I didn't like the fit of them. Yet all the same I wanted some plan and policy in my life, for I couldn't go on living in the mud of the present. My mind needed prospect and horizon. I had often made this reflection before in moments of disillusionment, but now it came upon me with the force of a revelation. I told myself that I was beginning to be cured of my weariness, for I was growing discontented, and discontent is a proof of vitality… As I fell asleep I was thinking of Goodeve and realising how much I liked him. His company might prove the tonic I required.

I rose early and went for a walk along the Arm to look for a possible trout. The May-fly season was over, but there were one or two good fish rising beyond a clump of reeds where the stream entered the wood. Then I breakfasted alone with Evelyn, for Flambard is not an early house. His horses were mostly at grass, but he lent me a cob of Sally's. I changed into breeches, cut a few sandwiches, and set out for the high Downs. I fancied that a long lonely day on the hills would do me as much good as anything.

It was a quiet dim morning which promised a day of heat. I rode through a mile of woods full of nesting pheasants, then over a broomy common, and then by way of a steep lane on to the turf of the Downs. I found myself on the track where Evelyn exercised his race-horses, for he trained at home, so I gave my beast its head, and had that most delectable of experiences, a gallop over perfect turf. This brought me well up on the side of Stobarrow, and by the time I reached its summit the haze was clearing, and I was looking over the Arm and the young Thames to the blue lift of Cotswold.

I spent the whole day on the uplands. I ate my sandwiches in a clump of thorns, and had a mug of rough cider at an alehouse. I rode down long waterless combes, and ascended other tops besides Stobarrow. For an hour I lay on a patch of thyme, drowsy with the heat and the aromatic scents. I smoked a pipe with an old shepherd, and heard slow tales of sheep and dogs and storms and forgotten fox-hunts. In the end I drugged myself into a sort of animal peace. Thank God, I could still get back when I pleased to the ancient world of pastoral.

But when on my return I came over the brink of Stobarrow I realised that I had gained little. The pastoral world was not mine; my world was down below in the valley where men and women were fretting and puzzling... I no longer thought of them as on a raft looking at misty seas, but rather as spectators on a ridge, trying to guess what lay beyond the next hill. Tavanger and Mayot and Goodeve – they were all at it. A futile game, maybe, but inevitable, since what lay beyond the hill was life and death to them. I must recapture the mood for this guessing game, for it was the mainspring of effort, and therefore of happiness.

I got back about six, had a bath, and changed into flannels. Sally gave me a cup of tea at a table in the hall which carried food for a multitude, but did not look as if it had been much patronised. Evelyn and the Lamingtons had gone to see the Wallingdon training stables; the young people had had tea in the tennis-court pavilion; Mayot had motored to Cirencester to meet a friend, and Tavanger had gone to Goodeve to look at the pictures, in which subject he was a noted connoisseur; Charles Ottery had disappeared after luncheon, and she had sent the Professor to bed till dinner.

Sally's face wore something between a smile and a frown.

"Reggie Daker is in bed, too. He was determined to try Sir Vidas over the jumps in the park, though Evelyn warned him that the horse was short of exercise and was sure to give trouble. The jumps haven't been mended for months, and the take-off at some of them is shocking. Well, Sir Vidas came down all right, and Reggie fell on his head and nearly cracked his skull. He was concussed, and unconscious for a quarter of an hour. Dr Micklem sewed him up, and he is now in bed, covered with bandages, and not allowed to speak or be spoken to till tomorrow. It's hard luck on poor Reggie, but it will keep him for a little from making a fool of himself about Pamela Brune. He hasn't a chance there, you know, and he is such a tactless old donkey that he is spoiling the field for Charles Ottery."

But it was not Reggie's misfortunes that made my hostess frown. Presently I learned the reason.

"I'm very glad of the chance of a quiet talk with you," she said. "I want to speak to you about Professor Moe. You saw him when he arrived last night. What did you think of him?"

"He seemed a formidable personage," I replied. "He looked very ill."

"He *is* very ill. I had no notion how ill he was. He makes light of it, but there must be something mortally wrong with his lungs or his heart. He seems to be always in a fever, and now and then he simply gasps for breath. He says he has been like that for years, but I can't believe it. It's a tragedy, for he is one of the greatest minds in the world."

"I never heard of him before."

"You wouldn't. You're not a scientist. He's a most wonderful mathematician and physicist – rather in the Einstein way. He has upset every scientific law, but you can't understand just how unless you're a great scientist yourself. Our own people hush their voices when they mention him."

"How did you come across him?"

"I met him last year in Berlin. You know I've a *flair* for clever people, and they seem to like me, though I don't follow a word they say. I saw that he was to be in London to read a paper to some society, so I thought I'd ask him to Flambard to show him what English country life was like. Rather to my surprise he accepted – I think London tired him and he wanted a rest."

"You're worried about him? Are you afraid that he'll die on your hands?"

"No-o," she answered. "He's very ill, but I don't think he'll die just yet. What worries me is to know how to help him. You see, he took me into his confidence this morning. He accepted my invitation because he wanted the quiet of the country to finish a piece of work. A tremendous piece of work – the work of his life... He wants something more. He wants our help. It seems that some experiment is necessary before he can be quite sure of his ground."

"What sort of experiment?"

"With human beings – the right kind of human beings. You mustn't laugh at me, Ned, for I can't explain what he told me, though I thought I understood when he was speaking... It has something to do with a new theory of Time. He thinks that Time is not a straight line, but full of coils and kinks. He says that the Future is here with us now, if we only knew how to look for it. And he believes he has found a way of enabling one to know what is going to happen a long time ahead."

I laughed. "Useful for Evelyn and George. They'll be able to back all the Ascot winners."

But Sally did not laugh.

"You must be serious. The Professor is a genius, and I believe every word he says. He wants help, he told me. Not people like Evelyn and George. He has very clear ideas about the kind of man he needs. He wants Mr Mayot and Mr Tavanger and perhaps Charles Ottery, though he's not quite sure about Charles. Above all, he wants you and Bob Goodeve. He saw you last night, and took a tremendous fancy to you both."

I forbore to laugh only out of deference to Sally's gravity. It seemed a reduction to the absurd of Goodeve's talk the night before and my reflections on the Downs. I had decided that I must be more forward-looking, and here was a wild foreigner who believed that he had found the exact technique of the business.

"I don't like it," I said. "The man is probably mad."

"Oh, no, he isn't. He is brilliantly sane. You have only to talk to him to realise that. Even when I couldn't follow him I could see that he was not talking nonsense. But the point is that he wants to put it all before you. He is certain that he can make a convert of you."

"But I don't know the first thing about science. I have often got up a technical subject for a case, and then washed it out of my mind. I've never been instructed in the first principles. I don't understand the language."

"That is just why Professor Moe wants you. He says he wants a fresh mind, and a mind trained like yours to weigh evidence. It wasn't your *beaux yeux*, Ned, that he fell for, but your reputation as a lawyer."

"I don't mind listening to what he has got to say. But look here, Sally, I don't like this experiment business. What does he propose?"

"Nothing in the least unpleasant. It only means one or two people preparing themselves for an experience, which he says he can give them, by getting into a particular frame of mind. He's not sure if he can bring it off, you know. The experiment is to be the final proof of his discovery. He was emphatic that there was no danger and no unpleasantness, whether it was successful or not... But he was very particular about the people he wanted. He was looking at us all this morning with the queerest appraising eyes. He wants you and Bob especially, and Mr Mayot and Mr Tavanger, and possibly Charles. Oh, yes, and he thinks he may want me. But nobody else. He was perfectly clear about that."

I must say that this rather impressed me. He had chosen exactly those whom I had selected at dinner the previous night as the care-full as opposed to the care-free. He wanted people whose physical vitality was low, and who were living on the edge of their nerves, and he had picked them unerringly out of Sally's house-party.

"All right," I said. "I'll have a talk to him after dinner. But I want you to be guided by me, and if I think the thing fishy to call it off. If the man is as clever as you say, he may scare somebody into imbecility."

Before I dressed I rang up Landor, and was lucky enough to find him still in London. Landor, besides being a patent-law barrister pretty near the top of his branch, is a Fellow of the Royal Society, and a devotee of those dim regions where physics, metaphysics, and mathematics jostle each other. He has published and presented me with several works which I found totally incomprehensible.

When I asked him about Professor Moe he replied with a respectful gurgle. "You don't mean to say you've got him at Flambard? What astounding luck! I thought he had gone back to Stockholm. There are scores of people who would walk twenty miles barefoot to get a word with him."

Landor confirmed all that Sally had said about the Professor's standing. He had been given the Nobel Prize years ago, and was undoubtedly the greatest mathematician alive. But recently he had soared into a world where it was not easy to keep abreast of him. Landor confessed that he had only got glimmerings of meaning from the paper he had read two days before to the Newton Club. "I can see the road he is travelling," he said, "but I can't quite grasp the stages." And he quoted Wordsworth's line about "Voyaging through strange seas of thought alone."

"He's the real thing," I asked, "and not a charlatan?"

I could hear Landor's cackle at the other end of the line.

"You might as well ask a conscript to vouch for Napoleon's abilities as ask me to give a certificate of respectability to August Moe."

"You're sure he's quite sane?

"Absolutely. He's only mad in so far as all genius is mad. He is reputed to be a very good fellow and very simple. Did you know that he once wrote a book on Hans Andersen? But he

21

looked to me a pretty sick man. There's a lot of hereditary phthisis in his race."

Dinner that evening was a pleasanter meal for me. I had more of an appetite, there was a less leaden air about my companions in fatigue, the sunburnt boys and girls were in good form, and Reggie Daker's woebegone countenance was safe on its pillow. Charles Ottery, who sat next to Pamela Brune, seemed to be in a better humour, and Mrs Lamington was really amusing about the Wallingdon stables and old Wallingdon's stable-talk. I had been moved farther down the table, and had a good view of Professor Moe, who sat next to our hostess. His was an extraordinary face – the hollow cheeks and the high cheek-bones, the pale eyes, the broad high brow, and the bald head rising to a peak like Sir Walter Scott's. The expression was very gentle, like a musing child, but now and then he seemed to kindle, and an odd gleam appeared in his colourless pits of eyes. For all his size he looked terribly flimsy. Something had fretted his body to a decay.

He came up to me as soon as we left the dining-room. He spoke excellent English, but his voice made me uneasy – it seemed to come with difficulty from a long way down in his big frame. There was a vague, sad kindliness about his manner, but there was a sense of purpose too. He went straight to the point.

"Some time you are going to give me your attention, Sir Edward, and I in return will give you my confidence. Her ladyship has so informed me. She insists, that gracious one, that I must go to bed, for I am still weary. Shall our talk be tomorrow after breakfast? In the garden, please, if the sun still shines."

III

I find it almost impossible to give the gist of the conversation which filled the next forenoon. We sat in wicker chairs on the flags of the Dutch garden in a grilling sun, for heat seemed to be the one physical comfort for which the Professor craved. I shall always associate the glare of a June sky with a frantic effort on my part to grasp the ultimate imponderables of human thought.

The Professor was merciful to my weakness. He had a great writing-pad on his knee, and would fain have illustrated his argument with diagrams, but he desisted when he found that they meant little to me and really impeded his exposition. Most scientists use a kind of shorthand – formulas and equations which have as exact a meaning for them as an ordinary noun has for the ordinary man. But there was no chance for this shorthand with me. He had to begin from the very beginning, taking nothing for granted. I realised his difficulty. It was as if I had had to argue an intricate case, not before a learned judge, but before an intelligent ignoramus, to whom each technical legal term had to be laboriously explained.

There was another difficulty, which applied not to me only, but to the most intelligent auditor in the world. Suppose you are trying to expound to a man who has been stone-deaf from birth the meaning of sound. You can show him the physical effects of it, the brain and sense reactions, but the *fact* of sound you cannot bring home to him by any diagram or calculation. It is something for him without sensory vividness, altogether outside his realised universe. It was the same with the Professor's exposition of strange new dimensions, the discovery of which depended on logical processes. I could not grasp them imaginatively, and, not having lived as he had done with the arguments, I could not comprehend them intellectually.

But here – very crudely and roughly – is the kind of thing he tried to tell me.

He began by observing that in the blind instinct of man there was something which the normal intellect lacked – a prevision of future happenings, for which reason gave no warrant. We all of us had occasionally dim anticipations of coming events, lurking somewhere in our nerves. A man walking in the dark was aware subconsciously of a peril and subconsciously braced himself to meet it. He quoted the sentences from Bergson which I have put at the head of the chapter. His aim was to rationalise and systematise this anticipatory instinct.

Then he presented me with a theory of Time, for he had an orderly mind, and desired to put first things first. Here he pretty well bogged me at the start. He did not call Time a fourth dimension, but I gathered that it amounted to that, or rather that it involved many new dimensions. There seemed to be a number of worlds of presentation travelling in Time, and each was contained within a world one dimension larger. The self was composed of various observers, the normal one being confined to a small field of sensory phenomena, observed or remembered. But this field was included in a larger field and, to the observer in the latter, future events were visible as well as past and present.

In sleep, he went on, where the attention was not absorbed, as it was in waking life, with the smaller field of phenomena, the larger field might come inside the pale of consciousness. People had often been correctly forewarned in dreams. We all now and then were amazed at the familiarity with which we regarded a novel experience, as if we recognised it as something which had happened before. The universe was extended in Time, and the dreamer, with nothing to rivet his attention to the narrow waking field, ranged about, and might light on images which belonged to the future as well as to the past. The sleeper was constantly crossing the arbitrary frontier which our mortal limitations had erected.

At this point I began to see light. I was prepared to assent to the conclusion that in dreams we occasionally dip into the future, though I was unable to follow most of the Professor's proofs. But now came the real question. Was it possible to attain to this form of prevision otherwise than in sleep? Could the observer in the narrow world turn himself by any effort of will into the profounder observer in the world of ampler dimensions? Could the anticipating power of the dreamer be systematised and controlled, and be made available to man in his waking life?

It could, said the Professor. Such was the result of the researches to which he had dedicated the last ten years of his life. It was as a crowning proof that he wished an experiment at Flambard.

I think that he realised how little I had grasped of his exposition of the fundamentals of his theory. He undertook it, I fancy, out of his scrupulous honesty; he felt bound to put me in possession of the whole argument, whether I understood it or not. But, now that he had got down to something concrete which I could follow, his manner became feverishly earnest. He patted my knee with a large lean hand, and kept thrusting his gaunt face close to mine. His writing-pad fell into the lily-pond, but he did not notice it.

He needed several people for his experiment – the more the better, for he wanted a variety of temperaments, and he said something, too, about the advantage of a communal psychical effort… But they must be the right kind of people – people with highly developed nervous systems – not men too deeply sunk in matter. (I thought of Evelyn and the Lamingtons and old Folliot.) He deprecated exuberant physical health or abounding vitality, since such endowments meant that their possessors would be padlocked to the narrower sensory world. He ran over his selection again, dwelling on each, summing each up with what seemed to me astounding shrewdness, considering that he had met them for the first time two days before. He wanted the hungry and the forward-looking. Tavanger and Mayot. "They will never be content," he said, "and their hunger is of the spirit, though maybe an earthy spirit…" Myself. He turned his hollow eyes on me, but was too polite to particularise what my kind of hunger might be… Charles Ottery. "He is unhappy, and that means that his hold on the present is loose…" Sally Flambard. "That gracious lady lives always *sur la branche* – is it not so? She is like a bird, and has no heavy flesh to clog her. Assuredly she must be one." Rather to my surprise he added Reggie Daker. Reggie's recent concussion, for some reason which I did not follow, made him a suitable object... Above all, there was Goodeve. He repeated his name with satisfaction, but offered no comment.

I asked him what form his experiment would take.

"A little training. No more. A little *ascesis*, partly of the body, but mainly of the mind. It must be disciplined to see what it shall see."

Then, speaking very slowly, and drawing words apparently from as deep a cavern as that from which he drew his breath, he explained his plan.

There must be a certain physical preparation. I am as unlearned in medical science as in philosophy, but I gathered that recently there had been some remarkable advances made in the study of the brain and its subsidiary organs. Very likely I am writing nonsense, for the Professor at this point forgot about tempering the wind to the shorn lamb, and poured forth a flood of technicalities. But I understood him to say that, just as the cortex of the brain was the seat of the intellectual activities, so the subcortical region above the spinal cord was the home of the instinctive faculties. He used a lot of jargon, which, not being an anatomist, I could not follow, but he was obliging enough to draw me a diagram in his pocket-book, the writing-pad being in the lily-pond.

In particular there was a thing which he called an "intercalated cell," and which had a very special importance in his scheme. Just as the faculty of sight, he said, had for its supreme function the creation of an extended world, a world of space perception, so the instinct which had its seat in this cell specialised in time-perception... I had been reading lately about telegnosis, and mentioned that word, but he shook his head impatiently. The faculty he spoke of had nothing to do with telegnosis. "You have not understood my exposition," he said. "But no matter. It is enough if you understand my purpose."

It was desirable to stimulate the functioning of this cell. That could only be done in a small degree. A certain diet was necessary, for he had discovered that the cell was temporarily atrophied by the wrong foods. Also there was a drug, which acted upon it directly.

At this I protested, but he was quick to reassure me. "On my honour," he cried, "it is the mildest drug. Its bodily effect is as innocuous as a glass of tonic water. But I have proved experimentally that it lulls the other faculties, and very slightly stimulates this one of which I speak."

Then he revealed his main purpose.

"I am still groping at the edge of mysteries," he said. "My theory I am assured is true, but in practice I can only go a very little way. Some day, when I am ashes, men will look at the future as easily as today they look out of a window at a garden. At present I must be content to exemplify my doctrine by small trivial things. I cannot enable you to gaze at a segment of life at some future date, and watch human beings going about their business. The most I hope for is to show you some simple matter of sense-perception as it will be at that date. Therefore I need some object which I am assured will be still in existence, and which I am also assured will have changed from what it now is. Name to me such an object."

I suggested, rather foolishly, the position of the planets in the sky.

"That will not do, for now we can predict that position with perfect certainty."

"A young tree?"

"The visible evidence of change would be too minute. I cannot promise to open up the future very far ahead. A year – two years maybe – no more."

"A building which we all know, and which is now going up?"

Again he shook his head. "You may be familiar with the type of the completed structure, and carry the picture of it in your memory... There is only one familiar object, which continues and likewise changes. You cannot guess? Why, a journal. A daily or weekly paper."

27

He leaned towards me and laid a hand on each of my knees.

"Today is the sixth of June. Four days from now, if you and the others consent, I will enable you to see for one instant of time – no longer – a newspaper of the tenth day of June next year."

He lay back in his chair and had a violent fit of coughing, while I digested this startling announcement... He was right on one point – a newspaper was the only thing for his experiment; that at any rate I saw clearly. I own to having been tremendously impressed by his talk, but I was not quite convinced; the thing appeared to be clean out of nature and reason. You see, I had no such stimulus to belief as a scientist would have had who had followed his proofs... Still, it seemed harmless. Probably it would end in nothing – the ritual prepared, and the mystics left gaping at each other... No. That could scarcely happen, I decided; the mystagogue was too impressive.

The Professor had recovered himself, and was watching me under drooped eyelids. All the eagerness had gone out of his face, but that face had the brooding power and the ageless wisdom of the Sphinx. If he were allowed to make the experiment something must happen.

Lady Flambard had promised to abide by my decision... There could be no risk, I told myself. A little carefulness in diet, which would do everybody good. The drug? I would have to watch that. The Professor seemed to read my thoughts, for he broke in:

"You are worrying about the drug? It is of small consequence. If you insist, it can be omitted."

I asked how he proposed to prepare the subjects of his experiment. Quite simply, he replied. A newspaper – *The Times*, for example – would be made to play a large part in our thoughts... I observed that it already played a large part in the thoughts of educated Englishmen, and he smiled – the first time I had seen him smile. There was an air of satisfaction about him, as if he knew what my answer would be.

"I see no objection to what you propose," I said at last. "I warn you that I am still a bit of a sceptic. But I am willing, if you can persuade the others."

He smiled again. "With the others there will be no difficulty. Our gracious hostess is already an enthusiast. Before luncheon I will speak to Mr Tavanger and Mr Mayot – and to Mr Ottery when he returns. I shall not speak to them as I have spoken to you."

"Why?" I asked.

"Because they are longing for such a revelation as I propose, whereas you care not at all. But I would beg of you to say a word on my behalf to Sir Robert Goodeve. His co-operation I especially seek."

He raised with difficulty his huge frame from the wicker chair, blinking his eyes in the hot sun, and leaning on a sundial as if he were giddy. I offered my arm, which he took, and together we went under the striped awning, which shaded one part of the terrace, into the coolness of the great hall.

You know the kind of banality with which, out of shyness, one often winds up a difficult conversation. I was moved to observe, as I left him, that in four days I hoped to be introduced to a new world. He made no answer. "To enter, waking, into the world of sleep," I added fatuously.

Then he said a thing which rather solemnised me.

"Not only the world of sleep," he said. "It is the world to which we penetrate after death."

As I watched his great back slowly mounting the staircase, I had a sudden feeling that into the peace of Flambard something fateful and tremendous had broken.

IV

I do not know what Professor Moe said to Tavanger and Mayot. I knew both men, but not intimately, for they were a little too much of the unabashed careerist for my taste, and I wondered how, in spite of his confidence, he was going to interest their most practical minds.

After luncheon I wanted to be alone, so I took my rod and went down to the Arm, beyond the stretch where it ran among water-meadows.

It was a still, bright afternoon, with a slight haze to temper the glare of the sun. The place was delicious, full of the scents of mint and meadowsweet, yellow flag-irises glowing by the water's edge, and the first dog-roses beginning to star the hedges. There was not much of a rise, but I caught a few trout under the size limit, and stalked and lost a big fellow in the mill pool. But I got no good of the summer peace, and my mind was very little on fishing, for the talk of the morning made a merry-go-round in my head.

I had moments of considering the whole business a farce, and wondering if I had not made a fool of myself in consenting to it. But I could not continue long in that mood. The Professor's ardent face would come before me like a reproachful schoolmaster's, and under those compelling eyes of his I was forced back into something which was acquiescence, if not conviction. There was a shadow of anxiety at the back of my mind. The man was an extraordinary force, with elemental powers of brain and will; was it wise to let such an influence loose on commonplace people who happened to be at the moment a little loose from their moorings? I was not afraid of myself, but what about the high-strung Sally, and the concussed Reggie, and Charles Ottery in the throes of an emotional crisis? I kept telling myself that there was no danger, that nothing could happen... And then I discovered, to my amazement, that, if that forecast proved true, I should be disappointed. I wanted something to happen. Nay, I believed at the bottom of my heart that something would happen.

In the smoking-room, before dinner, I found Charles Ottery and Reggie Daker – a rather pale and subdued Reggie, with a bandage round his head and a black eye. They were talking on the window seat, and when I entered they suddenly stopped. When they saw who it was, Charles called to me to join them.

"I hear you're in this business, Ned," he said. "I got the surprise of my life when the Professor told me that you had consented. It's a new line of country for a staid old bird like you."

"The man's a genius," I replied. "I see no harm in helping him in his experiment. Did you understand his argument?"

"I didn't try. He didn't argue much, but one could see that he had any quantity of scientific stuff behind him. He hopes to make us dream while we're awake, and I thought it such a sporting proposition that I couldn't refuse. It must all be kept deadly secret, of course. We have to get into the right atmosphere, and tune our minds to the proper pitch, and it would never do to rope in a born idiot like George Lamington. He'd guy it from the start."

"You were convinced by the Professor?" I asked.

"I won't say convinced. I was interested. It's an amusing game anyhow, and I want to be amused."

Charles spoke with a lightness which seemed to me to be assumed. He had obviously been far more impressed than he cared to admit. I could see that, since Pamela was giving him a difficult time, he longed for something to distract him, something which was associated with that world of new emotions in which he was living.

The lady's other suitor made no concealment. Reggie was honestly excited. He was flattered, perhaps, by being made one of the circle, and may have attributed his choice to his new role as an authority on books. At last he was being taken seriously. Also his recent concussion may have predisposed him to some research into the mysteries of mind, for as he explained, he could not remember one blessed thing that happened between putting Sir Vidas at a fence which be cleared with a yard to spare, and finding himself in bed with clouts on his head. He was insistent on the need of confidence in the experiment. "What I mean to say is, we've got to help the old boy out. If we don't believe the thing will come off, then it won't – if you see what I mean."

He dropped his voice as Evelyn Flambard and his terriers came noisily into the room.

As I was going upstairs to dress, I found Goodeve's hand on my shoulder.

"I hear you're on in this piece," he whispered jovially, as if the whole thing was a good joke.

"And you?" I whispered back.

"Oh, I'm on. I rather like these psychical adventures. I'm a hopeless subject, you know, and calculated to break up any *séance*. I haven't got enough soul – too solidly tied to earth. But I never mind offering myself as a victim."

He laughed and passed into his bedroom, leaving me wondering how the Professor had so signally failed with the man who was his special choice. He had obtained Goodeve's consent, so there was no need of pressure from me, but clearly he had not made any sort of convert of him.

At dinner we all tried to behave as if nothing special was afoot, and I think we succeeded. George Lamington had never had so good an audience for his dreary tales. He was full of racing reminiscences, the point of which was the preternatural cunning with which he had outwitted sundry rivals who had tried to beguile him. I never knew anyone whose talk was so choked with adipose tissue, but he generally managed to wallow towards some kind of point, which he and Evelyn found dramatic... During most of the meal I talked to his wife. She could be intelligent enough when she chose, and had a vigorous interest in foreign affairs, for she was an Ambassador's daughter. When I first knew her she had affected a foreign accent, and professed to be more at home in Paris and Vienna than in London. Now she was English of the English, and her former tastes appeared only in intermittent attempts to get George appointed to a Dominion Governorship, where he would most certainly have been a failure. For the present, however, the drums and trumpets did not sound for her. The recent addition to the Lamington fortunes had plunged her deep in the upholstery of life. She was full of plans for doing up their place in Suffolk, and, as I am as ignorant as a coal-heaver about bric-à-brac, I could only listen respectfully. She had the mannerism of the very rich, whose grievance is not against the price of things, but the inadequacy of the supply.

The Professor's health appeared to have improved, or it may have been satisfaction with his initial success, for he was almost loquacious. He seemed to have acute hearing, for he would catch fragments of conversation far down the table, and send his great voice booming towards the speaker in some innocent interrogation. As I have said, his English was excellent, but his knowledge of English life seemed to be on the level of a South Sea islander. He was very inquisitive, and asked questions about racing and horses which gave Evelyn a chance to display his humour. Among the younger people he was a great success. Pamela Brune, who sat next to him, lost in his company her slight air of petulance and discontent, and became once again the delightful child I had known. I was obliged to admit that the Flambard party had improved since yesterday, for certain of its members seemed to have shaken off their listlessness.

While youth was dancing or skylarking on the terrace, and the rest were set solidly to bridge, we met in the upper chamber in the Essex wing, which had been given me as a sitting-room. At first, while we waited for the Professor, we were a little self-conscious. Tavanger and Mayot, especially, looked rather like embarrassed elders at a children's party. But I noticed that no one – not even Reggie Daker – tried to be funny about the business.

The Professor's coming turned us into a most practical assembly. Without a word of further explanation he gave us our marching orders. He appeared to assume that we were all ready to surrender ourselves to his directions.

The paper chosen was *The Times*. For the next three days we were to keep our minds glued to that news-sheet, and he was very explicit about the way in which we were to do it.

First of all, we were to have it as much as possible before our eyes, so that its physical form became as familiar to each of us as our razors and cigarette cases. We started, of course, with a considerable degree of knowledge, for we were all accustomed to look at it every morning. I remember wondering why the Professor had fixed so short a time as three days for this intensive contemplation, till he went on to give his further orders.

This ocular familiarity was only the beginning. Each of us must concentrate on one particular part to which his special interest was pledged – Tavanger on the first City page, for example, Mayot on the leader page, myself on the Law Reports – any part we pleased. Of such pages we had to acquire the most intimate knowledge, so that by shutting our eyes we could reconstruct the make-up in every detail. The physical make-up, that is to say; there was no necessity for any memorising of contents.

Then came something more difficult. Each of us had to perform a number of exercises in concentration and anticipation. We knew the kind of things which were happening, and within limits the kind of topic which would be the staple of the next day's issue. Well, we had to try to forecast some of the contents of the next day's issue, which we had not seen. And not merely in a general sense. We had to empty our minds of everything but the one topic, and endeavour to make as full as possible a picture of part of the exact contents of *The Times* next morning – to see it not as a concept but as a percept – the very words and lines and headings.

For example. Suppose that I took the Law Reports pages. There were some cases the decisions on which were being given by the House of Lords today, and would be published tomorrow. I could guess the members of the tribunal who would deliver judgement, and could make a fair shot at what that judgement would be. Well, I was to try so to forecast these coming pages that I could picture the column of type, and, knowing the judges' idiosyncrasies, see before my eyes the very sentences in which their wisdom would be enshrined... Tavanger, let us say, took the first City page. Tomorrow he knew there would be a report of a company meeting in which he was interested. He must try to get a picture of the paragraph in which the City Editor commented on the meeting... If Mayot chose the leader page, he must try to guess correctly what would be the subject of the first or second leader, and, from his knowledge of *The Times* policy and the style of its leader-writers, envisage some of the very sentences, and possibly the headings.

It seemed to me an incredibly difficult game, and I did not believe that, for myself, I would get any results at all. I have never been much good at guessing. But I could see the general lay-out. Everything would depend upon the adequacy of the knowledge we started with. To make an ocular picture which would have any exactitude, I must be familiar with the Lord Chancellor's mannerisms, Tavanger with the mentality and the style of the City Editor, and Mayot with the policy of the paper and the verbal felicities of its leader-writers... Some of us found the prescription difficult, and Reggie Daker groaned audibly.

But there was more to follow. We were also to try to fling our minds farther forward – not for a day, but for a year. Each morning at seven – I do not know why he fixed that hour – we were to engage in a more difficult kind of concentration – by using such special knowledge as we possessed to help us to forecast the kind of development in the world which June of next year would show. And always we had to aim at seeing our forecasts not in vague concepts, but in concrete black and white in the appropriate corner of *The Times*.

I am bound to say that, when I heard this, I felt that we had been let in for a most futile quest. We had our days mapped out in a minute programme – certain hours for each kind of concentration. We would meet the Professor in my sitting-room at stated times... I think that he felt the atmosphere sceptical, for on this last point his manner lost its briskness and he became very solemn.

"It is difficult," he said, "but you must have faith. And I myself will help you. Time – all time – is with us *now*, but we are confined to narrow fields of presentation. With my help you will enlarge these fields. If you will give me honestly all your powers, I can supplement them."

Lastly he spoke of the necessary régime. Too much exercise was forbidden, for it was desirable that our health should be rather an absence of ailments than a positive, aggressive well-being. There were to be no cold baths. We might smoke, but alcohol was strictly forbidden – not much of a hardship, for we were an abstemious lot. As to diet, we had to behave like convalescents – no meat, not even fish – nothing which, in the Professor's words, "possessed automobility." We were allowed weak tea, but not coffee. Milk, cheese, fruit, eggs and cereals were to be our staples.

It all reminded me rather eerily of the ritual food which used to be given to human beings set apart for sacrifice to the gods.

"Our gracious hostess has so arranged it that the others will not be curious," said the Professor, and Sally nodded a mystified head.

I went to bed feeling that I should probably get a liver attack from lack of exercise, if I did not starve from lack of food. Next morning I found a *Times* on the tray which brought my morning tea. Sally must have sent ten miles to a main-line station to get it.

V

It is difficult to write the consecutive story of the next three days. I kept a diary, but on consulting it, I find only a bare record of my hours of meditation on that confounded newspaper, and of our conferences with the Professor. I began in a mood which was less one of scepticism than of despair. I simply did not believe that I could get one step forward in this preposterous business. But I was determined to play the game to the best of my capacity, for Moe's talk last night had brought me fairly under his spell.

I did as I had been told. I emptied my mind of every purpose except the one. I read the arguments in the case – it was an appeal by an insurance company – and then sat down to forecast what the report of the judgement would be, as given by *The Times* next day. Of the substance of the judgement I had not much doubt, and I was pretty certain that it would be delivered by the Lord Chancellor, with the rest of the Court concurring. I knew Boland's style, having listened often enough to his pronouncements, and it would have been easy enough to forecast the kind of thing he would say, using some of his pet phrases. But my job was to forecast what *The Times* reporters would make him say – a very different matter. I collected a set of old copies of the paper and tried to get into their spirit. Then I made a number of jottings, but I found myself slipping into the manner of the official *Law Reports*, which was not what I wanted. I remember looking at my notes with disfavour, and reflecting that this guessing game was nothing but a deduction from existing knowledge. If I had made a close study of *The Times* reports, I should probably get a good deal right, but since I had only a superficial knowledge I would get little. Moe's grandiose theories about Time had nothing to do with it. It was not a question of casting the mind forward into a new field of presentation, but simply of a good memory from which one made the right deductions.

After my first attempt I went for a walk, and tried to fix my mind on something different. I had been making a new rock-garden at Borrowby, and I examined minutely Sally's collection of Tibetan alpines. On my return the butler handed me a note. The Professor had decided to have conferences with each of us separately, and my hour was three in the afternoon.

Before that hour I had two other bouts of contemplation. I wrestled honourably with the incurably evasive, and filled several sheets of foolscap with notes. Then I revised them, striking out phrases which were natural enough to Boland, but unsuitable for a newspaper summary. The business seemed more ridiculous than ever. I was simply chewing the cud of memories – very vague, inexact memories.

The Professor received me in Sally's boudoir. Now, the odd thing was that in his presence I had no self-consciousness. If anyone had told me that I should have been unburdening my mind in a ridiculous game to a queer foreigner, with the freedom of a novice in the confessional, I should have declared it impossible. But there it was. He sat before me with his gaunt face and bottomless pits of eyes, very grave and gentle, and without being asked I told him what I had been doing.

"That is a beginning," he said, "only a beginning. But your mind is too active as yet to *perceive*. You are still in the bonds of ratiocination. Your past knowledge is only the jumping-off stage from which your mind must leap. Suffer yourself to be more quiescent, my friend. Do not torture your memory. It is a deep well from which the reason can only draw little buckets of water."

I told him that I had been making notes, and he approved. "But do not shape them as you would shape a logical argument. Let them be raw material out of which a picture builds itself. Your business is perception, not conception, and perception comes in flashes." And then he quoted what Napoleon had once said, how after long pondering he had his vision of a battle plan in a blinding flash of white light.

He said a great deal more which I do not remember very clearly. But one thing I have firm in my recollection – the compelling personality of the man. There must have been some strange hypnotic force about him, for as he spoke I experienced suddenly a new confidence and an odd excitement. He seemed to wake unexpected powers in me, and I felt my mind to be less a machine clamped to a solid concrete base, than an aeroplane which might rise and soar into space. Another queer thing – I felt slightly giddy as I left him. Unquestionably he was going to make good his promise and supplement our efforts, for an influence radiated from him, more masterful than any I have ever known in a fellow mortal. It was only after we had parted that the reaction came, and I felt a faint sense of antagonism, almost of fear.

In my last effort before dinner I struggled to follow his advice. I tried to picture next day's *Times*. The judgement, from its importance, would occupy a column at least; I saw that column and its heading, and it seemed to me to be split up into three paragraphs. I saw some of the phrases out of my notes, and one or two new ones. There was one especially, quite in Boland's manner, which seemed to be repeated more than once – something like this: "It is a legal commonplace that a contract of insurance is one *uberrimae fidei*, which is vitiated by any non-disclosure, however innocent, of material facts." I scribbled this down, and found, when I re-read it, that I had written *uberrimi*, and deplored my declining scholarship.

At dinner our group were as glum as owls. I did not know how the Professor had handled the others, but I assumed that his methods had been the same as with me, and certainly he had produced an effect. We all seemed to have something on our minds, and came in for a good deal of chaff, the more as we refrained from so many dishes. Reggie Daker escaped, for he was a convalescent, but Evelyn had a good deal to say about Goodeve's abstinence. Goodeve was supposed to be entering for a tennis contest which the young people had got up, while George Lamington started the legend that I was reducing my weight for the next Bar point-to-point. Happily this interest in our diet diverted their attention from our manners, which must have been strange. All seven of us were stricken with aphasia, and for myself I felt that I was looking on at a movie-show.

The Professor gathered us together in my sitting-room a little before midnight. As I looked at the others I had an impression of a kindergarten. Compared with him we all seemed ridiculously young, crude, and ignorant. Mayot's alert intelligence was only the callow vivacity of a child; Tavanger's heavy face was merely lumpish; even Goodeve looked the bright schoolboy. As for Sally and Reggie and Charles Ottery, something had happened to them which drained the personality from their faces, and made them seem slight and wispish. Moe himself brooded over us like a vital Buddha. I had an uneasy sense of looking at a man who lived most of his time in another world than ours.

He did not instruct us; he talked, and his talk was like a fierce cordial. Looking back at what I can remember of it, it does not seem to make any kind of sense, but it had an overwhelming effect on his hearers. It was as if he were drawing aside curtain after curtain, and, though we could not see into the land beyond the curtains, we were convinced of its existence. As I have said, I cannot make sense of my recollection of it, but while I was listening it seemed to be quite simple and intelligible...

He spoke of the instinct which gave perceptions, and of its immense power as compared to our petty reason which turned percepts into concepts. He spoke of what he called the "eye of the mind," and said the very phrase pointed to some intuition in the ordinary being of a gift which civilisation had atrophied... Then Reggie Daker became important. The Professor elicited from the coy Reggie that in his childhood he had been in the habit of seeing abstract things in a concrete form. For Reggie the different days of the week had each a special shape, and each of the Ten Commandments a special colour. Monday was a square and Saturday an oval, and Sunday a circle with a segment bitten out; the Third Commandment was dark blue, and the Tenth a pale green with spots. Reggie had thought of Sin as a substance like black salt, and the Soul as something in the shape of a kidney bean...

It all sounds the wildest nonsense, but the Professor made out of Reggie's confidences a wonderful thing. His images might seem ridiculous, but they showed perception struggling to regain its rightful place. He had some theory of the relation between the concrete vision and the abstract thought, which he linked somehow or other to his doctrine of Time. In the retrospect I cannot remember his argument, but he convinced me absolutely... He had a lot to say about the old astrologers and magic-makers who worked with physical charms and geometrical figures, and he was clear that they had had a knowledge of mysteries on which the door had long been locked. Also he talked about certain savage beliefs in ancient Greece and in modern Africa – which he said were profundity and not foolishness... He spoke, too, about the world of dreams, and how its fantasy had often a deeper reality than waking life. "We are children on the seashore," he said, "watching the jetsam of the waves, and every fragment of jetsam is a clue to a land beyond the waters which is our true home."

Not for a moment did any of us think him mad. We sat like beggars, hungrily picking up crumbs from a feast. Of one thing I was presently convinced. Moe had cast a stronger spell over the others than over myself. I found my mind trying feebly to question some of his sayings, to link them with the ordinary world of thought; but it was plain that the rest accepted everything as inspired and infallible gospel.

I dare say I was tired, for I slept more soundly than I had done for weeks. I was called at seven, and set myself, according to instructions, to a long-range forecast – what would be likely to happen on June tenth a year ahead. It sounds a futile job, and so I found it. My head soon grew dizzy with speculations, some of them quite outside the legal sphere which I had marked out as my own. But I found one curious thing. I had lost the hopelessness which had accompanied my contemplations of the previous day. I *believed* now that I could make something of the task. Also I found my imagination far more lively.

I convinced myself that in a year's time there would be a new Lord Chancellor and a new Lord of Appeal. I beheld them sitting in the Lords, but the figure on the Woolsack was so blurred that I could not recognise it. But I saw the new Lord clearly, and his face was the face of young Molsom, who had only taken silk two years ago. Molsom's appointment was incredible, but, as often as the picture of the scarlet benches of the Upper House came before me, there was Molsom, with his dapper little figure and his big nose and his arms folded after his habit. I realised that I was beginning to use the "mind's eye," to see things, and not merely to think them.

The Times was brought to my bedside at eight, and I opened it eagerly. There was the judgement in my case, delivered, as I had expected, by Boland. It ran not to a whole column, but to less than three-quarters; but I had been right on one point – it was broken up into three paragraphs. The substance of the judgement was much as I had foreseen, but I had not been lucky in guessing the wording, and Boland had referred to only two of the cases I had marked down for him...

But there was one amazing thing. He had used the sentence about *uberrimae fidei* – very much in the form I had anticipated. More – far more. *The Times* had that rare thing, a misprint: it had *uberrimi*, the very blunder I had made myself in my anticipatory jottings.

This made me feel solemn. My other correct anticipations might be set down to deductions from past knowledge. But here was an indubitable instance of anticipatory perception.

From that hour I date my complete conversion. I was as docile now as Sally, and I stopped trying to reason. For I understood that, behind all the régime and the exercises, there was the tremendous fact of Professor Moe himself. If we were to look into the future it must be largely through his eyes. By the sheer power of intellect he had won a gift, and by some superabundant force of personality he was able to communicate in part that gift to others.

I am not going to attempt to write in detail the story of the next two days, because external detail matters little; the true history was being made in the heads of the seven of us. I went obediently through the prescribed ritual. I pored over *The Times* as if my salvation depended upon it. I laboured to foresee the next day's issue, and I let my mind race into the next year. I felt my imagination becoming more fecund and more vivid, and my confidence growing hourly. And always I felt behind me some mighty impetus driving me on and holding me up. I was in the charge of a Moses, like the puzzled Israelites stumbling in the desert.

I spent the intervals with a rod beside the Arm, and there I first became conscious of certain physical symptoms. An almost morbid nervous alertness was accompanied by a good deal of bodily lassitude. This could not be due merely to the diet and lack of exercise, for I had often been sedentary for a week on end and lived chiefly on bread and cheese. Rather it seemed that I was using my nervous energy so lavishly in one direction that I had little left for the ordinary purposes of life… Another thing. My sight is very good, especially for long distances, and in dry-fly fishing I never need to use a glass to spot a fish. Well, in the little fishing I did that day, I found my eyes as good as ever, but I noted one remarkable defect. I saw the trout perfectly clearly, but I could not put a fly neatly over him. There was nothing wrong with my casting; the trouble was in my eye, which had somehow lost its liaison with the rest of my body. The fly fell on the water as lightly as thistledown, but it was many inches away from the fish's nose.

That day the Professor made us fix our minds principally on the lay-out of June tenth, next year. He wanted to have that date orientated for us with relation to other recurrent events – the Derby, Ascot, the third reading of the Budget, the conference of Empire Journalists and so forth. Also he provided us with sheets

43

of blank paper, the size of *The Times*, which were to be, so to speak, the screen on which the magic lantern of our prevision cast its picture. He was very careful, almost fussy, about this business. The sheets had nothing printed on them, but they had to be exactly right in size, and he rejected the first lot that Sally provided.

But I cannot say that I paid much attention to these or any other details. I was in a mood of utter obedience, simply doing what I was told to do to the best of my power. I was in the grip of a power which I had no desire to question, and which by some strong magic was breaking down walls for me and giving me a new and marvellous freedom. For there was no doubt about it – I could now set my mind at will racing into the future, and placing before me panoramas which might or might not be true, but which had all the concrete sharpness of reality. There were moments when I seemed almost to feel one sphere of presentation give place to another, as the driver of a car changes gear.

Dinner that night – Sally had sent the Professor to bed after tea – was as lively as the meal of the previous evening had been dull – lively, that is, for the rest of the party, not for us seven. For we seven suddenly developed a remarkable capacity for making sport for the populace, by a kind of mental light-heartedness, similar to my clumsiness with the trout. Our minds seemed to have jolted out of focus. There is a species of *bêtise*, which I believe at Cambridge is named after some don, and which consists in missing completely the point of a metaphor or a joke, in setting the heavy heel of literalness on some trivial flower of fancy. It is a fault to which the Scots are supposed to be prone, and it is the staple of most of the tales against that nation. The classic instance is Charles Lamb's story of how he was once present at a dinner given in honour of Burns, at which a nephew of the poet was to be present. As the company waited on the arrival of the guest, Lamb remarked that he wished the uncle were coming instead of the nephew: upon which several solemn

Scotsmen arose to inform him that that was impossible, because Burns was dead.

That night we seven became unconscious Caledonians. Reggie Daker began it, by asking a ridiculous question about a story of Evelyn's. At first Evelyn looked wrathful, suspecting irony, and then, realising Reggie's guilelessness, he turned the laugh against that innocent. The extraordinary thing was that we all did it. Sally was the worst, and Charles Ottery a good second. Even Mayot fell into the trick – Mayot, who had a reputation for a quick and caustic wit. George Lamington was talking politics. "A Bengali Cabinet in England," George began, and was interrupted by Mayot with, "But, hang it, man, there's no Bengali Cabinet in England!" The fact that I noted our behaviour would seem to prove that I was not so deeply under the spell as the others.

We made sport, as I have said, for the company, and some of them enjoyed the pleasant sense of superiority which comes when people who have a reputation for brains make fools of themselves. Yet the mirth struck me as a little uneasy. There was a sense somewhere that all was not well, that odd things were going on beneath the surface. Pamela Brune, I remember, let her eyes rest on Charles Ottery as she left the room, and in those eyes I read bewilderment, almost pain.

Next morning we began the drug. There were in all three doses – the first with morning tea, the second at three in the afternoon, and the third after dinner. For myself I felt no particular effects, but I can testify that that day, the last day of our preparation, my mood changed.

For the first time I found some dregs of fear in my mind. My confidence in Moe was in no way abated, but I began to feel that we were moving on the edge of things, not mysterious only but terrible. My first cause for uneasiness was the Professor himself. When I met him that morning I was staggered by his looks. His colour was like white wax, and the gauntness of his face was such that it seemed that not only flesh had gone but muscle and blood, so that there remained only dead skin stretched tight over dead bone. His eyes were alive, and no longer placid pools, but it was a sick life, and coughing shook him as an autumn wind shakes the rafters of a ruined barn. He professed to be well enough, but I realised that his experiment was draining his scanty strength. The virtue was going out of him into us, and I wondered if before the appointed time the dynamo might not fail us.

My other anxiety was Goodeve. He had begun by being the most sceptical of the lot of us, but I noticed that at each conference with Moe he grew more silent, his face more strained, and his eyes more unquiet. There was now something positively furtive in them, as if he were in dread of some menace springing out at him from ambush. He hung upon the Professor's words with dog-like devotion, very odd in a personality so substantial and well defined. By tacit consent none of us ever spoke of the experiment, as if we felt that any communication among ourselves might weaken the strong effluence from our leader's mind, so I could not put out any feelers. But the sight of Goodeve at luncheon increased my lurking fear that we were getting very near the edge of some indefinable danger.

I felt very drowsy all day, and dozed in a garden chair between the exercises. I usually dream a good deal of nights, but now I slept like a log – which may have been due to nervous fatigue, or more likely to the switching of the dream-world over into the waking hours. The strangest thing about the whole experience was that I never felt one moment of boredom. I was doing something infinitely monotonous, and yet my powers bent themselves to it as readily as if every moment were a new excitement. That, too, rather frightened me. If this stimulus was so potent for a flat nature like mine, what must be its power over more mercurial souls?

I must record what happened at tea. Nearly all the guests were there, and a cheerful party of young people had come over from a neighbouring house. Now Sally had a much-loved terrier, a

Dandie Dinmont called Andrew, who had been on a visit to the vet and had only returned that afternoon. Andrew appeared when tea was beginning, and was received by his mistress with every kind of endearment. But Andrew would not go near her; he fled, knocking over a table, and took refuge between Evelyn's legs, and nothing would draw him from his sanctuary. He used to be a friend of mine, but he met my advances with a snap and the most dismal howling. There he stood, pressed against Evelyn's shins, his teeth bared, his big head lowered and bristling. He seemed to have no objection to the others, only to Sally and me. Then Mayot came in with Tavanger, and again Andrew wailed to the skies. Charles Ottery and Reggie received the same greeting; Goodeve, too, who sat down next to Evelyn, and thereby drove Andrew yelping to a corner. After that he recovered a little and accepted a bit of bread and butter from Pamela Brune, by whose side he had ensconced himself. I was deeply interested in the whole performance, for it was not humanity that Andrew disliked, but that section of it which was engaged in the experiment. I was pondering on this marvel, when there came a howl like nothing on earth, and I saw Andrew streaking out of the drawing-room, slithering over rugs and barging into stools, with Evelyn after him. I also saw that Moe had just entered by another door, looking like a death-in-life.

The Professor sat himself by me, and drank his tea thirstily. The tiny cup seemed almost too great a weight for the mighty hand to raise. He turned to me with the ghost of a smile.

"That dog pays tribute to our success," he said. "The animal has instinct and the man reason, and on those terms they live together. Let a man attain instinct and the animal will flee from him. I have noted it before."

Some neighbours came to dinner, so we made a big party, and the silent conclave passed unnoticed, though Sally's partner must have wondered what had become of her famous sparkle, for she was the palest and mutest of spectres. I felt myself an observer set at a distance not only from the ordinary members of the party but from our coterie – which proves that I must have been less under Moe's spell than my companions. For example, I could not only watch with complete detachment the behaviour of the cheerful young people, and listen to George Lamington's talk of his new Lancia, but I could observe from without Sally's absent-mindedness and stammered apologies, and Goodeve's look of unhappy expectation, and Charles Ottery's air of one struggling with something on the edge of memory, and Tavanger's dry lips – the man drank pints of water. One thing I noticed. They clearly hated those outside our group. Sally would shrug her shoulders as if unbearably tried, and Mayot looked murderously now and then at Evelyn, and Charles Ottery, who sat next to Pamela Brune, regarded her with hard eyes. I was conscious of something of the same sort myself, for most of my fellows had come to look to me like chattering mannikins. They bored me, but I did not feel for them the overwhelming distaste which was only too apparent in the other members of the group. Their attitude was the opposite of Miranda's cry –

> *"O brave new world*
> *That has such people in't."*

I doubt if they thought the world brave, and for certain they had no illusion about its inhabitants.

It was a very hot night, and I went out beyond the terrace to sniff the fragrance of Sally's rock garden. As I sat dangling my legs over the parapet I felt a hand on my arm, and turned to find Pamela Brune.

"Come for a walk, Uncle Ned," she said. "I want to talk to you."

She slipped her arm through mine, and we went down the long alley between yews at the end of the Dutch garden. I felt her arm tremble, and when she spoke it was in a voice which she strove to make composed.

"What has happened to you all?" she asked. "I thought this Whitsuntide was going to be such fun, and it began well – and now everybody is behaving so oddly. Sally hasn't smiled for two days, and Reggie is more half-witted than ever, and you look most of the time as if you were dropping off to sleep."

"I am pretty tired," I replied.

"Oh yes, I know," she said impatiently. "There are excuses for you – and for Sally perhaps, for she has been overdoing it badly... But there is a perfect epidemic of bad manners abroad. Tonight at dinner I could have boxed Charles Ottery's ears. He was horribly rude."

"You haven't been very kind to him," I said lamely.

She withdrew her hand.

"What do you mean? I have always been civil...and he has been very, very unkind to me... I hate him. I'll never speak to him again."

Pamela fled from me down the shadowed alley like a nymph surprised by Pan, and I knew that she fled that I might not see her tears.

Later that night we had our last conference with Moe, for next morning at seven in my sitting-room we were to meet for the final adventure. It was a short conference, and all he seemed to do was to tighten the cords with which he had bound us. I felt his influence more sharply than ever, but I was not in such perfect thraldom as the others, for with a little fragment of my mind I could still observe and think objectively...

I observed the death-mask of the Professor. That is the only word by which to describe his face. Every drop of blood seemed to have fled from it, and in his deep pits of eyes there was no glimmer of life. It was a mask of death, but it was also a mask of peace. In that I think lay its compelling power. There was no shadow of unrest or strife or doubt in it. It had been purged of human weakness as it had been drained of blood. I remembered "grey-haired Saturn, quiet as a stone."

I thought – what did I think? I kept trying as a desperate duty to make my mind function a little on its own account. I cast it back over the doings of the past days, but I could not find a focus… I was aware that somehow I had acquired new and strange gifts. I had become an adept at prospecting the immediate future, for, though I made many blunders, I had had an amazing percentage of successes. But the Professor did not set much store apparently by this particular *expertise*, and my main task had been long-range forecasts a year ahead. These, of course, could not be verified, but I had managed to create a segment of a future world as shot with colour and as diversified with incident as the world of sense around me…

About that there were some puzzles which I could not solve. In guessing the contents of the next day's *Times* I had a mass of concrete experience to build on, but I had not that experience to help me in constructing what might happen across the space of a year, with all a year's unaccountable chances… Then I reflected that the power of short-range forecasts had come in only a small degree from the exercise of my reason upon past experience. That was but a dim light: it was the doemonic power of the Professor's mind which had given me those illuminations. Could the strong wings of that spirit carry seven humdrum folk over the barriers of sense and habit into a new far world of presentation?

That was my last thought before I fell asleep, and I remember that I felt a sudden horror. We were feeding like parasites upon something on which lay the shadow of dissolution.

VI

I was up and dressed long before seven. The drug, or the diet, or the exercises, or all combined, made me sleepy during the day, but singularly alert at first waking. Alert in body, that is – the feeling that I could run a mile in record time, the desire for something to task my bodily strength. But my brain these last mornings had not been alert. It had seemed a passive stage over which a pageant moved, a pageant of which I had not the direction... But this morning the pageant had stopped, the stage was empty, or rather it was brooded over by a vast vague disquiet.

It was a perfect midsummer morning, with that faint haze in the distance which means a hot noon. The park under my window lay drenched and silvered with dew. The hawthorns seemed to be bowed over the grasses under their weight of blossom. The birds were chattering in the ivy, and two larks were singing. Just under me, beyond the ha-ha, a foal was standing on tottering legs beside its mother, lifting its delicate nozzle to sniff the air. The Arm, where the sun caught it, was a silver crescent, and there was a little slow drift of amethyst smoke from the head keeper's cottage in a clump of firs. The scene was embodied, deep, primordial peace, and though, as I have said, my ordinary perception had become a little dulled, the glory of the June morning smote me like a blow.

It wakened a thousand memories, and memories of late had been rare things with me... I thought of other such dawns, when I had tiptoed through wet meadows to be at the morning rise – water lilies, and buckbean, and arrowhead, and the big trout feeding; dawn in the Alps, when, perched on some rock pinnacle below the last ridge of my peak, I had eaten breakfast and watched the world heave itself out of dusk into burning colour; a hundred hours when I had thanked God that I was alive... A sudden longing woke in me, as if these things were slipping away. These joys were all inside the curtain of sense and present perception, and now I was feeling for the gap in the curtain, and losing them. What mattered the world beyond the gap? Why should we reach after that which God had hidden?...

Fear, distaste, regret chased each other through my mind. Something had weakened this morning. Had the *mystica catena* snapped?... And then I heard a movement in my sitting-room, and turned away from the window. My mind might be in revolt, but my will was docile.

We sat in a semicircle round the Professor. It was a small room with linen-fold panelling, a carved chimney-piece, and one picture – a French hunting scene. The morning sun was looking into it, so the blinds were half-lowered. We sat in a twilight, except in one corner, where the floor showed a broad shaft of light. I was next to Sally at the left-hand edge of the circle. That is all I remember about the scene, except that each of us had a copy of *The Times* – not the blank paper we had had before, but that morning's *Times*, the issue for the tenth of June in that year of grace.

I must have slipped partly out of the spell, for I could use my eyes and get some message from them. I dare say I could have understood one of *The Times* leaders. But I realised that the others were different. They could not have made sense of one word. To them it was blank white paper, an empty slate on which something was about to be written. They had the air of dull, but obedient pupils, with their eyes chained to their master.

The Professor wore a dressing-gown, and sat in the writing-table chair – deathly white, but stirred into intense life. He sat upright, with his hands on his knees, and his eyes, even in the gloom, seemed to be probing and kneading our souls... I felt the spell, and consciously struggled against it. His voice helped my resistance. It was weak and cracked, without the fierce vitality of his face.

"For three minutes you will turn your eyes inward – into the darkness of the mind which I have taught you to make. Then – I will give the sign – you will look at the paper. There you will see words written, but only for one second. Bend all your powers to remember them."

But my thoughts were not in the darkness of the mind. I looked at the paper and saw that I could read the date and the beginning of an advertisement. I had broken loose; I was a rebel, and was glad of it. And then I looked at Moe, and saw there something which sent a chill to my heart.

The man was dying – dying visibly. With my eyes I saw the body shrink and the jaw loosen as the vital energy ebbed. Now I knew how we might bridge the gap of Time. His personality had lifted us out of our world, and, by a supreme effort of brain and will, his departing soul might carry us into a new one – for an instant only, before that soul passed into a timeless eternity.

I could see all this, because I had shaken myself free from his spell, yet I felt the surge of his spirit like a wind in my face. I heard the word "Now," croaked with what must have been his last breath. I saw his huge form crumple and slip slowly to the floor. But the eyes of the others did not see this; they were on *The Times* pages.

All but Sally. The strain had become more than she could bear. With a small cry she tilted against my shoulder, and for the few seconds before the others returned to ordinary consciousness and realised that Moe was dead, she lay swooning in my arms.

In that fateful moment, while the soul of a genius was quitting the body, five men, staring at what had become the simulacrum of a *Times* not to be printed for twelve months, read certain things.

Mayot had a vision of the leader page, and read two sentences of comment on a speech by the Prime Minister. In one sentence the Prime Minister was named, and the name was not that of him who then held the office.

Tavanger, on the first City page, had a glimpse of a note on the formation of a great combine, by the Anatilla Corporation, of the michelite-producing interests of the world.

Reggie Daker, on the Court page, saw an account of the departure of an archaeological expedition to Yucatan, and his name appeared as one of the members.

Goodeve and Charles Ottery – the one on the page opposite the leaders and the other on the first page of the paper – read the announcement of their own deaths.

II

MR ARNOLD TAVANGER

"For mee (if there be such a thing as I)
Fortune (if there be such a thing as shee)
Spies that I beare so well her tyranny,
That she thinks nothing else so fit for mee."

JOHN DONNE.

II

Mr Arnold Tavanger

I

Tavanger's life was a little beyond my beat. Your busy city magnate does not dine out a great deal, and as a rule he fights shy of political circles. Before that Flambard Whitsuntide I had met him occasionally at public dinners, and once I had had to cross-examine him in a case in the Commercial Court, and a very tough proposition I found him. I was attracted by something solid and dignified in his air, and I thought his taciturnity agreeable; your loquacious financier is the dullest of God's creatures. During the early autumn I found myself occasionally wondering whether Tavanger had seen anything under Moe's spell, for he had had the look of a convinced disciple. I was certain that he would play up to whatever vision he had been vouchsafed, for your financier is as superstitious as a punter and will act boldly on hints which he never attempts to rationalise. Then, in the beginning of the Michaelmas term, fortune brought us together.

I was invited to arbitrate in a case sent me by a firm of city solicitors who often briefed me. It concerned the ownership of a parcel of shares in a Rhodesian company. Tavanger had bought and paid for them, but there was some question about the title, and another party, representing a trust estate, had put forward a claim. It was a friendly affair, for the trustees only wished to protect themselves, and instead of making a case in court of it they had agreed, to save expense, to submit it to me as arbitrator – a growing practice in those days when there was little money to spend on litigation. The case, which turned on the interpretation of certain letters and involved a fairly obvious point of law, presented no great difficulty. I sat for four hours on a Saturday afternoon, and, after a most amicable presentation of both sides, I found for Tavanger.

This happened at the end of October, and interfered with a Saturday to Monday which I had meant to spend at Wirlesdon. It upset Tavanger's plans also, and, as we were leaving my chambers, he suggested that, since we were both left at a loose end, we should dine together. I agreed willingly, for I had taken a strong liking to Tavanger. He had given his evidence that afternoon with a downright reasonableness which impressed me, and I had enjoyed watching his strong, rather sullen face, enlivened by his bright humorous eyes. His father, I had been told, had come originally from Geneva, but the name had been anglicised to rhyme with "scavenger," and the man himself was as typical a Briton as you could picture. He had made a great reputation, and, incidentally, a great fortune, by buying wreckage and working it up into sound business. In whatever direction he moved he had a crowd of followers who trusted his judgement, but they trusted him blindly, for he was not communicative. He had done bold things, too, and more than once had defied City opinion and won. His name stood high for integrity as well as for acumen and courage, but he was not regarded as companionable. He was a bachelor, living alone in a big house in Kensington, and his hobbies were a hospital, which he ran brilliantly, and his collection of Dutch pictures. Nobody claimed to know him well, and I own to having been a little flattered when he showed a taste for my company. I had a notion that he might want to talk about Moe.

He didn't, for Flambard was never mentioned. But he had a good deal to tell me about the Rhodesian company, the Daphne

Concessions, which had been the subject of the arbitration. I had observed with some curiosity that he had taken special pains to acquire the seventeen thousand ordinary shares, and had paid a stiffish price for them, and I had wondered what purpose was at the back of his head. For when the papers had first come to me I had happened to meet the stockbroker who looked after my investments, and had asked him casually about the Daphne company. He had shaken his head over it. The shares were not quoted, he told me, and were presumably strongly held, but the mine had been going for five years without paying a dividend. Personally he did not believe in the future of michelite, but if I wanted a gamble there were plenty of shares of the chief producing company, the American Anatilla, to be had at round about sixteen shillings.

I am ashamed to say that I had only a very hazy idea what michelite was, and from Tavanger I sought information. I learned that it was a metal used chiefly in the manufacture of certain kinds of steel, and that it could also be applied to copper and iron. It gave immense hardness and impenetrability, and complete freedom from corrosion, and could therefore be used, like ferrochrome, for the construction of aeroplanes, projectiles, and armour-plates; but the product was less costly than chrome steel and easier to work. Tavanger thought that its use must soon be greatly extended, especially in the automobile industry. The difficulty lay in smelting the ore, a process which required very special fluxes and was still an expensive one; nevertheless, in spite of the cost, many industries would find it indispensable. It was found in large, but still undefined, quantities in a very few areas. In the Urals, of course, the home of all minerals, but there the deposits were little worked. In two places in the Balkans and one in Transylvania, where the owners were a German company, the Rosas-Sprenger, which had been the pioneer in the whole business. In Central America – Nicaragua, I think – under the Anatilla Corporation. These two companies, the Anatilla and the Rosas-Sprenger, virtually controlled the product now on the market.

"Prosperous?" he said in reply to my question. "No, not yet. They live in hope. The Anatilla has Glaubsteins behind it, and can afford to wait. The Rosas-Sprenger, I fancy, has a bit of a struggle, but they have Sprenger with them, who first discovered how to smelt the stuff – I'm told he is one of the greatest living metallurgical chemists. Sooner or later their chance is bound to come, unless the engineering trade goes bust altogether."

"How about our friends of the afternoon?" I asked.

"Oh, the Daphne is not yet a serious producer. It has always been a bit short of working capital. But we have assets the others don't possess. They have to mine their ore, and have pretty high working costs, whereas we quarry ours – quarry it out of a range of hills which seems to be made of it. Also our stuff is found in a purer form, and the smelting is simpler – not easy or cheap, but easier and cheaper than theirs. When a boom comes we shall be in a favourable position... Would you like some shares? I daresay it could be managed."

"No, thank you," I said. "I have no time to watch speculations, so I stick to gilt-edged... You have a solid lump of the ordinary stock. Are you looking for more?"

He laughed. "For all I can get. I have taken a sudden fancy to michelite, and I usually back my fancies. The mischief is to know where to find the shares. Daphnes seem to be held by a legion of small folk up and down the world, none of whom want to sell. I have to stalk them like wild deer. You're not in this business and won't queer my pitch, so I don't mind telling you that I mean to have a controlling interest in Daphnes before I'm many months older."

After that we talked about Hobbema. As I walked back to my rooms I had two clear impressions in my mind. One was that I should not like to be up against Tavanger in any business on which his heart was set. There was that in the set of his jaw and the dancing light in his eyes which made him look immensely formidable. The second was that he knew something about the Daphne Concession which others did not know, and knew it with absolute certainty. As I went to bed it suddenly occurred to me that he might have got this knowledge at Flambard, but as to its nature I could make no guess.

II

I did not meet Tavanger again till the week after Christmas. An unexpected piece of business had brought me up from Devonshire, and it lasted so long that I was forced to spend the night in Town. It was that dead patch at the end of December when London seems more deserted than in August, and, since I felt disinclined to face the howling desert of a club, I dined at the Savoy. There I found Tavanger marooned for the same cause. He had been shooting in Norfolk, and had been dragged up to an urgent conference.

He looked a different man from my last recollection of him – leaner in body, thinner in the face, deeply weathered, with the light patches round the eyes which you get from long blinking in a strong sun. I asked him what he had been doing with himself, and he laughed.

"Wait till I have ordered my dinner and I'll tell you. I'm short of good food and trying to make up for it. I want to get my teeth into decent beef again... What about wine? It's cold enough for Burgundy."

When he had arranged a menu to his satisfaction he began an account of his recent doings. It lasted through the meal and long afterwards over a pipe in my rooms. Tavanger was a good narrator in his dry way, and instead of an evening of sleepy boredom I had excellent entertainment, for I heard a tale of activities which few middle-aged men would have ventured upon...

Having got a list of the chief shareholders in Daphne Concessions, he set out to bargain for their holdings in the

61

speediest way, by personal visitation. I gathered that time was of the essence of the business.

First of all he flew to Berlin. There he had an interview with the president of one of the big air services, and, having a good deal of purchase, obtained certain privileges not usually granted to the travelling public. The said president gave a dinner for him at the Adlon, at which he met two people with whom he had long conversations. One was Dilling, the airman, one of the few German aces who had survived the War, who was now busy blazing the trails in commercial aviation. He was specialising at the moment in trans-African flights, and hoped to lower the record from Europe to Cape Town. Tavanger made friends with Dilling, who was a simple soul wholly engrossed in his profession.

The other guest was Sprenger, the metallurgical chemist who had first discovered the industrial uses of michelite. Sprenger was an untidy little man of about sixty, the kind of genius who has never reaped the fruit of his labours and is inclined to be peevish. But he went on doggedly with these labours under considerable difficulties, living on certain small fees for patent rights and on a modest salary paid him by the not very flourishing Rosas-Sprenger company. Tavanger had a remarkable gift of winning people's confidence, and he made Sprenger talk freely, since the latter had no notion that his companion had any michelite interests, though he showed an intelligent appreciation of the metal's possibilities. Three things Tavanger discovered. The first was that Sprenger was ill-informed about the Daphne Concessions, from which it might be deduced that his company was equally in the dark. Therefore no immediate competition for the Daphne shares need be looked for from that quarter. The second was that he was desperately loyal to his own company, and would never be seduced into a rival concern. This solved one problem for Tavanger, who had been ready to pay a considerable price for Sprenger's services. The third was that the little chemist was toiling away at michelite problems, especially the major difficulty of the smelting costs, and was inclined to hope that he was on the brink of a great discovery. Any such discovery would of course belong to his company, but Tavanger ascertained that the Rosas-Sprenger had an agreement with the Anatilla to pool any devices for lessening costs. The Anatilla no doubt provided some of the working capital which enabled the German company to experiment.

The dinner convinced Tavanger that there was no time to be lost. He flew to Salonika by the ordinary Middle East service, and then changed into a seaplane which took him to Crete. The famous antiquary, Dr Heilbron, was busy there with his Minoan excavations. Heilbron had some years before been engaged in investigating the Zimbabwe remains, and had spent a considerable time in Rhodesia. For some reason or other he had been induced to put money into Daphne Concessions at the start, and owned a block of five thousand shares which he had almost forgotten about.

I could guess at the masterly way in which Tavanger handled Heilbron and got what he wanted. He appeared to be the ordinary traveller, who had dropped in on his way to Egypt to get a glimpse of the antiquary's marvellous work. Being well read, he no doubt talked intelligently on the Minoan civilisation. He let drop that he was a businessman with South African interests, and drew from Heilbron the story of his Daphne investment. The antiquary was comfortably off, but excavation consumes a good deal of money, and he seems to have jumped at Tavanger's offer to buy his shares, which he had long ago written off as worthless when he thought of them at all. Tavanger offered a good price for them, but insisted on Heilbron consulting his stockbroker. The answer was favourable, and the transfer was arranged by cable.

While in Crete Tavanger received another cable which perturbed him. The big block of Daphne shares which he had acquired was not all in his own name; the registered holders of a third were his nominees and quite obscure people. This had been done with a purpose. He wanted to know if the Anatilla people were coming into the market; if they did, they were not likely to approach him in the first instance, but to go for the humbler holders. The cable told him that an offer had been made to one of his nominees – a handsome offer – and that this had been traced by his intelligence department as coming through two firms who were known to handle a good deal of Glaubsteins' European business.

Tavanger had had a long experience of Glaubsteins' methods, and he was aware that they did not enter any market for fun. If they were buyers of Daphnes at all they were out for complete control, and, being people of his own stamp, would not let the grass grow under their feet. They had obviously started on the road which was to lead to a great combine. The bulk of the shareholders were in South Africa, and he was morally certain that at this moment representatives of Glaubsteins' were on steamers bound for the Cape. Well, it behoved him to get there before them, and that could not be done by returning to England and embarking in a South African boat. No more could it be done by the Messageries line and the East African route. A bolder course was required, and, faced with apparently insurmountable difficulties, Tavanger began to enjoy himself.

He cabled to the Aero president in Berlin and to Dilling, and then set his face for Egypt. Here he struck a snag. There was no direct air line from Crete to Cairo, and if he went back to Salonika the journey would take him six days. But he managed to pick up a coasting steamer from the Piraeus, and by bribing the captain induced it to start at once. The weather grew vile, and the wretched boat took five days to wallow through the Eastern Mediterranean, while Tavanger, a bad sailor, lay deathly sick in a smelly cabin. He reached Cairo, pretty much of a physical wreck, only one day earlier than by the comfortable Salonika route.

But, as it happened, that one day made all the difference, for it enabled him to catch Dilling before he started on his southward journey. With Dilling he had all sorts of trouble, for the airman, in spite of the recommendation of the Aero president, showed himself most unwilling to take a passenger. He was flying a new type of light machine, and he wanted as his companion a skilled mechanic. I don't know how Tavanger managed to overcome his reluctance; he called in some of his airmen friends at the Cairo station, and he got the British authorities to make an international favour of the thing, but I fancy the chief weapons were his uncommon persuasive power and his personal magnetism. Anyhow, after a hectic afternoon of argument, Dilling consented.

Then began a wild adventure. Tavanger had never flown much, only pottered between Croydon and the continent, and now he found himself embarked on a flight across the wildest country on earth, with a pilot who was one-fourth scientist and three-fourths adventurer, and who did not value his own or anybody else's life at two pins. Tavanger admitted to me that at first his feet were cold. Also, Dilling on a big flight was a poor companion. His eagerness affected his temper, and his manners were those of a slave-driver and his conversation mostly insults.

As long as they were in the Nile Valley things went well enough. But in the basin of the Great Lakes they ran into a chain of thunderstorms, and after that into head-winds and massive sheets of rain. The bucketing they got played the deuce with the light machine, and engine trouble developed. They had to make a forced landing in very bad forest ground on the skirts of Ruwenzori, where they found that something had gone wrong with the petrol pump and that some of the propeller and cylinder bolts had worked loose. For forty hours they toiled in a tropical jungle cloaked in a hot wet mist, Dilling cursing steadily. Tavanger said that before they had got the machine right he had learned a good deal about air mechanics. When they started again they found that they had two lizards and a snake in their fuselage!

After that they had many minor troubles, and Dilling's temper had become so vile, owing to his disappointment at the rate of speed, that Tavanger had much ado to keep the peace. He himself had contracted a chill, and for the last ten hours of the journey had a high temperature and a blinding headache. When they reached Bulawayo and he crawled out of his seat he could scarcely stand. Dilling, having made port, became a new man. He kissed Tavanger on both cheeks, and wept when he said goodbye.

Tavanger went to an hotel, sent for a doctor, and cured himself in two days. He could not afford to waste time in bed. Also he permitted himself to be interviewed by the local press, for his journey with Dilling, in spite of the delays, had been something of a feat. He told the reporters that he had come to South Africa for a holiday, but that he hoped, while in the country, to have a look round. This of course meant business, for Tavanger's was a famous name in the circles of high finance. He mentioned no particular line, but hinted at the need for the establishment in South Africa of a certain type of steel-making plant to meet local requirements, with a possible export trade to India. He had considerable steel interests in Britain, and all this sounded quite natural. He knew that it would be cabled home, and would be read by the Anatilla people, and it seemed to him the best camouflage. If rumours got about that he was enquiring about Daphnes, they would be connected with this steel scheme and not taken too seriously.

He now controlled twenty-two thousand odd of the hundred thousand ordinary shares. There were five people in South Africa – about a dozen possibles, but five in particular – from whom he hoped to acquire the balance which would give him a controlling interest. The first was a retired railway engineer, who lived at Wynberg, near Cape Town. The second was a lawyer who had a seat in the Union Parliament, and the third was a Johannesburg stockbroker. The other two were a mining engineer employed at a Rhodesian copper mine, and a fruit farmer in the Salisbury district. Tavanger decided that he had better begin at Cape Town, for that was the point which the Anatilla emissaries would reach first, and he must not be forestalled. The Anatilla people were of course in possession of all the information about the shareholders that he had himself.

So, reflecting that he was playing a game which seemed to belong to some crude romance of boyhood, Tavanger flew to Cape Town, and put up at the Mount Nelson. He had various friends in the city, but his first business was to study a passenger list of the incoming steamers. The tourist traffic to South Africa does not begin till after Christmas, so he found the lists small, and most of the people, with the help of the shipping clerks, he was able to identify. None of the passengers gave an American address, but he decided that the Anatilla representative was one or other of two men, Robson and Steinacker. Then he gave a luncheon to some of his friends, and proceeded to sound them cautiously about the retired railway man at Wynberg, whose name was Barrowman.

It turned out that he was a well-known figure, a vigorous youth of sixty whose hobbies were botany and mountaineering. Now, Tavanger in his youth had been an active member of the Alpine Club – he had begun climbing as a boy with his Swiss relations – and he was delighted to find a ready-made link.

It was arranged that he should meet Barrowman at dinner at the house of one of his friends at Muizenberg, and presently, on a superb moonlit night, with the long tides breaking beneath them on the white sands, he sat on the Muizenberg stoep next a trim little man who overflowed with pent-up enthusiasms. Barrowman had made a comfortable small fortune by his profession, and was now bent on sampling all the enjoyments which had been crowded out of a busy life. He was a bachelor, and had settled at Wynberg in order that he might be near Table Mountain, on whose chimneys and traverses he was the chief authority. Tavanger conjured up his early ardour, asked eagerly concerning the different routes and the quality of the rock, and gladly accepted Barrowman's offer to take him next day to the summit of the mountain.

They spent some very hot and fatiguing hours in kloofs which were too full of vegetable matter for comfort, and reached the summit by a difficult and not over-safe chimney. Tavanger was badly out of practice and training, and at one point was in serious danger. However, the top was won at last, and Barrowman was in the best of tempers, for it pleased him to find one, who was some years his junior and who had done most of the legendary courses in the Alps, so manifestly his inferior in skill and endurance. So as they ate their luncheon on the dusty tableland he expanded happily.

It appeared that he thought of retiring for good to England. He had climbed everything in South Africa worth climbing, including the buttresses of Mont Aux Sources, and he wanted to be nearer the classic ground of his hobby. Also he dreamed of an English garden where he could acclimatise much of the Cape flora... He would like, however, to realise some of his South African holdings. All his eggs were in the one basket, and, if he was going to settle at home, he ought to distribute them better. In England one could not watch South African stocks with the requisite closeness. "The trouble," he said, "is that it's a rotten time to change investments. Good enough for the buyer, but the devil for the seller... Do you know anything about these things?"

"A little," Tavanger answered. "You see, they're more or less my profession. I should be delighted to help you. If your things are sound, there is generally a fair market to be had, if you take a little pains to find it."

So three hours later in the Wynberg bungalow he went with Barrowman over his holdings. Most were good enough – town lots in Johannesburg, Bulawayo and Durban, investment company debentures, one or two deep-level gold properties which were paying high dividends; but there was a certain amount of junk, mostly land development companies where Barrowman had come in on the ground-floor. "Oh, and there's those Daphnes," Barrowman said wryly. "God knows why I ever got let in for them. There was a man at Salisbury who swore by them, and as I was rather flush of money at the time I plunged. I meant to realise in a month or two, but the darned things have never paid a penny, and no one will look at them. I've tried to get rid of them, but I was never bid more than five bob."

Tavanger took a lot of pains with Barrowman's list, and, since he seemed to possess uncanny knowledge of the markets of the world and was a fellow-mountaineer, Barrowman accepted all he said for gospel. He advised holding on to the town lots and the debentures, but taking the first favourable moment to sell the deep levels, the producing life of which was limited. As the dividends were high they would fetch a reasonable figure. As to the unsaleable junk, Barrowman had better hold on; you never knew how a dud might turn out. "I can get you a fair price for your Daphnes," he added. "They're not everybody's stock, but they might have their uses."

"What sort of price?" Barrowman asked. "I bought them at par, you know."

"I can get you sixteen and six," was the answer. "At least, I think I can... I tell you what I'll do. This is my own line of country, and as a speculation I'll buy them from you at that price. Call it a small return for your hospitality."

This was the price that Tavanger had paid in London, and Barrowman jumped at it. "I felt so generous," Tavanger told me, "that I took over also a block of shares in a thing called the Voortrekkers, a land company which owned a lot of Portuguese bush-veld, and had sat tight on its undeveloped holding for twenty years. Barrowman almost wept when I gave him my cheque for the lot. I really felt that I had done well by him, for, when you added the worthless Voortrekkers, I had paid pretty nearly par for the Daphne shares."

The next step was easy. The lawyer-politician, Dove by name, Tavanger had already met. He was frankly hard up, for he had spoiled a good practice by going into Parliament, and at the same time was determined to stick to politics, where his chief ambition lay. He knew all about Tavanger by repute, and actually sought him out to consult him. Tavanger was friendly, and declared himself anxious to help a man who had so sound a notion of the future of the Empire. A directorship or two might be managed – he controlled various concerns with South African boards – he would look into the matter when he got home. He counselled Dove to give as much time as he could to the Bar – he would do what he could to put work in his way. Thus encouraged, Dove opened his heart. He wanted money, not in the future but now – there were payments due on certain irrigated lands which he owned, and he did not want to have the mortgages foreclosed. But everything was at such ruination prices, and if he sold any of his sound investments it would be at a hideous loss. Tavanger asked him what he had, and in the list given him was a block of Daphne shares about which Dove was blasphemous. Tavanger appeared to consider deeply.

"I'll tell you what I'll do," he said at length. "I'll buy your Daphnes. I might make something of them. They're not worth half a crown to the ordinary operator, but they're worth more than that to me. To *me*, and I believe to scarcely anybody else. I'll give you sixteen and sixpence for them."

Dove stared and stammered. "Do you mean it? It's tremendous. But I can't take it, you know. It's pure charity."

"Not a bit of it," said Tavanger. "I quote you sixteen and six because I happen to know that that was the price paid for a block in London the other day by a man who was very much in my position. It's a gamble, of course, but that's my business."

As Tavanger was leaving the club, where he had been having an early lunch with Dove, he ran into Barrowman in the company of a lean, spectacled gentleman, whose particular quality of tan proclaimed that he had just landed from a sea voyage. Barrowman was effusive in his greetings and longings for another talk before Tavanger sailed. "I can't wait now," he said. "I've got to give a man luncheon. A fellow called Steinacker, an

American who has an introduction to me from one of my old directors."

Tavanger took the night mail to Johannesburg, feeling that he had won his first race by a short head.

The next proposition was tougher. The Johannesburg stockbroker, Nall by name, to whom he had taken the precaution of being introduced by cable from London, received him royally, insisted on putting him up in his big house in the Sachsenwaid, and gave a dinner for him at the Rand Club, to which most of the magnates of the place were bidden. Tavanger was of course a household name in these circles, and there was much curiosity as to what he was doing in South Africa. He stuck, both in private talk and in his interviews with the Press, to his original story: he was there for a holiday – had long wanted to fly Africa from north to south – was becoming interested in commercial aviation – hoped to get some notion of how South Africa was shaping – had some idea of a new steel industry. He made a speech at the Rand Club dinner in which he expounded certain views on the currency situation throughout the globe and the importance of discovering new gold-fields. For three days he feasted and talked at large, never saying anything that mattered, but asking innumerable questions. Nall watched him with a quizzical smile.

On the third evening, in the seclusion of the smoking-room, his host took off his glasses and looked at him with his shrewd eyes, a little bleared with the Rand dust.

"Seriously, Mr Tavanger, what are you here for? That steel business story won't wash, you know."

"Why not?" Tavanger asked.

"Because you have already turned down that proposition when it was made to you."

"May not a man have second thoughts?"

"He may, but not you – not after the reasons you gave last year."

Tavanger laughed. "All right. Have it your own way. Would you be surprised to learn that the simple explanation is true? I wanted a holiday. I wanted to fling my heels and get rid of London for a month or two. I was getting infernally stale. Are you clever enough to realise that the plain reason is often the right one?... But being here, I had to pretend that I had some sort of business purpose. It's a kind of *lèse-majesté* for people like me to get quit of the shop."

"Good," said Nall. "That is what I thought myself. But being here, I take it you're not averse to doing a little business."

"By no means. I have had my fling, and now I'm quite ready to pick up anything that's going. What have you to suggest? I had better say straight off that I don't want gold-mines. I don't understand that business, and I've always made it a rule never to touch them. And I don't want town lots. I carry enough of the darned things in the city of London."

"Good," said Nall again. "Now we understand each other. I wonder what would interest you."

That was the first of several long and intricate talks. If Tavanger brought up the subject of Daphnes, at once Nall would become suspicious and ask a fancy price – or refuse to sell at all, for there was no such motive as in the cases of Dove and Barrowman. His only hope was to reach the subject by the method of exhaustion. So Tavanger had to listen while all the assets of South Africa were displayed before him – ferrous and nonferrous metals, rubies in the Lebombo hills, electric power from the streams that descended the Berg, new types of irrigation, new fruits and cereals and fibres, a variety of fancy minerals. He professed to be interested in a new copper area, and in the presence of corundum in the eastern mountains. Then Nall mentioned michelite. In a level voice Tavanger asked about it, and was given a glowing account of the possibilities of the Daphne Concessions.

"That subject rather interests me," Tavanger said, "for I know a German chemist, Sprenger, who is the chief authority on it. They're up against every kind of snag, which they won't get over in our time, but it might be the kind of thing to buy and lock away for one's grandchildren."

Nall demurred. On the contrary, michelite was on the edge of a mighty boom, and in a year Daphnes would be soaring. When Tavanger shook his head, he repeated his view, and added, by way of confirmation, that he held twenty thousand Daphnes which he meant at all costs to stick to.

"I have some michelite shares, I think," said Tavanger, after an apparent effort of reminiscence, "and like you, I shall stick to them. Indeed, I wouldn't mind getting a few more. My children will curse me, but my grandchildren may bless me."

Again and again they went over the list, and Tavanger gave the impression that he was seriously interested in corundum, moderately in copper, and very mildly in michelite, though he thought the last not practical business at the moment. He adopted the pose of a man who had no desire for anything more, but might take a few oddments if his capricious appetite were tempted. Presently he discovered that Nall was very keen about the corundum affair, and was finding it difficult to get together the requisite working capital. Tavanger poured all the cold water he could on the scheme, but Nall's faith was proof against it.

"I want you to help, Mr Tavanger. I want your money, but still more I want your name."

Tavanger yawned. "You've been uncommonly kind to me," he said, "and I'd like to give you a hand. Also I rather fancy picking up some little thing wherever I go, just as a tripper buys souvenirs. But your Lebombo business is quite outside my beat."

"Is that final?" Nall asked.

"Yes… Well, no – I'll tell you what I'll do. You want ready money, and I have a little in hand. I'll put up ten thousand for the Lebombo, and I'll buy your Daphne shares. There's no market for them at present, you tell me. Well, I'll make you a fair offer. I'll give you sixteen and six, which was about the best price last year for Anatillas."

Nall wrinkled his brow.

"Why do you want them?" he asked.

"Because they are in my line, which corundum isn't. I have already some michelite shares, as I told you, and I believe it's a good investment for my family."

"I would rather not sell."

"Then the whole deal is off. Believe me, my dear fellow, I shall be quite happy to go home without putting a penny into South Africa. I came out here literally for my health."

Then Nall tried to screw up the price for Daphnes, but there he met with such a final negative that he relinquished the attempt. The result was that two days later Tavanger took the train for Delagoa Bay, with ten thousand more Daphnes to his credit and a liability for ten thousand pounds, his share in the underwriting of the coming flotation of the Lebombo Corundum Corporation.

From Lourenço Marquez he sailed to Beira, and ascended to the Rhodesian plateau. There he stepped off the plank into deepish waters. The two remaining holders of Daphnes lived in the country north of Salisbury, both a long distance from railhead, but fairly near each other. Tavanger decided to take Devenish first, who had a fruit farm in the hills about forty miles from a station. He was a little puffed up by his successes, and anticipated no difficulties; he did not trouble to enquire about Devenish or the other man, Greenlees, or to get introductions to them; he was inclined now to trust to his unaided powers of persuasion, and meant to drop in on them as a distinguished stranger touring the country.

It was early summer in those parts, when rain might be looked for, but so far the weather had been dry. The roads were in good order and Tavanger hired a car in Salisbury in which he proposed to make the trip. But he had not gone twenty miles before the heavens opened. The country had been smoking with bush-fires, but these were instantly put out by a torrential deluge. The roads had never been properly engineered and had no real bottom, and in an hour or two the hard red grit had been turned into a foot or two of gummy red mud, while the shallow fords had swollen to lagoons. With immense difficulty the car reached the dorp on the railway line, which was the nearest point to Devenish's farm. Tavanger put up at the wretched hotel, and made enquiries. He got hold of an old transport driver called Potgieter, who told him that the car was as useless as a perambulator. His only chance of getting to Devenish next day was by cape-cart and a span of mules, and that, unless the rain stopped, was not very rosy.

Tavanger left the car and the driver in the dorp, and started next morning with Potgieter in the same relentless deluge. The transport-rider was an old hand at the game, but even he confessed that he had never travelled in worse conditions. The road was mostly impossible, so they took to the open veld among ant-heaps and meerkat holes which threatened to wrench the wheels off. The worst trouble was with the streams that came down from the hills on their left, each a tawny torrent. Also they struck many patches of marsh, which they had to circumnavigate, and in one vlei they spent an hour getting the wheels of the cart out of the mire. The mist hung close about them, and if Potgieter had not known the road like his own hand, they would have been wandering in circles. At a native village half-way, they heard that a bigger stream in front was impassable, but they managed to cross with the mules swimming, while Potgieter performed miracles with his long whip. But the end came when they were still five miles from their destination. The cape-cart smashed its axle in an extra deep mud-hole, and the rest of the journey was performed on foot, with Potgieter driving the mules before him. Soaked to the bone and mud to the eyes, Tavanger presented himself at Devenish's little farm. Instead of arriving in a lordly way in a touring car, he appeared out of the mist, a very weary, hungry, and dishevelled tramp.

As it turned out it was the best thing that could have happened. Devenish was a simple, hospitable soul with a taste for letters, who had lately taken to himself a like-minded wife. He was profoundly suspicious of the dwellers in cities, especially the financial folk who played tricks with the market for his fruit and tobacco. He had inherited his Daphne holding from an uncle, and had personally never bought or sold a share in his life. Had Tavanger arrived in a smart car with the air of a moneyed man of affairs, Devenish would have looked on him with deep distrust. But this muddy and famished stranger, who was obviously an educated man, he took to his heart, prepared a hot bath for him, lent him dry clothes, and fed him handsomely on broiled chicken, green mealies and Afrikander sausages.

That night, while Potgieter puffed his deep-bowled pipe and dozed, Tavanger and Devenish talked of books and home. As luck would have it Mrs Devenish came from that part of Norfolk where Tavanger for a long time had had a shoot, and they were able to identify common friends. The fruit-farmer was very much in love with his job, but both he and his wife were a little starved of conversation with their own kind, and the evening was a great occasion for them. Mrs Devenish played Schubert on the cottage piano, and they all went to bed very good friends. Not a word had been spoken of business, for Tavanger had sized up his host and realised that he must proceed cautiously.

But the thing proved to be simplicity itself. Next morning came one of those breaks in the rain, when a hot sun shone on a steaming earth. Devenish conducted his guest round his property – the orchards of peach and apricot and naartje, the tobacco lands, the dam shining like a turquoise amid the pale emerald of the alfalfa fields. He told him the tale of his successes and his difficulties; even with the bad prices of tobacco he was covering costs (he had some private income to live on), but he badly needed more capital for development. He wanted to make a second dam and lay out a new orchard for a special kind of plum, but he was determined not to mortgage his farm. Where was the money to come from? Tavanger enquired tactfully about his possessions, and heard about the seven thousand Daphne shares which he had inherited. Devenish had already made some attempt to sell these, for he had no views on the subject of michelite, but had found them unsaleable except at a price which he regarded as a swindle. He was such an innocent that he believed that if a share was nominally worth a pound any man who offered him less was trying to cheat him... The upshot was that Tavanger bought the seven thousand Daphnes, but had to buy them at par. He realised that he might argue till Doomsday before he got Devenish to understand the position, and that any attempt at bargaining would awake suspicions in his host. He had never met a man so compounded of caution and ignorance.

Devenish had a blacksmith's shop on his farm, and his overseer was a good mechanic, so the cape-cart was fetched from the mud-hole and given a new axle. The rain kept off that day, but the next morning when they started for Greenlees' mine it began again in grim earnest. They had about fifty miles to go through a wild bit of country, which did not contain even a native village, and the road was at its best only a scar on the veld, and, when it ran through bush, scarcely wider than a foot-track. Devenish insisted on providing them with plenty of food, which was fortunate, for they took three days to reach Greenlees...

This was the best part of Tavanger's story, but I must confine myself to the bare outline. They struck a river at what was usually a broad shallow ford, but was now a lake of yeasty water. It was the only possible place, for above and below the stream ran a defile among rocks, and the whole outfit was nearly drowned before they made the crossing. But they found themselves on an island, for another branch of the river, broader, deeper and swifter, confronted them a hundred yards farther on. This proved hopeless, and Potgieter tried to recross the first branch, with the notion of making a circuit and finding an easier ford farther up. But the water was rising every minute, and even the transport-rider's stout heart failed him. He announced that there was nothing to be done except to wait for the river to fall. Happily the island was high ground, so there was no risk of its being overflowed.

They spent two nights and a day in that dismal place, which in twelve hours had shrunk to the limits of about a couple of acres. It was covered with low scrub, but this was no shelter from the unceasing rain. Potgieter made a scherm for the mules out of wait-a-bit thorns, and inside it rigged up a sort of tent with the cover of the cape-cart. It was as well that he did this, for the two men were not the only refugees on the island. Various kinds of buck had been cut off by the flood, and bush-pig, and the mules were in a perpetual ferment, which Potgieter said was due to lions. Tavanger more than once thought he saw a tawny, slinking shadow in the undergrowth. They got a sort of fire going, but there was no decent fuel to burn, and the best they could do was a heap of smoking twigs. Potgieter shot a brace of guinea-fowl, which they cooked for dinner in the scanty ashes. He would not let Tavanger stir from the scherm, for he said that the island would be full of storm-stayed snakes and other unhallowed oddments. So the wretched pair had to twiddle their thumbs for thirty-six hours in an atmosphere like a Turkish bath, coughing and choking by the greenwood fire, and subsisting for the most part on Devenish's cold viands. Unluckily they had neither tea nor coffee, and their tobacco ran out. Tavanger got a furious cold in his head and rheumatic pains in his back, but the worst discomfort was the utter boredom; for Potgieter had no small talk, and slept most of the time.

Late on the second night the rain ceased, and revealed a wonderful sky of stars. On the second morning the river had fallen sufficiently to be forded, and mules and men, very stiff and miserable, started off for Greenlees. But their troubles were not over, for the valley they presently struck seemed to have melted into primeval slime, and when they got on to the higher ground they had to make lengthy detours to circumvent landslips. It was almost dark when they reached the mine, and it took Greenlees some time, Tavanger said, to realise that they were human. When he did, when he understood who Tavanger was – having spent some time in a London office he knew him by repute – and recognised Potgieter as a man with whom he had once hunted, he was hospitable enough. In an empty *rondavel* he filled two wooden tubs with scalding water, into which he put a tin of mustard and a can of sheep-deep, declaring that it was the only way to stave off pneumonia.

Greenlees proved the simplest of the five to deal with, for he was an enthusiast about michelite. He was a Scotsman from Berwickshire, who had had a sound university training and knew a good deal about metallurgical chemistry as well as about engineering. He had been employed at the Daphne mine when it first began, and had believed so firmly in its prospects that he had scraped up every penny he could muster at the time and bought a biggish holding. Then he had quarrelled with the manager, but his faith in the concern had not wavered. He declared that it was abominably managed, that the costs were far too high, and the marketing arrangements rudimentary, but nevertheless, he was convinced that before long it would be one of the most lucrative concerns in the country. He anticipated, for one thing, some discovery which would bring down the smelting costs. "I'll hold on," he said, "though I should have to go wanting the breeks to do it."

Tavanger, seeing the sort of man he had to deal with, put his cards on the table. He told Greenlees frankly that he meant to control Daphne. He described, as only Tavanger could describe, the manoeuvres by which he had acquired the big London block, his journey to South Africa ("God, but you're the determined one," said Greenlees), his doings at the Cape and in Johannesburg, and his wild trek in the Rhodesian rains.

"I want to buy your holding, Mr Greenlees," he concluded. "I will pay any price you fix, and will contract to sell you the shares back on demand any time after next June at the price I gave for them. What I want is control of the stock till then, and for the privilege I am ready to pay you a bonus of one thousand pounds."

Of course Greenlees consented, for he saw that Tavanger was a believer like himself, and so far he had not met another. He asked various questions. Tavanger said nothing about the coming combine, but let him think that his views were the same as his own, a belief that presently a scientific discovery would make michelite a commodity of universal use. He mentioned having talked with Sprenger in Berlin, and Greenlees nodded respectfully.

They sat late into the night discussing the future. Greenlees explained the system at work at the Daphne mine, and how it could be bettered, and Tavanger then and there offered him the managership. It was a London company, and its annual shareholders' meeting fell in January; Tavanger proposed drastically to reconstruct both the English and South African boards and to reform the management.

"What about having a look at the place?" Greenlees asked. "You could easily look in on your way down country."

Tavanger shook his head. "I'm not a technical expert," he said, "and I would learn very little. I've always made it a rule never to mix myself up with things I don't understand. But I reckon myself a fair judge of men, and I shall be content to trust you."

As they went to bed Greenlees showed him a telegram. "Did you ever hear of this fellow? Steinacker or Stemacker his name is. He wants to see me – has an introduction from the chairman of my company. I wired to him to come along, and he is turning up the day after tomorrow."

This was the story which Tavanger told me that night in my rooms. His adventures seemed to have renewed his youth, for he looked actually boyish, and I understood that half the power of the man – and indeed of anyone who succeeds in his line – lay just in a boyish readiness to fling his cap on the right occasion over the moon.

"I deserve to win out, don't you think?" he said, "for I've risked my neck by air, land and water – not to mention black mambas... I should like to have seen Steinacker's face when he had finished gleaning in my tracks... The next thing is to get to grips with Glaubsteins. Oh yes, I'll keep you informed. You're the only man I can talk to frankly about this business, and half the fun of an adventure is to be able to gossip about it."

III

I saw nothing of Tavanger again till the end of February, when he appeared as a witness for the defence in a case in which I led for the plaintiff, and I had the dubious pleasure of cross-examining him. I say "dubious," for he was one of the most formidable witnesses I have ever met, candid, accurate, self-possessed and unshakable. Two days later I had to make a speech – an old promise to him – at the annual meeting, in the hall of the Fletchers' Company, of the children's hospital of which he was chairman. There I saw a new Tavanger, one who spoke of the hospital and its work as a man speaks of his family in a moment of expansion, who had every detail at his fingers' end and who descanted on its future with a sober passion. I was amazed, till I remembered that this was one of his two hobbies. He was Master of the Company, so he gave me tea afterwards in his private room, and expanded on the new dental clinic which he said was the next step in the hospital's progress.

"I mean to present the clinic," he told me, "if things turn out well. That is why I'm so keen about this Daphne business..."

He stopped and smiled at me.

"I know that I'm reputed to be very well off, and I can see that you're wondering why I don't present it in any case, since presumably I can afford it. Perhaps I can, but that has never been my way. I have for years kept a separate account which I call my 'gambling fund,' and into it goes whatever comes to me by the grace of God outside the main line of my business. I draw on that account for my hobbies – my pictures and my hospital. Whatever I make out of Daphnes will go there, and if my luck is in I may be able to make the hospital the best-equipped thing of its kind on the globe. That way, you see, I get a kind of sporting interest in the game.

"Oh, we have brisked up Daphnes a bit," he said in reply to my question. "I'm chairman now – my predecessor was an elderly titled nonentity who was easily induced to retire. We had our annual meeting last month, and the two vacancies on the directorate which occurred by rotation were filled by my own men. We've cleaned up the South African board too. Greenlees is now chairman, as well as general manager of the mine. He has already reduced the costs of mining the stuff, and we're getting a bigger share of the British import... No, there's been no reduction of price, though that may come. We stick to the same price as the other companies. There is a modest market for our shares, too, when they're offered, which isn't often. The price is about fifteen shillings, pretty much the same as Anatillas.

"I own fifty-two thousand shares out of the hundred thousand ordinaries," he went on, "just enough to give me control with a small margin. They have cost me the best part of seventy thousand pounds, but I consider them a good bargain. For Glaubsteins have opened the ball. They're determined to get Daphne into their pool, and I am quite willing to oblige them – at my own price." Tavanger's smile told me the kind of price that would be.

"Oh yes, they're nibbling hard. I hear that Steinacker managed to pick up about ten thousand shares in South Africa, and now they are stuck fast. They must come to me, and they've started a voluptuous curve in my direction. You know the way people like Glaubsteins work. The man who approaches you may be a simple fellow who never heard of them. They like to have layers of agents between themselves and the man they're after. Well, I've had offers for my Daphnes through one of my banks, and through two insurance companies, and through" – he mentioned the name of a solid and rather chauvinistic British financial house which was supposed to lay a rigid embargo on anything speculative. His intelligence department, he said, was pretty good, and the connection had been traced.

"They've offered me par," he continued. "The dear innocents! The fact is, they can't get on without me, and they know it, but at present they are only manoeuvring for position. When we get down to real business, we'll talk a different language."

As I have said, I had guessed that Tavanger was working on a piece of knowledge which he had got at Flambard, and I argued that this could only be a world-wide merger of michelite interests. He knew this for a fact, and was therefore gambling on what he believed to be a certainty. Consequently he could afford to wait. I am a novice in such matters, but it seemed to me that the only possible snag was Sprenger. Sprenger was a man of genius, and though he was loyal to the German company, I had understood from Tavanger that there was a working arrangement between that company and the Anatilla. At any moment he might make some discovery which would alter the whole industrial status of michelite, and no part of the benefit of such a discovery would go to the Daphne Concessions. I mentioned my doubt.

"I realise that," said Tavanger, "and I am keeping Sprenger under observation. Easy enough to manage, for I have many lines down in Berlin. My information is that for the moment he has come to a halt. Indeed, he has had a breakdown, and has been sent off for a couple of months to some high place in the Alps. Also Anatilla and Rosas are not on the friendliest terms at present. Glaubsteins have been trying to buy out the Germans, and since they have lent them money, I fancy the method of procedure was rather arbitrary. They'll get them in the end, of course, but just now relations are rather strained, and it will take a fair amount of time to ease them."

The word "time" impressed me. Clearly Tavanger believed that he had a free field up to the tenth of June – after which nothing mattered.

"I'm a babe in finance," I said. "But wouldn't it be wise to screw up Anatilla to a good offer as soon as possible, and close with it. It's an uncertain world, and you never know what trick fortune may play you."

He smiled. "You're a cautious lawyer, and I'm a bit of an adventurer. I mean to play this game with the stakes high. The way I look at it is this. Glaubsteins have unlimited resources, and they believe firmly in the future of michelite. So for that matter do I. They want to have control of the world output against the day when the boom comes. They can't do without me, for I own what is practically the largest supply and certainly the best quality. Very well, they must treat."

"Yes, but they may spin out the negotiations if you open your mouth too wide. There is no reason why they should be in a hurry. And meantime something may happen to lower the value of your property. You never know."

He shook his head.

"No. I am convinced they will bring things to a head by midsummer."

He looked curiously at something which he saw in my face. In that moment he realised, I think, that I had divined his share in that morning session at Flambard.

IV

A few weeks later I happened to run across a member of the firm of stockbrokers who did my modest business.

"You were asking about michelite in the autumn," he said. "There's a certain liveliness in the market just now. There has been a number of dealings in Daphnes – you mentioned them, I think – at rather a fancy price – round about eighteen shillings. I don't recommend them, but if you want something to put away you might do worse than buy Anatillas. For some reason or other their price has come down to twelve shillings. In my opinion you would be perfectly safe with them. Glaubsteins are behind them, you know, and Glaubsteins don't make mistakes. It would be a lock-up investment, but certain to appreciate."

I thanked him, but told him that I was not looking for any new investments.

That very night I met Tavanger at dinner and, since the weather was dry and fine, we walked part of the way home together. I asked him what he had been doing to depress Anatillas.

"We've cut prices," he replied. "We could afford to do so, for our costs of getting michelite out of the ground have always been twenty-five per cent lower than the other companies'. We practically quarry the stuff, and the ore is in a purer state. Under Greenlees' management the margin is still greater, so we could afford a bold stroke. So far the result has been good. We have extended our market, and though we are making a smaller profit per ton, it has increased the quantity sold by about twenty per cent. But that, of course, wasn't my real object. I wanted to frighten Anatilla and make them more anxious to deal. I fancy I've rattled them a bit, for, as you seem to have observed, the price of their ordinaries has had a nasty jolt."

"Couldn't you force them down farther?" I suggested. "When you get them low enough you might be able to buy Anatilla and make the merger yourself."

"Not for worlds!" he said. "You don't appreciate the difference between the financier and the industrialist. Supposing I engineered the merger. I should be left with it on my hands till I could sell it to somebody else. I'm not the man who makes things, but the man who provides the money for other people to make them with. Besides, Glaubsteins would never sell – not on your life. They've simply got to control a stuff with the possibilities of michelite. With their enormous mineral and metal interests, and all their commercial subsidiaries, they couldn't afford to let it get out of their hands. They're immensely rich, and could put down a thousand pounds for every hundred that any group I got together could produce. Believe me, they'll hang

85

on to michelite till their last gasp. And rightly – because they are users. They have a policy for dealing with it. I'm only a pirate who sails in and demands ransom because they've become a little negligent on the voyage."

I asked how the negotiations were proceeding.

"According to plan. We've got rid of some of the agency layers, and have now arrived at one remove from the principals. My last step, as I have said, woke them up. Javerts have now taken a hand in it, and Javerts, as you may or may not know, do most of the English business for Glaubsteins. They are obviously anxious to bring things to a head pretty soon, for they have bid me sixty shillings a share."

"Take it, man," I said. "It will give you more than a hundred per cent profit."

"Not enough. Besides, I want to get alongside Glaubsteins themselves. No intermediaries for me. That's bound to happen too. When you see in the press that Mr Bronson Jane has arrived in Europe, then you may know that we're entering on the last lap."

We parted at Hyde Park Corner, and I watched him set off westward with his shoulders squared and his step as light as a boy's. This Daphne adventure was assuredly renewing Tavanger's youth.

Some time in May I read in my morning paper the announcement of Sprenger's death. *The Times* had an obituary which mentioned michelite as only one of his discoveries. It said that no chemist had made greater practical contributions to industry in our time, but most of the article was devoted to his purely scientific work, in which it appeared that he had been among the first minds in Europe. This was during the General Election, when I had no time for more than a hasty thought as to how this news would affect Daphne.

When it was all over and I was back in London, I had a note from Tavanger asking me to dinner. We dined alone in his big house in Kensington Palace Gardens, where he kept his picture collection. I remembered that I could not take my eyes off a superb Vermeer which hung over the dining-room mantelpiece. I was in that condition of bodily and mental depression which an election always induces in me, and I was inclined to resent Tavanger's abounding vitality. For he was in the best of spirits, with just a touch of that shamefacedness with which a man, who has been holidaying extravagantly, regards one who has had his nose to the grindstone. He showed no desire to exhibit his treasures; he wanted to talk about michelite.

Sprenger was dead – a tragedy for the world of science, but a fortunate event for Daphne. No longer need a bombshell be feared from that quarter. He seemed to have left no records behind him which might contain the germ of a possible discovery; indeed, for some months he had been a sick and broken man.

"It's a brutal world," said Tavanger, "when I can regard with equanimity the disappearance of a great man who never did me any harm. But there it is. Sprenger was the danger-point for me, and he was Anatilla's trump card. His death brought Bronson Jane across the Atlantic by the first boat. His arrival was in the papers, but I dare say you haven't been reading them very closely."

It appeared that Jane had gone straight to Berlin, and, owing to the confusion caused by Sprenger's death, had succeeded in acquiring the control of Rosas for Anatilla. That was the one advantage he could get out of the catastrophe. It was a necessary step towards the ultimate combine, but in practice it would not greatly help Anatilla, for Daphne remained the keystone. Two days ago Jane had arrived in England, and Tavanger had seen him.

"You have never met Bronson Jane?" he asked. "But you must know all about him. He is the new thing in American big business, and you won't find a more impressive type on the globe... Reasonably young – not much more than forty – rather good-looking and with charming manners... A scratch golfer, and quite a considerable performer at polo, I believe... The kind of education behind him which makes us all feel ignoramuses – good degree at college, the Harvard Law School, then a most comprehensive business training in America and Europe... The sort of man who is considered equally eligible for the presidency of a college, the charge of a department of State, or the control of a world-wide business corporation. We don't breed anything quite like it on this side. He is over here for Glaubsteins, primarily, but he had to dash off to Geneva to make a speech on some currency question, and next week he is due in Paris for a conference about German reparations. Tomorrow I believe he is dining with Geraldine and the politicians. He dined here last night alone with me, and knew rather more about my pictures than I knew myself, though books are his own particular hobby. A most impressive human being, I assure you. Agreeable too, the kind of man you'd like to go fishing with."

"Is the deal through?" I asked.

"Not quite. He was very frank. He said that Glaubsteins wanted Daphne because they could use it, whereas it was no manner of good to me. I was equally frank, and assented. Then he said that if I held out I would be encumbered with a thing I could not develop – never could develop, whereas Glaubsteins could bring it at once into their great industrial pool and be working day and night on its problems. All the more need for that since Sprenger was dead. Again I assented. He said that he believed firmly in michelite, and I said that so did I. Finally, he asked if I wanted anything more than to turn the thing over at a handsome profit. I said I wanted nothing more, only the profit must be handsome.

"So we started bargaining," Tavanger continued, "and I ran him up to eighty shillings. There he stuck his toes into the ground, and not an inch could I induce him to budge. I assume that that figure was the limit of his instructions, and that he'd have to cable for fresh ones. He'll get them, I have no doubt. We've to meet again when he comes back from Paris."

"It seems to me an enormous price," I said. "In a few months you've forced the shares up from under par to four pounds. If it was my show I should be content with that."

"I want five pounds!" he said firmly. "That is the figure I fixed in my mind when I first took up the business, and I mean to have it."

He saw a doubt in my eye and went on. "I'm not asking anything unreasonable. Anatilla must have their merger, and in a year or two Daphnes will be worth more than five pounds to them – not to everybody, but to them. My terms are moderation itself compared with what Brock asked and got for his tin-pot railway in the Central Pacific merger, or Assher for his rotten newspaper. I'm giving solid value for the money. You should see Greenlees' reports. He says there is enough michelite in prospect to supply every steel plant on earth for a century."

We smoked afterwards in the library, and I noticed a sheaf of plans on the table. Tavanger's eye followed mine.

"Yes, that's the lay-out for the new clinic. We mean to start building in the autumn."

V

I was in my chambers, dictating an opinion, when my clerk brought me Tavanger's card. I had seen or heard nothing of him since that dinner at his house, and the financial columns of the press had been silent about michelite. All I had noticed was a slight rise in Anatilla shares owing to the acquisition of Rosas, the news of which had been officially published in America. Bronson Jane seemed to be still in England, judging from the press, and he had been pointed out to me on the other side of the table at a City dinner. It was a fine June evening, and I was just about to stretch my legs by strolling down to the House.

"The weather tempted me to walk home," said Tavanger, when I had dismissed my clerk and settled him in my only armchair, "and it suddenly occurred to me that I might catch you here. Can you give me ten minutes? I've a lot to tell you."

"It's all over? You've won, of course," I said. His air was so cheerful that it must mean victory.

He laughed – not ironically, or ruefully, but with robust enjoyment. Tavanger had certainly acquired a pleasant boyishness from this enterprise.

"On the contrary," he said, "I have found my Waterloo. I have abdicated and am in full retreat."

I could only stare.

"What on earth went wrong?" I stammered. "Who was your Wellington?"

"My Wellington?" he repeated. "Yes, that's the right question to ask. I struck a Wellington who was not my match perhaps, but he had the big battalions behind him. It wasn't Bronson Jane. I had him in a cleft stick. It was a lad who was raised, I believe, in a Montana shack."

Then he told me the story. Sprenger had been under agreement with Anatilla to communicate to them from time to time the data on which he was busy. To these Glaubsteins had turned on their own research department, and they had put in charge of it a very brilliant young metallurgical chemist called Untermeyer. He had been working on michelite for the better part of two years, chiefly the problems of a simpler and more economical method of smelting. Well, as luck would have it, he stumbled on the missing link in the process which poor Sprenger had been searching for – had an inkling of it, said Tavanger with awe in his tone, just after Sprenger's death, and proved it beyond a peradventure on the very night when Bronson Jane had dined in Kensington Palace Gardens. Jane's cable for permission to make a higher bid for the Daphne shares was answered by a message which put a very different complexion on the business.

Glaubsteins had lost no time. They had cabled to take out provisional patents in every country in the world, and they had opened up negotiations with the chief American steel interests. There could be no doubt about the success of the new process. Even in its present form it brought down smelting costs by half, and it was doubtless capable of improvement. Michelite, instead of being a commodity with a restricted market, would soon have a world-wide use, and those who controlled michelite would reap a rich harvest.

Michelite *plus* the new patented process. That was the whole point. The process had been thoroughly proven, and Tavanger said that there was no doubt that it could be fully protected by patents. The steel firms would work under a licence from Glaubsteins, and one of the terms of such a licence would be that they took their michelite from Anatilla. The steel industry on one side became practically a tied-house for Glaubsteins, and Daphne was left in the cold.

"It's a complete knock-out," said Tavanger. "Our lower mining costs and our purer quality, which enabled us to cut the price, don't signify at all. They are all washed out by the huge reduction in smelting costs under the new process. Nobody's going to buy an ounce of our stuff any more. It's quite true that if michelite gets into general use Glaubsteins will want our properties. But they can afford to wait and starve us out. They have enough to go on with in the Anatilla and Rosas mines. There never was a prettier calling of a man's bluff."

I asked what he had done.

"Chucked in my hand. It was the only course. Bronson Jane was quite decent about it. He gave me par for my Daphne shares, which was far better than I could have hoped. Also, he agreed to my condition about keeping on Greenlees in the management. I am only about twenty thousand pounds to the bad, and I've had a lot of sport for my money. Funny to think that three weeks ago I could have got out of Daphne with a cool profit of one hundred and forty thousand."

"I am sorry about the clinic," I said.

"You needn't be," was the answer. "I mean to present it just the same. This very afternoon I approved the final plans. It will be provided for out of my 'gambling fund,' according to my practice. I shall sell my Vermeer to pay for it... It's a clinic for looking after children's teeth, but in the circumstances it would have been more appropriate if it had been for looking after their eyes. The gift is a sacrifice to the gods in token of my own blindness."

Tavanger had suddenly become serious.

"I think you guessed all along that I saw something that morning at Flambard. Well, I did, and I believed in it. I saw the announcement of the world-merger arranged by Anatilla. That is to say, I knew with perfect certainty that one thing was going to happen. If I hadn't known it, if I had gone in for Daphnes as an ordinary speculation, I would have been content to take my profit at two or three or four pounds. As it is, that infernal atom of accurate knowledge has cost me twenty thousand.

"But it was worth it," he added, getting up and reaching for his hat, "for I have learned one thing which I shall never forget, and which I commend to your notice. Our ignorance of the future has been wisely ordained of Heaven. For unless man were to be like God and know everything, it is better that he should know nothing. If he knows one fact only, instead of profiting by it he will assuredly land in the soup."

III

THE RT. HON. DAVID MAYOT

"I once did see
In my young travels through Armenia,
An angrie Unicorne in his full carier
Charge with too swift a foot a Jeweller,
That watcht him for the Treasure of his browe;
And ere he could get shelter of a tree,
Naile him with his rich Antler to the Earth."

GEORGE CHAPMAN, *Bussy D'Ambois.*

III

The Rt. Hon. David Mayot

I

I must make it clear at the outset that I was not in Mayot's confidence during the year the events of which I am about to record. Goodeve and Reggie Daker confided in me, and, through a series of accidents, I stumbled into Tavanger's inner life. Also I came to have full knowledge of Charles Ottery's case. But I only knew Mayot slightly, and we were opponents in the House, so, although our experiences at Flambard brought us a little nearer, we were far from anything like intimacy. But I realised that, under Moe's spell, he had seen something which had affected him deeply, and I studied closely his political moves to see if I could get a clue to that something. As a matter of fact, before Christmas I guessed what the revelation had been, and my guess proved correct. Later, when the whirligig of politics had brought Mayot and myself into closer touch, I learned from him some of the details which I now set forth.

First of all let me state exactly what he saw. For a second of time he had a glimpse of the first *Times* leader a year ahead; his eyes fell somewhere about the middle of it. The leader dealt with India, and a speech of the Prime Minister on the subject. By way of variation the writer used the Prime Minister's name in one sentence, and the name was Waldemar. Now, the Labour Party was then in office under Sir Derrick Trant, and Mr Waldemar was the leader of the small, compact, and highly efficient Liberal group. Within a year's time, therefore, a remarkable adjustment of parties would take place, and the head of what was then by far the smallest party would be called upon to form a Government.

This for a man like Mayot was tremendous news – how tremendous will appear from a short recital of the chief features in his character. He was that rare thing in the class to which he belonged, a professional politician. A trade-union secretary looks to a seat in Parliament as a kind of old-age pension, and the ranks of Labour are for the most part professional. But nowadays the type is uncommon – except in the case of a few famous families – among the middle and upper classes. Mayot would have made a good eighteenth-century politician, for the parliamentary game was the very breath of his nostrils. All his life he had been the typical good boy and prize pupil. At school he had not been regarded as clever, but he had worked like a beaver; at the University there were many who called him stupid, but nevertheless he had won high honours in the schools. It was the same with games. He was never a good cricketer, but he was in his School Eleven, and at Cambridge, by dint of assiduousness professional coaching in the vacations, he managed to attain his Blue – and failed disastrously in the 'Varsity match. He seemed to have the knack of just getting what he wanted with nothing to spare, but, since the things that he wanted were numerous and important, he presented a brilliant record to the world.

He was the only son of a well-to-do Lancashire manufacturer, and had no need to trouble about money. He was devouringly ambitious – not to do things, but to be things. I doubt if he cared much for any political cause, but he was set upon becoming a prominent statesman. He began as a Tory democrat, an inheritor of some threads of Disraeli's mantle. He went to Germany to study industrial problems, lived at a settlement in Rotherhithe, even did a spell of manual labour in a Birmingham factory – all the earnest gestures that are supposed to imply a tender heart and a forward-looking mind. He got into

Parliament just before the War as a Conservative Free-trader for a Midland county constituency where his father had a house, and made himself rather conspicuous by a mild support of the Government's Irish Home Rule policy. In the War he lay very low; he had opportunely remembered that his family had been Quakers, and he had something to do, from well back at the base, with a Quaker ambulance. After peace he came out strong for the League of Nations, bitterly criticised the Coalition, was returned in '22 as an Independent, made a spectacular crossing of the floor of the House, and in '23 was the Labour member for a mining area in Durham, with a majority of five figures. He was an under-secretary of the Labour Government of '29, and, when Trant became Prime Minister, he entered his Cabinet as President of the Board of Trade. As such he was responsible for the highly controversial Factory Bill to which I have referred earlier in this story.

A rich bachelor, he had no other interest than public life, or rather every other interest was made to subserve that end. He used to say grandly, in Bacon's phrase, that he had "espoused the State," which was true enough if husband and wife become one flesh, for he saw every public question through the medium of his own career. In many ways he was not a bad fellow; indeed, you would have said the worst of him in calling him an *arriviste* and a professional politician.

The first point to remember is that he had not a very generous allowance of brains, but made his share go a long way. He carefully nursed his reputation, for he knew well that he had no great margin. He cherished his dignity, too, cultivated a habit of sardonic speech, and obviously longed to be respected and feared. A few simple souls thought him formidable and most people esteemed his industry, for he toiled at every job he undertook, and left nothing to chance. For myself, I never could take him quite seriously. He was excellent at a prepared statement, which any Treasury clerk could do as well as a Minister, but when you got to grips with him in debate he funked and rode off on a few sounding platitudes. Also I cannot imagine any man, woman or child being moved by his harangues, for he had about as much magnetism as a pillar-box.

The second thing to remember is that he knew that he was second-rate, in everything except his industry and the intensity of his ambition. Therefore he was a great student of tactics. He was determined to be Prime Minister, and believed that by a close study of the possible moves of the political cat he might succeed. So far he had done well, for he would never have had Cabinet rank if he had remained a Tory. But one realised that he was not quite easy, and that his eyes were always lifting anxiously over the party fence. Let me add that most people did not suspect his gnawing ambition, or his detachment from anything that might be called principles, for there was a heavy, almost unctuous, earnestness about his oratorical manner. He was clever enough, when the ice was thin, not to be too fluent, but to let broken sentences and homely idioms attest the depth of his convictions.

Believing firmly in Moe, he believed in the fragment of revelation which had been vouchsafed him, and was set on making the most of it. Waldemar, the Liberal leader, would be Prime Minister a year hence, and he pondered deeply how he could turn this piece of news to his advantage... The first thing was to discover how it could possibly come about. He naturally thought first of a coalition between Labour and Liberal, but a little reflection convinced him of its unlikelihood, for Trant and Waldemar were the toughest kind of incompatibles.

Waldemar was a relic of Victorian Liberalism, a fanatical Free-trader, an individualist of the old rock. He was our principal exponent of the League of Nations, and had made an international reputation by his work for world peace. By profession a banker, he looked like a most impressive cleric – Anglican, not Nonconformist – with his lean, high-boned face, his shaggy eyebrows, and his superb, resonant voice. He was far the best speaker in the House, for he could reel off, without preparation, model eighteenth-century prose, and he was also a formidable debater; but he was a poor parliamentarian, for his mind lacked flexibility. He awed rather than conciliated, and, with his touch of fanaticism, was apt to be an inept negotiator.

Derrick Trant was his exact opposite. He was the most English thing that God ever made, and, like most typical Englishmen, was half Scots. He had drifted into the Labour Party out of a quixotic admiration for the doings of the British rank-and-file in the War, and he proved extraordinarily useful in keeping that precarious amalgam together. For all sections both liked and trusted him, the solid Trade Union lot and the young bloods alike, for his simplicity and single-heartedness. He had clearly no axe to grind, and the ordinary Labour man was willing to be led by one whose ancestors had fought at Crécy; the extremists respected his honesty, and the moderates believed in his common sense. He represented indeed the greatest common denominator of party feeling. He had instincts rather than principles, but his instincts were widely shared, and his guileless exterior concealed a real shrewdness. I have heard him again and again in the House pull his side out of a mess by his powers of conciliation. He made no secret of his dislike of Waldemar. It was the secular antipathy of the nationalist to the internationalist, the Englishman to the cosmopolitan, the opportunist to the doctrinaire, the practical man to the potential fanatic.

Mayot soon decided that there was nothing doing in that quarter. The alliance, which would put Waldemar into office, must be with the Tories. At first sight it seemed impossible. The party to which I have the honour to belong had been moving steadily towards Protection, and had preached a stringent policy of safeguarding as the first step towards the cure of unemployment. Waldemar had taken the field against us. and seemed to hope to engineer a Liberal revival on a Free-trade basis, and so repeat the triumph of 1906. On the other hand, there was the personality of our leader to be remembered. Geraldine was by far the greatest parliamentarian of our time and the adroitest party chief. Like Mayot, he was a professional, and the game was never out of his mind. Being mostly Irish in blood, he had none of Trant's Englishness or Waldemar's iron dogmas; his weapons were endless ingenuity, audacity and humour. He wanted to return to power, and might use the Liberals to oust the Government. But in that case why should Waldemar be Prime Minister? Geraldine would never kill Charles to make James king... Mayot could reach no conclusion, and resolved to wait and watch.

The parliamentary session through six blistering weeks dragged itself to a close. The Budget debate was concluded after eight all-night sittings, the Factory Bill passed its third reading and went to the Lords, and there was the usual massacre of lesser measures. It had been Mayot's habit to go to Scotland for the autumn vacation, for he had a good grouse moor and was a keen shot. But that year he changed his plans and resolved to stalk Waldemar.

Now, Waldemar was something of a valetudinarian, and every year, after the labours of the session, was accustomed to put himself for some weeks in the hands of an eminent physician who dwelt in the little town of Erdbach in the Black Forest. Moreover, Waldemar was not like Geraldine and Mayot himself; he had hobbies other than politics, and, just as Sir Derrick Trant was believed to be more interested in Gloucester cattle, wild white clover and dry-fly fishing than in Parliament, so Waldemar was popularly supposed to prefer the study of birds to affairs of State. Mayot, professing anxiety about his blood pressure, became an inmate of Dr Daimler's *kurhaus*, and prepared himself for his task by a reading of small popular works on ornithology.

At Erdbach he spent three weeks. I happened to meet him there, for I stopped at the principal hotel for two days while motoring to Switzerland, and ran across him in Waldemar's company while taking an evening walk. Waldemar had no particular liking for Mayot, but he had nothing definitely against him except his politics, and the two had never been much pitted against each other in the House. When I saw them they seemed to have reached a certain degree of intimacy, and Mayot was listening intelligently to a discourse on the Alpine swift, and trying to identify a specimen of tit which Waldemar proclaimed was found in Britain only in the Spey valley. The Liberal leader was in a holiday mood, and he was flattered, no doubt, by Mayot's respectful docility.

He talked, it seemed, a great deal of politics, and one of Mayot's suspicions was confirmed. He was slightly more civil about the Tories than about the Government. Geraldine, indeed, he profoundly distrusted, but he was quite complimentary about certain of Geraldine's colleagues. And he made two significant remarks. British politics, he thought, were moving back to the old two-party division, and in his opinion the most dangerous reactionary force was Sir Derrick Trant. Trant was the legitimate leader and the natural exponent of diehard Conservatism – a class-consciousness which would in the long run benefit the capitalist, and a chauvinism which might plunge his country into war... After a rather tedious three weeks Mayot returned to his neglected grouse, with a good deal of vague information about birds, and a clear conviction that there had been several *pourparlers* between Waldemar and the Tories. He seemed to have got the pointer he wanted.

But a fortnight later he changed his mind. Geraldine's chief lieutenant, a man of whom Waldemar had spoken with approval, addressed a political demonstration in the park of an Aberdeenshire castle. The speech, which became famous as the "Issachar speech," was a violent attack upon the Liberals. Labour was dismissed as a confusion of thought based upon honourable inclinations, but Liberalism was denounced as a deliberate blindness, an ossification of heart and an atrophy of brain. What were the boasted "Liberal principles," the speaker asked, but dead and decomposing relics? Waldemar was described as Issachar, an "ass between two burdens," one being his precious dogmas and the other a deadweight of antediluvian jealousies and fears.

Mayot, who read the speech one evening after coming in from a grouse-drive, decided with a sigh that he must try a cast on another line.

II

The autumn session began under the shadow of unemployment. The figures were the worst since the War, and it was generally believed would pass the three million point by Christmas. Industries which six months before had been slightly on the up-grade were now going back, and industries which had been slightly depressed were now going downhill with a rush. People began to talk of a national emergency Government, and a speech of Trant's was interpreted as a feeler. Mayot pricked up his ears and set himself to study the omens.

It was clear that there was no friendliness between Waldemar and Geraldine. The spirit of the Issachar speech was apparent in the first debate, and there were some brisk passages in the House between the two leaders. Then Geraldine went on the stump in Scotland and the industrial north. His one theme was unemployment, and he had enormous meetings everywhere, with enthusiastic overflows. He really felt the tragedy of the situation, and he gave the unemployed the feeling that he understood their case and would stick at nothing to find a remedy. There was no doubt that he made headway as against the inertness of the Prime Minister, who was in the hands of the Treasury officials, and the stubborn formalism of Waldemar.

At Durham he outlined his programme, the chief point in which was a new emigration policy. Thousands, he said, had been permanently disinherited from the work for which they had been trained; certain industries must face the fact of a permanent reduction to a lower level; what was to be done with the displaced? Trant had a transference scheme working, but it could only account for a fraction. The resources of the Empire must be brought in to meet the deficiencies of one part of it. The Dominions had virgin land, unharnessed power; Britain had the human material; the situation was ripe for a deal. Geraldine proposed to short-circuit the whole existing emigration machinery. He had been in Canada the year before, and had fixed upon two areas, one in British Columbia and the other on the Peace River, for a great national experiment. He proposed to buy or lease the land from the Canadian Government, exactly as a private citizen might acquire a Canadian estate. Then he proposed to call the best business talent in Britain and Canada to his aid, and to establish a new chartered company to develop the area. Roads and railways would be built, townships laid out, water and electric power provided, just as in a scheme of private development. Unskilled jobs in the preliminary construction would be found at once for thousands of the unemployed in Britain, and in the meantime others would be put into training for farm and industrial work later. The new settlements would be not only agricultural, but also industrial, and whole industrial units would be transplanted bodily from Britain. Each British district would contribute its quota of emigrants, and it was believed that, in a scheme which appealed so strongly to the imagination, so far from there being a disinclination to emigrate there would be a brisk competition to get on the quota. He foreshadowed a new chartered company of adventurers, like the Hudson Bay and the East India Companies, and he hoped to have it run by able business men whose reputation would be pledged to its success. It would be financed by a twenty million loan, issued with a guarantee by the British Government, and Geraldine believed that a good deal of money would be forthcoming for the purpose from the Dominions and even from the United States.

This policy, preached in depressed areas with Geraldine's eloquence to audiences deep in the mire of unemployment, had a considerable success. Waldemar was, of course, in violent opposition. He harped on the iniquities and corruption of chartered companies in the past, and he ingeminated the word "inflation." Trant pooh-poohed the whole thing. You could not cure an ill, he said, by running away from it; he was a simple Englishman, who disliked a grandiose Imperialism run for the benefit of Jews. But the most serious disapproval was in Geraldine's own party – the "big business" group, who were afraid of the effect of such a loan on the markets. The younger Tories as a whole were enthusiastic, and, what is more – significant, the Left Wing of Labour blessed it cordially. It was their own line of country, the kind of thing they had been pressing on their otiose leader. Trant's life was made a burden to him by endless questions in the House from his own people, and Collinson, a young Labour member from the Midlands, declared that Geraldine was the best Socialist of them all, since he alone had the courage to use in an emergency the corporate power and intelligence of the State.

Mayot considered hard. The omens pointed to an alliance between Waldemar and the Tory Right Wing. But how was that possible? The anti-Geraldine Tories were to a man Protectionists, and Waldemar and his party would die in the last ditch for Free Trade... What about a grouping of the Labour Left and the Tory Left? On the matter of ultimate principles, no doubt, there was a deep cleavage, for the most progressive young Tory would have nothing to do with Marxism. But after all, Marxism was becoming a very shadowy faith, and in practical politics it was easy to conceive Tory and Labour youth lining up. Both were natural Protectionists, and abominated Whiggism and all its ways. He noticed how in the House the two groups seemed to be friendly, and mingled constantly in the smoking-room. A volume of political essays had recently been published, to which Geraldine had written a preface, and the contributors included Collinson, Macleish, the Glasgow firebrand, and young Tories like Lord Lanyard and John Fortingall... But no! It was impossible, he decided. For the leader of such a combination would be Geraldine, whereas, as he knew, in eight months Waldemar would be Prime Minister. Victory would not follow such banners, so he tried another cast.

At this point Sally Flambard took a hand. She suddenly appeared as a political hostess, and I do not think that Mayot had anything to do with it. Her husband was of course a Tory of an antique school, but Sally had not hitherto shown any political interest. Now she discovered that she believed in constitutional government and the old ways, and profoundly distrusted both Labour and Geraldine. The move, I think, was only another phase of Sally's restless activity. She had had her finger in most pies, and wanted a new one. Also she had acquired a regard for Waldemar. Being a New Englander, she had in her bones an admiration for the type of statesman represented by the fathers of her country – large, grave, gnomic, rhetorical men – and Waldemar seemed to her to be a judicious compound of Daniel Webster and Abraham Lincoln.

Anyhow, she took to giving luncheon parties in Berkeley Square, at which much nonsense was spoken, especially by the hostess. You see, she misread Waldemar, and the initial mistake spoiled all her strategy. She thought that he was a natural leader and an original thinker, whereas he was primarily a mechanical instrument, discoursing – very beautifully no doubt – traditional music. She was convinced that she had only to bring him into touch with some of the solider Conservatives for them to feel that he was a demonic figure, a wedder of current realities to historic wisdom. So she got together some amazing gatherings of incompatibles. The materials, so far from being the essentials of good fare to be cooked by a skilful hand, were more like chemicals turned by their juxtaposition into explosives.

Mayot was to be the *trait d'union*, the adroit outsider, who could combine the ill-assorted guests, preparatory to Waldemar's treatment. I don't know where she got her notion of him – probably from himself. I attended two of the luncheons, and they gave me some idea of Mayot's game. The plan was to unite the Tory Right and Centre (*minus* Geraldine) with the Liberals through a common dislike of viewy extravagance and a common trust in Waldemar.

The result was high comedy. Waldemar, honest man, did his best. He tried to be civil to everybody in his pleasant old-fashioned way, but he had no single thing in common with nine out of ten of the Tories who sat at Sally's table. I could see Mayot trying to guide him into diplomatic paths, but Waldemar was far too hardset a being to play a part, even if he had wished to. He talked books and the classics to Sir Penton Furbast, the press magnate, who was more or less illiterate. He told stories of Gladstone, and expatiated on the glory that had died with him, to old Isaac Isaacson, whose life had been spent in a blind worship of Disraeli. Once he thought he had got hold of a batch of country gentlemen, and discoursed on a scheme he had for lightening the burdens on rural land by means of an ingenious tax on inflated stock-exchange values; but it was champagne, not country air, that gave them their high colour – all were noted market operators, and his talk scared them into fits. An impish fate seemed to brood over those luncheons. Waldemar talked disarmament to the chairman of the Navy League, and acidly criticised America to Wortley-Dodd, who had an American mother and mother-in-law. His only success was with me, for I had always rather liked him, and could talk to him about birds and the inaccuracies of the Greville Memoirs. But the real rock on which the thing shipwrecked was Protection. Every one of Sally's Tories was an earnest Protectionist, and, at the last luncheon just before Christmas, Waldemar told Ashley Bridges that Protection meant four million unemployed and the dissolution of the Empire, and Bridges retorted in so many words that he was a fool.

Sally's parties were a most valuable experience for Mayot. He was progressing in his quest by the time-honoured method of trial and error. By this time he was perfectly clear on one point. No alliance was conceivable between Waldemar and the Tory rank-and-file, for a strong dislike of Trant and a growing suspicion of Geraldine would never surmount the tariff difficulty. So he turned to the only remaining combination which would suit his book – the Liberals and the Labour Right.

I should have said that hitherto Mayot had never identified himself with any group in his party. He had been of the Centre, a Labour man *sans phrase*; one who would be able, without any compromising past, to incline, when the occasion arose, to the Right or to the Left. But clearly this detachment would soon be impossible. If Waldemar was to form a Government, it could only be with the help of the Labour Right, for it was difficult to imagine Collinson and his like having anything to do with one whom they had repeatedly described in public as a fatted calf. If he, Mayot, were to play a prominent part in that Government, it was therefore obligatory to get some hold on the section of his party which would support Waldemar. He must edge discreetly towards the Right Wing.

Discretion was essential, and secrecy. He could not afford as yet to break with the Left, and he must give no sign of disloyalty to Trant. He needed a confederate, and he found in old Folliot the man he wanted.

Folliot, as I have mentioned, was an elderly gossip, who had been a notable figure in the Edwardian era, but who since the War had become a bore. He appeared less regularly at smart dinner-parties, and fewer country houses were open to him. When I first came to London men drew near him, when the women had left the room, to hear his stories, and youth in the clubs made rather a cult of him. I remember congratulating myself on the privilege of being acquainted with one who had known all the great men in Europe for half a century. Now the poor old fellow was allowed to drink his port in lonely silence. He was a pathetic figure, and what chiefly grieved him was his exclusion from politics. He had never been anything of a serious politician, though he had twice sat for short terms in the House, but he had been a useful go-between. One of his virtues was that, though a notorious gossip, he could be trusted to be as secret as the grave in any business in which he was employed. He used never even to mention the things he had done – his negotiations as a young man with the Liberal-Unionists, or his very useful work over the House of Lords question in 1910 – only grinned and looked wise when the topics came up. Folliot had his own point of honour.

Lately he had come to affect Labour out of disgust at the neglect of his own people. He did not love Trant, who laughed at him, but he had some vogue among the feudal aristocracy of the trade unions, who liked what they regarded as a link with historic British policy. Mayot easily enlisted him, for he was a gullible old gentleman, and was flattered at being consulted. He discovered that he had a mission to restore the two-party system by a union of all soberly progressive forces. He himself had begun life as a follower of Hartington, and so had never cared for the straiter sect of the Carlton Club, and had always had his doubts about Protection. He foresaw a chance of reviving that decorous Whiggism for which he had always hankered, based upon the two solidest things in Britain – the middle-class Liberal and the intelligent working man.

So during the early part of the new year he was happily busy. He gave a great many dinners, sometimes at his flat and sometimes at Brooks', to which were bidden trade-union members of Parliament, one or two members of the Government who were supposed to be disaffected towards Trant, and a number of carefully selected Liberals. Waldemar came once or twice and Mayot was invariably present. These dinners seem to have gone off very well, and no hint of them leaked into the press. It was a game which Mayot could play to perfection. He could see that already he was regarded with favour by the Liberal stalwarts, and a certain type of Labour man was coming to look with a new respect upon one who could interpret his honest prejudices and give them an air of political profundity. By the end of January he was very well satisfied. He had decided that he had forecast correctly the process which would lead to Waldemar's premiership, and had put himself in a position to reap the full advantage of his foreknowledge. What he hoped for, I think, was the Exchequer.

III

But with February came one of the unlooked-for upheavals of opinion which make politics such a colossal gamble. The country suddenly awoke to the meaning of the unemployment figures. These were appalling, and, owing to the general dislocation of world credit and especially to the American situation, held no immediate hope of improvement. The inevitable followed. Hitherto sedate newspapers began to shout, and the habitual shouters began to scream. Hunger-marchers thronged the highways to London; there were mass-meetings in every town in the North; the Archbishops appointed a day for public prayer; and what with deputations, appeals, and nagging questions in the House, the life of Trant became a burden.

The crisis produced a prophet, too. It is curious how throughout our history, whenever there is a strong movement from below, the names of the new leaders are usually queer monosyllables. It was so in Jack Cade's rebellion, and in Venner's business during the Commonwealth, and in the early days of the Labour movement; and now we had the same phenomenon, as if the racial maelstrom at the foot of the ladder had thrown up remnants of a long-hidden world. The new prophet bore the incredible name of Chuff. From Tower Hill to Glasgow Green he stumped the land, declaring that our civilisation had broken down, that the crisis was graver than at the outbreak of the War, and demanding that the Government should act at once or admit their defeat. The remarkable thing about Chuff was that he was not an apostle of any single nostrum. He was a rather level-headed young man, who had once been a sailor, and he was content to bring home to the national conscience the magnitude of the tragedy; the solution, he said, he left to cleverer people. He had real oratorical gifts, and what with Chuff on the platform and Collinson and his friends in the House, there was high confusion in domestic politics.

Opinion was oddly cross-divided, but presently it sorted itself out into two groups. The Activists demanded instant and drastic action, and the Passivists – the name was given them by their opponents and made prejudice owing to its resemblance to Pacifists; they called themselves Constitutionalists – counselled patience, and went on steadily with local relief works, transference, the expediting of one or two big public utilities, and the other stock remedies. The Activists were a perfect Tower of Babel, all speaking different tongues. Some wanted an immediate application of Marxian Socialism. A big section, led by Collinson, had a fantastic scheme of developing the home markets by increased unemployment pay – a sort of lifting up of one's self by the hair. Most accepted Geraldine's emigration policy; and a powerful wing advocated a stringent tariff with a view to making the Empire a self-contained economic unit. The agreed point, you might say, of all sections was direct and immediate action, a considerable degree of State Socialism, and a very general repudiation of Free Trade.

Activism, as I have said, cut clean across parties. Roughly its strength lay in the Labour Left and the Tory Left, and it was principally a back-bench movement, though Geraldine gave it a somewhat half-hearted blessing. Lord Lanyard and Collinson appeared on the same platforms in the country, and one powerful Tory paper supported the cause and sent special commissioners into the distressed areas to report. There was a debate on the Ministry of Labour estimates, in which the Labour Whips found themselves confronted with something very like a revolt. The Government was saved by the Liberals, but John Fortingall's motion was only lost by seven votes. This incident made the Passivists sit up and organise themselves. They had on their side Trant and the Labour Right and Centre, the whole of

Waldemar's following, and the bulk of the Tories, Geraldine sitting delicately on the fence. But the debating ability – except for Waldemar and Mayot – was conspicuously with their opponents.

It was now that Mayot became something of a figure. The path was being prepared for a Labour-Liberal coalition with Waldemar as leader – though he could not quite realise how the latter event would come about. In such a combination, if it took office, Trant might become Foreign Secretary, while he must make sure of the Exchequer. He made sure by hurling himself into the controversy with a vigour hitherto unknown in his career. He, who had always been a little detached and a good deal of a departmentalist, who had moreover been very respectful to his own extremists, now became a hard-hitting fanatic for moderation. He picked up some of Waldemar's apocalyptic mannerisms, and his parliamentary style acquired a full-throated ease. It shows how much the man was in earnest about his ambitions, that in a few weeks he should have forced himself to acquire a host of new arts. At that time I was so busy at the Bar that I was very little in the House, but, my sympathies being rather with the Activists, I had one or two brushes with Mayot. I found him a far more effective antagonist than before, for, though he was no better at argument, he could do what is usually more effective – denounce with apparent conviction.

Events in March played into his hands, for India suddenly boiled over, and the new constitution which we had laboriously established there seemed to be about to fail. There was a good deal of rioting, which had to be suppressed by force, and a number of patriots went to gaol. This split the Activist group asunder, for Collinson went out bald-headed against what he called the "fascist" policy of the Government, and most of the Labour Left followed him, while the young Tories took precisely the other line and shudderingly withdrew from their colleagues, like a prim virgin who opportunely discovers deeps of infamy in her lover. Lanyard, indeed, who had humanitarian leanings,

111

seized the occasion to become an Independent, and no longer received the party Whips, but John Fortingall and the others returned hastily to the fold. The Government handled the Indian situation with firmness, said its supporters – with cheap melodrama and blind brutality, said its critics – and it had behind it three-fourths of its own people, all the Liberals, and every Tory except Lanyard. Peace had revisited the tents of Israel.

Mayot in those days was a happy man, for the world was ordering itself exactly according to his wishes. The course of things was perfectly clear. Unemployment was the issue that blanketed all others, and unemployment had to all intents obliterated party lines. India had broken up the Activist phalanx. The advocacy of quack remedies was left to a few wild men. Geraldine's grandiose emigration dream had faded out of the air, and the Tories were back in their old Protectionist bog, in which he was confident that the bulk of the country would never join them. He thought that he had trained himself to look at facts with cold objective eyes, and such was his reading of them. The economic situation was very grim, and likely to become grimmer, and the solution must be some kind of national emergency Government in which Waldemar would take the lead, for he alone had the requisite prestige of character and was in the central tradition of British policy. Trant would be glad to be a lieutenant instead of a leader, and he himself, as the chief liaison officer between Liberal and Labour, would have his choice of posts. His only anxiety concerned Flotter, now at the Exchequer. But Flotter was nearer the Left than himself, and farther from the Liberals, and could never command his purchase. Flotter was a dismal old man, whose reputation had been steadily decreasing, whereas in recent months he himself had added cubits to his political stature.

So Mayot began to talk discreetly in private about the National Government which facts were making imperative. I heard him airing his views one night at a dinner of Lady Altrincham's, and at a luncheon of Folliot's, where I sat next to him, he did me the honour to throw a fly over me. I asked him what his selections would be, and he replied that such a Government would have all responsible Labour to choose from, and all the Liberal talent.

"What about us?" I asked.

He looked wise. "That is harder, since Geraldine sticks to his Protection. But we should be glad to have some of you – on terms. You yourself, for instance."

"What puzzles me is, how you distinguish a National Government from a Coalition," I said. "Remember the word Coalition still stinks in the nostrils of most people."

"A Coalition," he said gravely, "only shares the loot, but a National Government pools the brains."

I grinned, and thanked him for the compliment.

IV

Just before the Easter recess I lunched with Sally Flambard. Her craze for Waldemar had gone, she had never liked Geraldine, and, save for Mayot, she had had very little to do with the Labour people. But now she had discovered Trant. She had been staying at a house in his own county, and he had come to dine, and she had at once conceived for him one of her sudden affections. There was a good deal of reason for that, for Trant was an extraordinarily attractive human being, whatever his defects might be as a statesman. Evelyn liked him too, though deploring his party label, for they were both sportsmen and practical farmers. The consequence was that Trant had become for the past month a frequent guest in Berkeley Square. It was a pleasant refuge for him, for he was not expected to talk politics, and he met for the most part people who did not know the alphabet of them.

Trant and I had always been good friends, and on that April Wednesday when we found ourselves side by side, I had from him – what I usually got – a jeremiad on the boredom and futility of his profession.

"I'm not like you," he lamented. "You've got a body of exact knowledge behind you, and can contribute something important – legal advice, I mean. But here am I, an ordinary ill-informed citizen, set to deal with problems that no mortal man understands and no human ingenuity can solve. I spend my time clutching at imponderables."

I said something to the effect that his modesty was his chief asset – that at least he knew what he did not know.

"Yes," he went on, "but, hang it, Leithen, I've got to fight with fellows who are accursedly cocksure, though they are cocksure about different things. Take that ass Waldemar ..."

Trant proceeded to give an acid, and not unjust, analysis of Waldemar and the way he affected him. The two men were as antipathetic as a mongoose and a snake. He was far too loyal to crab any of his own side to an opponent, but I could see that he was nearly as sick of Collinson and his lot, and quite as sick of Mayot. In fact, it looked as if there was now no obvious place for Trant in his party, since he was at war with his own Left Wing, and Mayot had virtually taken over the leadership of the Right and Centre. At that time we were all talking about the alliance of Liberal and Labour, and this conversation convinced me that it would not include Trant.

Then he began to speak of ponderable things like fishing. He was just off to a beat on the Wye, and lamented the bad reports of the run of fish. Just as we were leaving the table he said something that stuck in my memory. He asked me what was the best text of the Greek Anthology, attributing to me more scholarship than I possessed... Now, Trant had always been bookish, and had a number of coy literary ambitions. I remembered that once, years before, he had confessed to me that, when he was quit of public life, he meant to amuse himself with a new translation of the Anthology. Meleager, I think, was his special favourite.

I walked down to the House that afternoon with one assured conviction. Trant was about to retire. His air had been that of a schoolboy who meant to defy authority and hang the consequences. He had the manner of one who knew he was going to behave unconscientiously and dared anybody to prevent him. Also there was his Greek Anthology scheme.

By this time I had a pretty shrewd idea of Mayot's purpose. That afternoon I sat next to him in the tearoom and tried to sound him. He looked at me sharply.

"Have you heard anything?" he asked, and I told him "Not a word," but the whole situation seemed to me fluid.

"Trant won't go till he has made certain of his successor," said Mayot. "And that won't be yet awhile."

But Trant did go, leaving the succession gloriously unsettled. A fortnight later the papers published a letter from him to Flotter, the chairman of his party. It was a dignified performance, and there was finality in every syllable. Trant said he had placed his resignation in His Majesty's hands and that it had been graciously accepted. He proposed to retire altogether from public life, and would not be a candidate at the next election. He made no complaints, but offered his most grateful thanks to his party for their unfailing loyalty in difficult times, and expressed his warm hopes for a brilliant future... I had a line from him from the Spey, chiefly about fishing; but it ended with: "You did not think Master Silence a man of this mettle? Thank God it's over. Now I shall have peace to make my soul."

I ran across Mayot next day, and he was fairly walking on his toes with excitement. His face was prim with weighty secrets. "The Consuls must see to it that the Republic takes no hurt," he said impressively. He was swollen with delicious responsibilities, and clearly believed that his hour had come.

The next event was the party meeting. Mayot was generally fancied as Trant's successor, but to everybody's surprise, Flotter, the Chancellor of the Exchequer, was elected by nine votes. Flotter was of Mayot's persuasion, but he was slightly nearer to

115

the Left perhaps; at any rate, he had not been so controversial a figure as Mayot, so he had the support of Collinson's merry men. Mayot did not seem to take the defeat much to heart, for he was looking well ahead. In a few weeks Waldemar would be Prime Minister, and he was the chief link between Waldemar and Labour.

I was, of course, not in the confidence of the Cabinet, and can only judge by results. But I fancy that the decision to ask for a dissolution must have been chiefly Mayot's. You see, he knew one fact which was hidden from all the world, and he had to consider how this fact was coming to birth. If Flotter took office at once he would not readily be induced to resign, though he was an old man, not very strong in body, and never credited with much ability. An election was desirable on every ground for both the Labour and the Tory Parties were deeply divided, and the verdict of the polls would clear the air. Mayot had no doubt that the country was on the whole on the side of the kind of cautious progress represented by Waldemar and himself. The Tory Left had not been making much headway; Collinson and his group were discredited because of their attitude on India; and the appeal of the redoubtable Chuff had lost its first freshness. His chief fear was Geraldine, whose tactical skill he profoundly respected. But an immediate election would spike Geraldine's guns, since he had no new policy to urge, and, if he improvised one, would not have time to elaborate it.

So Flotter was sent for by the King, and asked for a dissolution, which was granted. His Budget resolutions were hastily passed by a House whose interests were elsewhere, and in the second week of May the campaign began.

V

I have fought in my time seven elections, and can recollect a good many more, but I never knew one like this. My own seat was safe enough, and I was able to speak for our side up and down the land during the hottest May that I ever remember. But the whole thing was a nightmare, for in twenty-four hours all creeds and slogans were mixed up in a wild kaleidoscope. Very few candidates knew quite where they stood, and desperate must have been the confusion of the ordinary voter. Laboriously devised programmes became suddenly waste paper.

The supreme fact was that Waldemar went mad, or had a call, or saw a vision like Paul on the road to Damascus. You can take which explanation you choose. He had been lying low for some weeks, touring about the country and scarcely opening his mouth. He must have discovered the horrors of unemployment for himself, just as Geraldine had discovered them seven months before when he started his emigration scheme. Out of the provinces came Waldemar, like Mahomet from the desert, to preach a new gospel.

It was a complete reversal of all that he and Mayot had stood for. He was still a Free Trader, he proclaimed, and would have nothing to do with a self-contained Empire, chiefly on the ground that it would be a barrier to that internationalism on which the future of humanity depended. But he was quite prepared to prohibit the import of certain rival commodities altogether as an emergency measure, and he had a great scheme for State purchase in bulk and the regulation of prices. He went farther. He, who had once moaned "inflation" when Geraldine's loan was proposed, was now a convert to a huge loan for emergency public works. Moreover, he swallowed wholesale most of Collinson's stuff about increasing our home power of consumption, and proposed measures which made the hair of the ordinary economist stand on end.

But it was not so much what Waldemar said as the way he said it. The old Activism was a stagnant pool compared to his furious torrent. He preached his heresies with the fire and conviction of an Israelitish prophet, and brought into the contest the larger spirit of an earlier age. He was quite frank about his conversion. He had had his eyes opened, and, like an honest man and a

117

patriot, must follow the new light. It was the very violence of the revolution in his creed that made it so impressive. We had got into the habit of saying that the day of oratory was over, and that all that mattered was that a leader should be able to broadcast intelligibly. Waldemar disproved this in two days. He was a great orator, and he swept over the North and the Midlands like a flame. Gladstone's Midlothian campaign was beaten hollow. He motored from town to town in a triumphal procession, and every gathering he addressed was like a revivalist meeting, half the audience in tears and the rest too solemnised to shout. Wild as his talk was, he brought hope to those who had none, and stirred up the political waters as they had not been moved since the War.

It was an awful position for everybody else. His own party, with a few exceptions, accepted him docilely, though they had some difficulty in accustoming themselves to the language. You see, the Liberals, having been long in the wilderness, were prepared to follow any Moses who would lead them across Jordan. There was a half-hearted attempt to make a deal about seats, so as to prevent unnecessary fights between Liberal and Labour, but it was a little too late for that, and we had the curious spectacle in many constituencies of official opponents saying precisely the same thing. Geraldine was in an awkward fix, for he had been a bit of an Activist and had his young entry to consider. He did the only thing possible – relapsed upon sobriety *plus* Protection, and did the best he could with tariffs and the Empire. But his form was badly cramped, and he had to face the unpleasing truth that he, the adroit tactician, had been tactically caught bending. His party, however, was well disciplined, and managed, more or less, to speak with one voice, though it was soon clear that many former Tory voters were being attracted by Waldemar.

The Labour people were in a worse hole. Flotter, who was very little use in an election, steered a wary course, welcoming some of Waldemar's ideas, but entering a *caveat* now and then to preserve his consistency. His programme was a feeble stammering affair, for he was about as much of a leader to his party as a baggage pony in a mountaineering expedition. It was Collinson who took charge. He ranged the Labour Left solidly under Waldemar's banner, and became Waldemar's most efficient henchman. In the whirlwind tour before the poll he never left his leader's side.

For the unhappy Mayot there was no place. Miracles do not happen in batches. What in the case of one man may be ascribed to the vouchsafement of divine light will in a second case be put down to policy. Mayot simply could not turn in his tracks. If he had, he would have become a public laughing-stock. His denunciation of Activism had been too wholehearted, his devotion to economic sanity too complete. So he did nothing. He never spoke outside his own constituency, where he was opposed by the formidable Chuff, who stood as a Labour Independent. I gather that he talked a lonely Waldemarism, which Waldemar himself was busily engaged in tearing to tatters.

I got the final results at a Perthshire inn. Mayot was badly beaten: a small thing in itself, for another seat would have been found for him if he had mattered anything to any party – which he did not. There had been the expected defection of Tory voters. The Liberals had done well at our expense owing to Waldemar's name, and all the Labour Left were back with big majorities. So far as I remember, the figures were 251 Labour, 112 Liberals, 290 Tories, and 12 Independents. The country had approved a Coalition.

I went down to stay with Trant for a weekend in the May-fly season. The new Cabinet had just been announced – Waldemar, Prime Minister; Collinson at the Ministry of Labour; Flotter back at the Exchequer; and Lord Lanyard at the Foreign Office.

Trant, in disreputable clothes, was soaking gut and tying on flies.

"There has been a good deal of trouble," he told me. "Our party didn't want Waldemar. They thought that the leader should come from them, and I gather that Waldemar would have been quite willing to stand down if there had been anybody else. But there wasn't. You couldn't put Flotter in charge.

"Poor old Mayot," he went on, his pleasant face puckered into a grin. "Politics are a brutal game, you know. Here is an able fellow who makes one mistake and finds himself on the scrap-heap. If he hadn't been so clever he would be at No. 10 today... Of course he would. If he had even been like Flotter, and trimmed from sheer stupidity, he would have been Prime Minister... I must say I rather respect him for backing his fancy so steadily. He was shrewd enough to spot the winner, but not the race it would win. Thank God, I never pretended to have any cleverness...'

IV

MR REGINALD DAKER

"As when a Gryfon through the wilderness,
With wingéd course o'er Hill or moarie Dale,
Pursues the Arimaspian."

JOHN MILTON, *Paradise Lost.*

IV

Mr Reginald Daker

I

I can tell this story out of the fullest knowledge, for Reggie Daker had long made it a habit to pour out to me his inmost mind. But he was such an inconsequent being that it was not always easy to follow the involutions of that mind. So if my narrative has ragged edges it is because of its principal figure, who had a genius for discontinuity.

He had read in that upper room at Flambard quite clearly an announcement of an expedition to Yucatan, of which he was a member, and which was alleged to have left England on June ninth the following year. Now, Reggie believed in Moe more implicitly than any of us, for one of his chief traits was a profound credulity. But he did not in the least believe in the announcement. Or rather let me put it that, while he was quite certain that the words he read would be in *The Times* a year hence, he was not less certain that they did not concern him. Nothing would induce him to go to Yucatan or any place of the kind. He did not trouble to consider how he was to square his belief in the accuracy of this piece of foreknowledge with his determination that it should not be true in fact. He only knew that he was not going to budge from England.

He did not know where Yucatan was, for he had the vagueness about geography which distinguishes the products of our older public schools and universities, and he had not the curiosity to enquire. He fancied that it must be in the East; places ending in "tan" were always in the East; he remembered Afghanistan, Baluchistan, Gulistan. But, east or west, it mattered nothing to him. A man could not be hustled off abroad unless he wanted to, and nothing was farther from his inclinations.

Reggie was one of a type created by the post-war world. My nephew Charles, who was seven years his senior, and had been much battered by campaigning, said that it comforted him to look at Reggie, for it made him realise that the War chapter was really closed. His mother had died when he was a baby, and his father fell in the Yeomanry fight at Suvla, leaving him a small family property in the Midlands. A sudden industrial expansion made this property valuable, and in the boom year after peace his trustees sold it for a big sum, so that Reggie went to Oxford with a considerable income and no encumbrances. He was not distinguished at the University except for his power to amass friends. He had the family gift of horsemanship, and for a time showed extraordinary energy in riding in "grinds" and country steeplechases. Reggie, with his kit in a brown-paper parcel, might have been seen catching very early trains for remote places. But the craze passed, though his love of horses endured, and Reggie settled down to make a comfortable nest for himself in life.

His intellectual powers were nothing to boast of, but no man had a finer collection of interests. He had a knack of savouring the quality of a variety of things, never going far below the surface, but getting the maximum of pleasure for the minimum of pains. He dabbled in everything – art, literature, field sports, society, even a little corner of philanthropy. He was modest, eager, enthusiastic, and as generous a soul as God ever made. Also he had a pretty talent for sheer farcical fun. The result was that he was widely popular, for in his innocent way he oxygenated the air around him. He had been a member of Pop at Eton, though he had no athletic or scholastic distinctions, and he went down from the University with a larger equipment of friends – not acquaintances merely, but friends – than any of his contemporaries.

He cast about for a job, for he had a conscience of a sort, but, as I have already mentioned, he was a difficult creature to fit into any niche. He was too mercurial, and after a week or two managed to tumble out. But all the time he had his own private profession. His purpose was to make an art of English life. The ritual of that life had been badly dislocated by the War, but enough remained to fascinate Reggie. He was in love with every detail of the ordered round which carried youth of his type from January to January. He adored London in all her moods – the snugness of her winters, new faces at dinner-parties, the constant meetings of friends, plays and books, glossy ponies and green turf at Roehampton, cricket matches and race meetings, the view over St. James's Park in May, Piccadilly in summer, Kensington Gardens in their October russet. Nor did he appreciate less the rural background to London's life – riverside lawns, a cutter on the Solent in a fresh breeze, smoky brown coverts in the December dusks, purple Scots twilights when the guns moved homeward from the high moors. Reggie was supremely content with the place where his lines had been cast. It seemed to him that, if he lived to the age of Methuselah, he could not exhaust England.

He had a pleasant little house near the Brompton Road, where an elderly couple looked after his wants. He belonged to two good clubs – one a young man's and the other an old man's – and enjoyed them both. He hunted regularly with the Saturday Bicester, had a rod on a dry-fly stream in Berkshire, went every year on a round of Scots visits, and, being an excellent shot, was a welcome guest at covert shoots. Indeed, Reggie was a welcome guest anywhere, for he had the gift of making whatever he did seem better worth doing to those who companioned him. His enthusiasm, which was never boring, put colour and light into other people's worlds. I have come down to breakfast before a day's partridge shooting, apathetic about the prospect, and have been compelled by Reggie to look forward to it with the ardour of a boy. Small wonder he was popular; many people remain young, but few can communicate youthfulness.

You must understand that he was no undiscriminating epicurean. Every day he was developing a more perfect technique of appreciation. It sounds a selfish and effeminate mode of spending one's time, and certainly there was nothing of the strenuous life about Reggie. He had no inclination to buffet opponents about the head and build up the Empire. But he was so warm-hearted and friendly that people were very ready to condone a slight lack of virility, the more so as he had considerable repute as a bold man to hounds. For myself, though now and then he exasperated me, on the whole it did me good to contemplate anyone so secure and content.

Reggie was wise enough to see that he needed some string to unite his many interests and give some sort of continuity to his life. So he was on the look-out for a regular job, occasionally found one, and invariably lost it. Then he decided that his avocation lay in the sale of old books. He had always been rather bookish, and had picked up a good deal of general information on the subject. It fitted in perfectly with his other tastes and the general tenour of his existence. He took to frequenting sales, cultivated dealers and collectors, enlarged his American acquaintance, and on a country-house visit made a point of investigating the library.

So at the time of the Flambard Whitsuntide party he had started in a modest way as a dealer in old books, specialising in the English seventeenth century. He had had a few successes, and was full of hope. Here was a profession which in no way interfered with his rule of life, was entrancing in itself, and might repair the ravages which the revenue authorities were making in his private income.

He came to lunch with me in London in July, and I realised that the impression made by Moe was fast disappearing. "Terrible business," said Reggie. "I'm hanged if I quite know what happened, for, looking back, I think we were all asleep. Oh, I read *The Times* all right. It said I had started off to a place called Yucatan with an expedition. Rotten idea!"

I asked him if he believed in the reality of his vision.

"Of course," he replied. "I can't explain how – no one can, except poor old Moe, and he's dead – but I read the words in the paper as clearly as I am seeing you."

"You think they are true – will be true?"

"I think that they will appear in *The Times* of June tenth next year. True in that sense. But not true in the sense that I shall have gone to Yucatan. Catch me doing anything so idiotic! Forewarned, forearmed, you know."

And Reggie plunged into an account of the pirated pre-first edition of the *Religio Medici*, of which he had heard of a copy.

II

So he went off to Scotland for the Twelfth, quite easy in his mind. He rarely thought about the Moe business, and, when he did, it was only to reflect with some amusement that in ten months' time an eminent newspaper would be badly out in its facts. But he was thinking a great deal about Pamela Brune.

We have all our own Scotlands, and Reggie's was not mine, so we never met north of the Tweed. He would have abhorred the rougher kind of deer forest, for he would never have got up the mountains, and he was no salmon fisherman. The kind of place he liked was a civilised country house where the comforts of life were not forgotten. He was a neat shot at driven grouse, and loved a day on a mild moor where you motored to the first butts and had easy walks to the others. He liked good tennis and golf to be available on by-days, and he liked a large house-party with agreeable women. Reggie was the very opposite of the hard-bitten sportsman; sport was for him only one of the amenities of life, a condiment which should not be taken by itself, but which in combination gave flavour to the dish. So he selected his visits carefully, and was rarely disappointed.

This year he had an additional purpose; he went where he thought it likely that he might meet Pamela Brune. He believed himself to be very much in love, and he still had hopes; for in the last few weeks of the season Pamela had been a little kinder. She had been rather gentle and abstracted, and he hoped that her heart might be softening towards him.

He did not meet Pamela Brune, for reasons which I shall have to record elsewhere. But he had a very pleasant two months in comfortable dwellings, varied with a week in a yacht among the Western Isles. It was a fine autumn in the north, and Reggie returned with a full sketch-book – he dabbled in water-colours – and a stock of new enthusiasms. He had picked up a lot of folk-lore in the Hebrides, had written a good deal of indifferent verse in Pamela's honour, had conceived a scheme for the making of rugs with Celtic designs coloured by the native Highland dyes, and had learned something about early Scottish books – David Lyndesay and the like – on which he hoped to specialise for the American market. He meant to develop these lines in the pleasant London winter to which he was looking forward.

Only one visit had been a failure. He had known Lamancha for some years as a notable connoisseur of pictures, and he had gladly accepted an invitation to Leriot. But Lamancha in Scotland was a very different person from Lamancha in London. Reggie found a party of men only, and with none of them, not even his host, did he appear to have much in common. They shot all day on the famous Leriot moors, and there be acquitted himself reasonably well, though he found the standard higher than elsewhere. But it was the evenings that proved out of joint. Eight sleepy men gossiped in the smoking-room till they stumbled to bed, and the talk was of two things only. All except Reggie had served in the War, and half the evenings were spent in campaign reminiscences which bored him profoundly. "Worse than golf shop," he complained to me. But the conversation of the other half scared him, for it was all about adventures in outlandish parts of the globe. It seemed that everyone but himself had sojourned in the oddest places. There was Maffit who had solved the riddle of the Bramaputra gorges, and Beavan who had been the first to penetrate the interior of New Guinea and climb Carstensz, and Wilmer who had been with the second Everest expedition, and Hurrell who had pursued his hobby of birds to the frozen tundras of the Yenesei. Apparently they were not garrulous; but they spoke of their doings with a quiet passion which frightened Reggie. They were all men of some distinction in English life, but they talked as if what they were now doing was the merest triviality, and the real world for them lay across the seas. Even Lamancha, who was supposed to have the ball at his feet in politics, confessed that he would give up everything for the chances of being the first man to cross the great desert of southern Arabia.

To me later Reggie waxed eloquent on his discomfort.

"You never saw such a set of toughs," he said. "Real hearties."

I grinned at the word, and pointed out that "hearty" scarcely described the manner of Lamancha or Hurrell or Beavan.

"Oh, I don't mean that they were the cheery, backslapping type of lad. Their style was more like frozen shell-fish. But they were all the lean, hard-bitten, Empire-building breed. To listen to them you would think it was a kind of disgrace to enjoy life at home as long as there was some filthy place abroad where they could get malaria and risk their necks. They made me feel an abject worm... And, hang it all, you know, they began to infect me with their beastly restlessness. I was almost coming to believe that I was a cumberer of the ground, and should take up the white man's burden or do something silly. They were such cocksure pagans – never troubled to defend their views, but took it for granted that everybody but a hermaphrodite must share them."

There had been one exception, a middle-aged man called Tallis, who had a place in Wales. He was an antiquary of sorts, and appeared in his time to have done his bit of globe-trotting, but he was now settled at home, and had inherited a fine library about which he was willing to talk. But the rest had been repellent, and what scared Reggie was that they had not been repellent enough. He had been attracted against his will; he had felt himself being slowly drawn into an atmosphere utterly at variance with all his tastes. He uneasily remembered Flambard. These men were mostly Oriental travellers, and somewhere in the East lay Yucatan… Reggie cut short his visit to Leriot, and fled for safety to Town.

There he found what seemed to be complete sanctuary, and presently the memory of Leriot and its outlanders grew dim. He lapped himself in urban peace. By Christmas he had realised that Pamela Brune was not for him, and, being a philosophic soul, accepted the fact with resignation. He found many consolations in his life. The economic troubles which hit most people did not greatly affect a *rentier* like Reggie, whose modest but sufficient investments were widely and wisely distributed. He had enough exercise and fresh air to keep him fit – regular golf, an occasional day with the Bicester and an occasional covert-shoot, and he took care that the company he kept was very different from that of Leriot. The people he met on his shooting visits were mostly from the City, and their one aim was to recover a lost stability. The older men talked with longing of the comfortable Edwardian days, and Reggie wholeheartedly shared their regrets. All the world he mixed with seemed to be converted to his own view of life, Lamancha, making speeches in the House and presiding at public dinners, was very unlike the savage who at Leriot had sighed for the Arabian desert. Even Hurrell, whom he saw occasionally in one of his clubs, was a respectable black-coated figure, more concerned with a paper he was to read to the Royal Society than with the Siberian tundras.

Reggie had rarely spent more agreeable months. During November and December there was a good deal of frost, and London had never seemed at once so tonic and so cosy. Being a good-hearted fellow he did a little mild philanthropy, and sat on a committee which took care of several distressed mining villages, besides putting in one evening a week at his boys' club. For the rest he had his pleasant little dinners of selected friends, his club luncheons, his researches at the Museum, his plays and picture shows, and his steadily growing bibliophilic fervour. And behind everything he did was the delicious background of London, which linked up the centuries and made even the new and the raw seem long-descended – an atmosphere which at once soothed and stimulated – the last perfection of man's handiwork – the true setting for a civilised life.

He made real progress, too, with his book-selling, and it looked as if he had found at last the thing he could do well. It was the kind of subject which Reggie could cope with, for he had an excellent memory, and, when his interest was actively engaged, a real power of absorbing knowledge. Also the times suited him, for there was a slump in everything but books. Pictures, furniture, houses, land – there were plenty of sellers and few buyers; but in books the demand kept level with the supply. Hard-up country gentry put their libraries into the market, and it was often possible to buy these privately at modest prices. Reggie had several such lucky speculations, and found that often half a dozen volumes returned him his outlay with a handsome profit.

III

Then in January a little thing happened which had momentous consequences.

He picked up a cheap lot of books at a sale in the Midlands, and one of these was a copy of a little-known political poem of Thomas Gray, called, I think, *The Candidate*. It was printed in the familiar Caslon type of the Strawberry Hill press, and it had on the fly-leaf a long inscription to a certain Theophilus Tallis, in which comment was made on the poet and his work. The inscription was signed "HW," and on the inside of the cover was the armorial bookplate of Tallis of Libanus Hall. If this inscription were genuine, here was an "association" book of a high order. Reggie compared it with many specimens of Horace Walpole's handwriting, with the general style of which it seemed to agree. Could he establish the identity of Theophilus Tallis, and ascertain that he had been a friend of Walpole's, the authenticity would be complete... Then he remembered the man he had met at Leriot. His name was Tallis, and he had a place on the Welsh border. Reggie had scribbled down his club address, so he wrote to him there and asked him for information. In a day or two a reply came from Libanus Hall. The Theophilus in question was his great-grandfather, said the writer, and doubtless the book had strayed from his library. Such things often happened – an undergraduate would carry off a volume to Oxford and forget about it, or a guest would borrow and fail to return. The old Theophilus had left many papers which had never been examined, but in which the connection with Walpole could no doubt be traced. Let Reggie pay him a visit, for there were many things in his library to interest him.

So in the last week of January Reggie departed for the Welsh marches. The association of Tallis with Leriot gave him no anxiety, for recently he had been so lapped in urban life that he had forgotten about Leriot and its uneasy guests, and in any case Tallis had been different from the others. Tallis had not looked like them, for he was a man of a comfortable habit of body, with a round, high-coloured face – a hunting squire with a dash of the *bon vivant*. Reggie remembered with satisfaction how he had criticised Lamancha's port. It was true that he seemed to have travelled much, but his wandering years were over. He had merely hinted at his doings abroad, but he had spoken at length and with gusto about his collections and his library.

Libanus proved to be a dwelling after Reggie's heart, a Tudor manor-house, built round a border keep, according to the fashion of the Welsh marches. It stood on a shelf in a shallow river valley, backed with low, scrub-clad hills, and behind them were wide, rolling moorlands. It was a bachelor establishment, very well run, and Tallis was the perfect host. The collections did not interest Reggie – stone plaques, and queerly marked tiles, and uncouth stone heads which suggested a more primitive Epstein. He took them for Assyrian, and when Tallis called them "Mayan" the word conveyed nothing to him. But the library far surpassed his hopes. It had been founded in the seventeenth century, when Wales was full of lettered squires, by a certain John Tallis, who had obligingly kept a notebook in which he recorded his purchases and the prices he paid for them. It was especially rich in authors with a Welsh connection, like Henry Vaughan and the Herberts, but there was a fine set of Donne, two of the Shakespeare folios, and many of the Cavalier lyrists, besides a quantity of devotional and political *rariora*. The other collector in the family had been Theophilus Tallis in the reign of George III. He had specialised in illustrated books, mostly French, but he had also added to the shelves some notable *incunabula*, for he lived into the day of the Roxburghe and Heber libraries. Reggie hunted up Theophilus in the family archives, and found that he had been a friend of Gray and a frequent correspondent of Horace Walpole. There were batches of letters from both, which had never been published.

Tallis was also a master of foxhounds, a mountainy pack, with some of the old shaggy Welsh strain in them, which hunted about a hundred square miles of wild country at the back of Libanus. The river valley was pockety and swampy, but the short bent of the moors made splendid going. Reggie was well mounted by his host, it was soft, grey weather in which scent lay well, and he had several glorious days up on the roof of things. "You never saw such a place," he wrote to me. "Nothing much to lep, but you must ride cunning, as on Exmoor, if you want to keep up with hounds. I couldn't keep my eye on them for the scenery. One was on a great boss, with a hint far away of deeper valleys, and with lumps of blue mountain poking up on the horizon – foreshortened, you know, like ships coming into sight at sea. It fairly went to my head. Then the hunt was pure Sir Roger de Coverley – hard-riding farmers and squires that had never stirred from their paternal acres. I felt as if I had slipped through a chink of time into an elder England."

Reggie enjoyed every moment, for it was the precise ritual in which his fancy delighted. He and Tallis would get home in the twilight, and have poached eggs and tea by the library fire. Then would come a blessed time in slippers with a book or a newspaper; then a bath and dinner; and after that a leisurely ranging among the shelves and pleasant sleepy armchair talk. Tallis was an ideal host in other ways than as a provider of good sport, good quarters and good fare. He never obtruded his own interests, never turned the talk to the stone monstrosities in the hail which he had given half his life to collect, or expounded the meaning of "Mayan." With Reggie he was the bibliophile and the rural squire, prepared to agree with him most cordially when he proclaimed that there was no place on earth like his own land and wondered why anyone was foolish enough to leave it.

"Fate," said Tallis. "Something switches you abroad before you know where you are. I've always started unwillingly, but there has never been any alternative if I wanted to get a thing done."

Reggie shook his head, implying that he would prefer the thing to remain undone.

He was in this mood of comfort, sentimentality and complacency when Verona Cortal came to dine. Tallis was apologetic. "The Reeces at Bryncoch have a niece staying with them – she comes every year for a week or two's hunting – and I always give Jim Jack a hand to entertain her. She's rather a pleasant child, and deserves something nearer her age than an old buffer like me. I hope you don't mind. She's pretty knowledgeable about books, you know – been to college and that sort of thing." So the following evening Reggie found himself seated at dinner next to an attractive young woman with whom he had no difficulty in conversing. Miss Cortal was of the marmoreal blonde type, with a smooth white skin and a wealth of unshingled fair hair. Her eyes were blue, not the pale lymphatic kind, but a vivacious masterful blue. She was beautifully turned out, polished to a high degree, and to the last degree composed and confident. Reggie did not think her pretty; she was a trifle too substantial for one who was still under the spell of Pamela Brune's woodland grace; but he found her an entrancing companion.

For she seemed to share his every taste and prejudice. They talked of the countryside, for which she had a lively enthusiasm. Her own home was in Gloucestershire, to which her people had moved from the West Riding, where they had been local bankers till they amalgamated with one of the London banks. Her father was dead, but her brothers were in business in London, and she lived partly with them and partly with her mother in the country. Reggie had never met anyone, certainly no woman, who seemed to savour so intelligently the manifold delights of English life, as he understood them. Pamela had been blank and derisory when he tried to talk of such things, but this girl seemed instinctively to penetrate his moods and to give his imponderables a clean-cut reality. It was flattering to be so fully comprehended. They talked of books, and it appeared that she had taken a degree in history at Oxford, and was making a study of the Roman remains in Cotswold. They discovered that they had friends in common, about whose merits and demerits they agreed; and presently in a corner of the shabby drawing-room, while her aunt dozed and Jim Jack and Tallis were deep in hounds, they advanced to the intimacy which comes to those who unexpectedly find themselves at one in their private prepossessions. Reggie saw the Bryncoch car depart with the conviction that he had never before met quite so companionable a being.

It only needed some little thing to set Verona in a romantic light, and that something befell next day. The soft grey weather broke up into one of those clear, late-winter afternoons which are a foretaste of spring. The hounds, after various false starts in the morning, had run right to the top of the moorlands, and killed near the standing stones called the Three Brothers. Verona's mare got an overreach in a bog, and she and Reggie were left behind to make their way home alone in the gathering dusk. The girl looked well on horseback, and the excitement of the day and the winds of the moor had given her a wild-rose colour and abated the trimness of her get-up. As they jogged home Reggie wondered that he had not thought her pretty before; the polished young lady had gone, and in its place was something very girlish and young, something more primitive and more feminine. They rode slowly under a sky of lemon and amethyst, and stopped to watch the sunset flaming over the remote western hills, or to look east to where the shadows were creeping over the great hollow which was England. Then they descended by green drove-roads to the valley woods, and saw the lights' twinkle, miles apart, of their respective homes. It was dark now, and Reggie had to help with the limping mare in some of the dingles. On one such occasion she laid a light hand on his arm.

"What a day!" she said, in a rapt whisper. "This is what I love best – to come out of the wilds into ancient, habitable peace. You can only do it in England. What a land! Who was it called it 'Merlin's Isle of Gramarye'?"

"What a girl!" thought Reggie. "She knows what I want to think before I have thought it."

Two days later he went to Bryncoch to luncheon. Verona was delightful. At Libanus she had been the accomplished woman of the world; on the moors she had been touched with romance; but here she was a child, eager to show her playthings to another child. She dragged him through the library, and out of a wilderness of forestry journals and reports of agricultural societies unearthed volumes worthy of a bibliophile's eye. She acted showman to the architectural curiosities of the house, and after luncheon led him to the old-fashioned walled garden. "They used to be able," she told him, "to grow all kinds of hothouse fruits here out of doors. Do you know why?" She pointed out the flues which ran from a furnace at each corner through the immense brick walls. "That is how they beat the frost and the east winds. They kept the walls all winter at an even temperature. They could do it a hundred years ago, when coal cost little more than the price of carting it from the pit-heads over the hills."

"I love all these relics," she said with the prettiest sentiment. "I want the memory of them to survive. We should keep the past next door to us in our lives and be always looking back to it."

Reggie warmly approved, for it was his own philosophy. But he was a little surprised when she embarked on a most business-like discussion as to the price of coal, and what it would cost to do the same thing today. She quoted figures like an accountant. He was spurred to tell her of his own work, of his book-selling schemes, the successes he had had and his plans for the future. She listened eagerly and made what seemed to him some acute suggestions.

He went back to London next day with his mind in a pleasant confusion. He did not think that he was in love with Miss Cortal, but he decided that in her he had found a most congenial comrade. To have discovered someone so like-minded, so able to justify the faith they shared, gave him a welcome sense of security. Whatever was in store for him he had now a puissant ally.

IV

I do not want to give the impression that Reggie was a vapid, sentimental young man. He was very much the other way. He had plenty of shrewdness, and had all the reticences of his kind. No virginity was ever more fastidiously guarded than the sacred places of the English male in youth. He would perish sooner than confess the things nearest to his heart. If anyone had told Reggie in his presence that he was an artist in life, a connoisseur of evasive sensations, the charge would have been hotly denied. He believed himself to be a normal person, who rejoiced in running with the pack. I guessed his creed, but it was only from casual unguarded phrases and his manner of life, never from his own confession. He would have blushed to say the things which Verona was always saying. But in her mouth they delighted him, for she put into words what he was incapable of expressing himself – incapable partly from shamefacedness and partly from simple lack of the gift for definition. She was magnificently explicit, and carried it off. I have been told that, when you can adequately formulate a grief, you have removed half the sting of it, and I fancy that in the case of the pleasing emotions the same explication doubles the pleasure. That is the virtue of the poets, since they do for the ordinary man what he cannot do for himself. Verona was Reggie's bard. She gave a local habitation and a name to his airy nothings, and in so doing she confirmed him in his faith. He felt that the things he cared for were given a new stability when she became their most competent prophet.

They had arranged to meet in London, and next week he dined at the Cortals' large, dull house in Eaton Square. I happened to be a guest, for my nephew Charles was connected with the Cortals in business, and I had been their counsel in a complicated House of Lords appeal. It was the first occasion on which I met the daughter of the house.

It was a big dinner-party, representative of the family's many interests, starred with celebrities, none of whom were quite of the first order, except Geraldine, the Tory leader. There was a corps commander in the late War, who had taken up politics and hankered after a British variant of Fascism; Lord Lavan, who had governed some Dominion; a Royal Academician, who painted mystical topical allegories, a sort of blend of Blake and Frith; a director of the Bank of England; Smithers, the Cambridge economist; one or two city magnates; Claypole, the buxom novelist, whom his admirers regarded as an English Balzac; a Cotswold master of hounds up in London to visit his dentist; nothing young except Reggie.

The dinner was the elaborate affair which used to be in fashion when I first came to London – two dishes in every course, and the old-fashioned succession of wines instead of the monotonous champagne of today. Mrs Cortal sat beaming at her end of the table, with the blank amiability of the stone deaf, and the duties of hostess fell upon her daughter. I did not then realise her power over Reggie, but I watched her with admiration. She sat between Geraldine and Claypole, and she kept a big section of the table going. Her manner was a gentle alertness, quick to catch the ball of talk and return it, but never for one moment asserting itself. She had a pleasant trick of turning to a speaker with bright eyes and slightly raised brows, a trick which was an invitation to confidences. Being opposite her, I had a chance on such occasions of observing her face in profile, and it struck me that when she grew older she would have a look of Queen Victoria – the same ripeness and authority. Her performance was extraordinarily efficient, for she managed to make her neighbours talk as freely as if it had been a *tête-à-tête*, and at the same time broadcast the results to a considerable part of the company. Claypole's bubbling utterances were clarified by her into good conversation, and used as baits to entice Geraldine. The novelist's pose was that of a detached observer of life, a kindly and half-contemptuous critic of the ordinary struggle for success, whereas Geraldine was frankly an adept at the game, who made no concealment of his devotion to it. Claypole's mild cynicism, as interpreted by Verona, was just the thing to rouse the latter, who was adroitly led into spirited confessions of faith. There is no talker to compare with Geraldine when he is stirred, with his Irish humour, his dazzling overstatements, and his occasional flights into serious passion, and I have rarely heard him better than under Verona's stimulus. Claypole was flattered, for he was not in the habit of consorting with ex-Prime Ministers; the others were flattered, for they seemed to be privileged to share a great man's confidences. I saw Reggie's eyes fixed on the girl in respectful wonder.

When the women rose I had a talk with one of her brothers. There were two of them, very much alike except that one was fair and one was dark; both were clean shaven, and both wore eyeglasses. One was a director of the bank which had absorbed the family business, and the other was a partner in a well-known financial house. It was the latter who took the chair beside me, and presently I found myself able to place the Cortal family. The brothers belonged to the type which in my irreverent youth we called the "blood stockbroker" – the people who wanted to be gentlefolk first and city men afterwards, but were determined to be a complete success in both rôles. They had been to the best public school and the most fashionable college, and had acquired a manner blended of the guardsman, the country squire and the man of affairs. Young Mr Michael talked hunting to me and the prospects of the National, touched upon spring salmon and his last year's experience in Scotland, and told an excellent story which he had heard that afternoon in White's; but he also said some shrewd things about politics, and when I asked him a question about certain rumours in the City I got a crisp and well-informed reply. The Cortals were assuredly a competent family, though I decided that there was most quality in the girl. There had been something Napoleonic in that graceful profile which I had studied during dinner.

Afterwards in the drawing-room I saw Verona and Reggie in a corner. They were smiling on each other like old friends, and she was saying something to him with an affectionate, almost maternal air. I had decided that she would make an excellent wife for an ambitious politician, but now I began to wonder if she were not the wife for Reggie. Far more suitable than Pamela Brune, whose rarity and subtlety required a different kind of mate. Reggie needed somebody to form him and run him, somebody who would put order into the attractive chaos of his life. Those firm white hands of hers might do much with such plastic stuff.

That dinner was followed by many meetings between the two. Verona dined with him in his little house, they went to the play together, she mounted him with her own pack, the Myvern, and they had several days with the Bicester. The first dinner in Eaton Square was soon succeeded by another, this time a family party – the four Cortals, a maiden aunt, a married uncle and several cousins. Reggie was the only stranger, and he was there as an adopted member of the clan, Verona's chosen friend. Not a suitor but a friend. There was as yet no suggestion of love-making. It was one of these newfangled, cold-blooded companionships between the sexes.

But at this dinner it was apparent that the Cortal family had taken up Reggie seriously. He had already expounded his book-selling ambitions to Verona, as the kind of activity which made an appropriate background for the life he desired, and she had approved. Now it appeared that the whole family knew of it, and were acutely interested. There was a good opportunity, said the uncle – his name was Shenstone, and he was a member of a shipping firm which had done well during the War – for men like Reggie, who had the entry to many corners of English society, to establish himself as an honest broker between those who had, and wished to sell, and those who had not, and wished to buy. At present, he said, both sides went to the big dealers, and there was no human touch, but the human touch was needed in what should be more than a matter of cold business.

"Take pictures," said Mr Shenstone, who was a connoisseur. "I see very little fun in picking up what I want at a big sale at Christie's. What I like is to run something to earth in some odd corner of England, and get it by friendly negotiation. When I look at it on my walls, I remember the story behind it as well as its artistic merits. It stands for an episode in my life, like a stag's head which recalls a good stalk. I must say I am always grateful to anyone who puts me in the way of this sporting interest in collecting."

The others agreed. Mr Algernon, the elder brother, expanded the theme. "Reggie," he declared (they had very soon got on to Christian name terms), "can be the link between supply and demand, and a benefactor to both sides. He might be a sort of English Rosenbach. In every shire there are families who just manage to keep going. They have family possessions which they are far too proud to send to a sale, except in the very last resort. But very often they would gladly sell a picture or a book privately, if they knew how to do it, and such a sale might make all the difference to their comfort."

The maiden aunt assented, and told how a family of her acquaintance in Shropshire had been saved from penury by a discovery in a garret, through the medium of a visiting Cambridge don, of three Shakespeare quartos. One of the cousins recounted a similar event in Westmorland.

"Money is tight, no doubt," continued Mr Algernon, "but there's more of it about than people imagine. Fortunes are made on a falling as well as on a rising market. And people who have it do not know how to invest it. Industrials are too precarious, Government stocks have lost caste, and, since every part of the globe is under the weather, there is not the old attraction about foreign securities. I believe that there will be a growing tendency for people who have an ample margin of income to do what the Germans did when the mark was tumbling, and buy objects of art. But it must be something which is going to increase in value. Now, the fashion in pictures fluctuates, but not in books. There are only, say, twenty copies of an old book known to exist, and the numbers cannot be added to. An association book – say one which Walter Scott presented to Wordsworth with an autograph inscription – can never be duplicated. These things are better than bank-notes – they are solid bullion. The Americans have recognised this. A new millionaire in the States, as soon as he has made his pile, starts to found a library, though he may be scarcely literate. He knows what is certain to appreciate. He remembers the Huth and the Britwell sales."

"And think of the charm of the business!" said Verona. "You are dealing in spiritual as well as in commercial values. And the cleanness of it!"

"But it needs careful handling," said Mr Shenstone. "You cannot depend upon yourself, Mr Daker. You must get a staff together, and lay down your lines carefully, for what you want is an intelligence department and a scientifically arranged clearing-house. You have to organise the buying side, and know just where to lay your hands on what you want. And you have to organise your customers – to get into touch with the people on both sides of the Atlantic who are hungering for your services. Your watchword must be organisation."

"Rationalisation," said Mr Michael with a pleasant smile. "You must be in the fashion, my dear Reggie."

Reggie was flattered that his ideas should be taken so seriously by such a company, for he had the reverence for the businessman which is often an obsession with the unbusinesslike. He was excited, too. He saw himself becoming a figure, a power, a man of wealth, all that he had ruled out as beyond his compass – and this without sacrifice of the things he loved... But, as he caught Verona's beaming eyes, he had far down in his heart a little spasm of fear. For he seemed to see in them a hint of fetters.

V

The transformation of Reggie into a businessman was begun at once, and it was Verona who took charge of it. Politics at the moment were exciting, and in order to attend critical divisions I had to dine more than I liked at the House. The result was a number of improvised dinner-parties there, and at one of them I found Verona. No doubt Reggie had talked to her about me, so she treated me as if I were his elder brother. I thought her attractive, but I am bound to say a little formidable also, for I have rarely met any woman who knew her own mind so clearly.

The first thing to do was to get Reggie to organise his life. "You cannot achieve anything," she said sagely, "unless you make a plan." It was idle to think of running a business from the house in Brompton, so she had induced him to take an office – a pleasant little set of rooms which were fortunately vacant in the Adelphi neighbourhood. She had got him a secretary, a girl who had been at college with her, and she had started a system of card indexes, on which she dwelt lovingly. There was one for books, another for possible buyers, and a third for his acquaintances. She made a great point about codifying, so to speak, Reggie's immense acquaintance, for it was his chief asset in the business. Properly managed, it should give him access to quarters into which no dealer could penetrate. She nodded her head, and emphasised her points by tapping her right-hand fingers on her left-hand palm, exactly like a pretty schoolmistress. And several times she said "we," not "he," when she mentioned the undertaking.

She thought that he had better limit its scope. *Incunabula* and missals and such-like might be put aside as too ambitious. He should specialise on his old love, the seventeenth century, with excursions into the eighteenth and early nineteenth. There was already a vigorous interest in the Augustans, and she predicted a revival in the post-Romantics and the Victorians. Above all, he should specialise in "association books" and manuscripts, which were the kind of thing to which he was likely to have access. More was needed than an intelligence bureau: they wanted a research department to verify *provenances*. There would have to be a good deal of work in the Museum, and for this she could enrol several young women who had been with her at Oxford. She was compiling a list of experts in special branches, university dons and so forth, to whom they could turn in special cases for advice... Also they must make friends with the dealers, for it was no use antagonising the professionals; they could work in with them up to a point, and put little things in their way. Reggie knew a good many, and they were having some carefully selected luncheon-parties to extend his acquaintance. As for buyers, her brothers could help, for, being in the City, they knew where money was. Especially with America, she thought; both Algernon and Michael had a great deal of American business passing through their hands, and were frequently in New York. The American rich, she said, were an easier proposition than the English, for they talked freely of their hobbies instead of hiding them away like a secret vice.

I confess that I was enormously impressed by the girl's precision and good sense, and I was still more impressed when a few days later I ran across Reggie in the Athenaeum, a club which he had taken to frequenting. She had made a new man of him, a man with a purpose, tightened up and endowed with a high velocity. His eagerness had always been his chief charm, but now, instead of being diffused through the atmosphere, it seemed to have been canalised and given direction. "I'm one of the world's workers," he announced. "Office hours ten to five, and longer if required. I hop about the country too, like a bagman. I never knew that a steady grind was such fun."

"How is your colleague?" I asked.

"Marvellous!" It was his favourite adjective. "By Jove, what a head she has! Already she has forgotten more about my job than I ever knew!"

"What do you call yourself?"

"Ah, that's a puzzler. We must have a little private company, of course. We rather thought of 'The Interpreter's House.' Bunyan, you know. You see the idea – the place where things are explained to people and people are explained to themselves. It was Verona's notion. Jolly good, I think."

It seemed an ambitious name for a dealer in old books, but it was not for me to damp Reggie's ardour. I could only rejoice that someone had managed to break him to harness, a task in which his friends had hitherto conspicuously failed. I met him

145

occasionally in the company of the Cortal brothers, and I fancied that these glossy young men had something of the air of horsebreakers. They peered at the world through their glasses with a friendly proprietary air, and clearly regarded Reggie as their property. I was never quite at ease in their presence, for their efficiency was a little too naked; they were too manifestly well equipped, too elaborately men of the world. But Reggie was fascinated. He, whose clothes had never been his strong point, was now trim and natty, and wore, like them, the ordinary City regimentals.

I asked my nephew Charles what he thought of the brothers, and he laughed. "The shiny Cortals!" he replied. "Good enough chaps in their way, I believe. Quite a high reputation in their own line. Can't say I care much for them myself. Their minds are too dashed relevant, if you know what I mean. No margin to them – no jolly waste – everything tidied up and put to its best use. I should think more of them if now and then they condescended to make a bloomer. Their gentility is a little too self-conscious, too. Oh, and of course they haven't a scrap of humour – not what you and I would call humour."

One night I dined with one of the livery companies, and sat next to the uncle, Shenstone, who was prime warden. Under the influence of some wonderful Madeira he became talkative, and I realised that the harness laid upon Reggie's back was going to be something more than a business set. For Shenstone spoke of him as if he were a member of the family, with just that touch of affectionate candour with which one speaks of a promising but still problematical relative. "Dear old Reggie," said the uncle. "Best of good fellows and full of stuff, you know. Slackly brought up, and needs to learn business habits, but improving every day." I forbore to mention Verona's name, for I feared confidences. But I understood that Reggie was no more the unattached spectator of life; he had been gathered into the fold of a tightly knit and most competent clan.

Just before I went abroad for Easter I dined again in Verona's company, and had the privilege of a long and intimate talk. I learned why the name of "Interpreter's House" had been selected. Verona had visions which soared far beyond the brokerage of old books. She wanted to make the firm a purveyor of English traditions, a discreet merchant of English charm. It would guide strangers of leisure into paths where they could savour fully the magic of an ancient society. It would provide seekers with a background which, unless they were born to it, they could never find. It would be a clearing-house for delicate and subtle and indefinable things. It would reveal and interpret the sacred places of our long history. In a word, it would "rationalise" and make available to the public the antique glamour of these islands.

It all sounds preposterous, but there was nothing preposterous about her exposition. She had a trick, when excited, of half-closing her lids, which softened the rather hard vitality of her eyes, and at such times she lost her usual briskness and was almost wistful. "*You must* understand what I mean. We are all agreed that England is Merlin's Isle of Gramarye." (I quote her exact words.) "But to how many is that more than a phrase? It is so hard to get behind the veil of our noisy modernism to the lovely and enduring truth. You know how sensitive Reggie is to such things. Well, we want to help people who are less fortunate. Strangers come to London – from the provinces – from America – steeped in London's romance which they have got from books. But the reality is a terrible anticlimax. They need to be helped if they are to recapture the other Londons which are still there layer on layer, the Londons of Chaucer and the Elizabethans, and Milton and Dr Johnson and Charles Lamb and Dickens... And Oxford...and Edinburgh... and Bath...and the English country. We want to get past the garages and petrol pumps and county council cottages to the ancient rustic England which can never die."

"I see. Glamour off the peg. You will charge a price for it, of course?"

She looked at me gravely and reprovingly, and her lids opened to reveal agate eyes.

"We shall charge a price," she said. "But moneymaking will not be our first object."

I had offended her by my coarse phrase, and I got no more confidences that evening. It was plain that Reggie was being equipped with several kinds of harness; his day was mapped out, he was inspanned in a family team, and now his vagrant fancies were to be regimented. I thought a good deal about him on my holiday, while I explored the spring flowers of the Jura. One of my reflections, I remember, was that Moe's moment of prevision had failed badly so far as he was concerned. Reggie was not likely to undertake any foreign adventure, having anchored himself by so many chains to English soil.

VI

Some time in May I began to have my doubts about the success of the partnership.

May is the pleasantest of months for a London dweller. Wafts of spring are blown in from its green cincture, the parks are at their gayest, there is freshness in the air, and the colours, the delicate half-shades of the most beautiful city on earth, take on a new purity. Along with late October, May had always been Reggie's favourite season. First there would be the early canter in the Park. Then a leisurely breakfast, the newspaper, and his first pipe, with the morning sun making delectable patterns on the bookshelves. He would write a few letters and walk eastward, dwelling lovingly on the sights and the sounds – the flower-girls, the shoppers, the bustle of the main streets, the sudden peace of the little squares with their white stucco and green turf and purple lilacs and pink hawthorns. Luncheon at one of his clubs would follow, or perhaps an agreeable meal at a friend's house.

In the afternoon he had many little tasks – visits to the Museum, the sales or the picture galleries, researches in bookshops, excursions into queer corners of the City. He liked to have tea at home, and would spend the hours before dinner over books, for he was a discriminating but voracious reader. Then would come dinner; with a group of young men at a club or restaurant; or at some ceremonial feast, where he enjoyed the experience of meeting new people and making friendly explorations; or best of all at home, where he read till bedtime.

He had his exercise, too. He played a little polo at Roehampton and a good deal of tennis. He was an ardent fisherman, and usually spent the weekends on a Berkshire trout stream, where he had a rod. He would have a delightful Friday evening looking out tackle, and would be off at cockrow on Saturday in his little car, returning late on the Sunday night with a sunburnt face and an added zest for life... I always felt that, for an idle man, Reggie made a very successful business of his days, and sometimes I found it in my heart to envy him.

But now all this had changed. I had a feverish time myself that May with the General Election, which did not, of course, concern Reggie. When I got back to Town and the turmoil was over, I ran across him one afternoon in the Strand, and observed a change in him. His usual wholesome complexion had gone; he looked tired and white and harassed – notably harassed. But he appeared to be in good spirits. "Busy!" he cried. "I should think I was. I never get a moment to myself. I haven't had a rod in my hand this year – haven't been out of London except on duty. You see, we're at the most critical stage – laying down our lines – got to get them right, for everything depends on them. Oh yes, thanks. We're doing famously for beginners. If only the American slump would mend..."

I enquired about Miss Cortal, as I was bound to do. No engagement had been announced, but such a relationship could only end in marriage. People had long ago made that assumption.

"Oh, Verona's very well. A bit overworked like me." There was an odd look in his eyes, and something new in his voice – not the frank admiration and friendliness of the pre-Easter period – something which was almost embarrassment. I set it down to the shyness of a man in first love.

I asked him to dine, but he couldn't – was full up for weeks ahead. He consulted a little book, and announced his engagements. They all seemed to be with members of the Cortal family. Luncheon was the same. On my only free days he was booked to Shenstone, the maiden aunt, and cousins from Norfolk who had taken a house in Town. He left me with the same hustled, preoccupied face... Next day I saw him on the Embankment walking home with the Cortal brothers. They were smiling and talking, but somehow he had the air of a man taking exercise between two genial warders.

I spoke to my cynical nephew about it. "The Shinies!" Charles exclaimed. "Not the Sheenies – there's nothing Jewish about Cortal Frères. When will the world realise that we produce in England something much tougher than any Hebrew? We call them the Shinies, because of their high varnish... Old Reggie is corralled all right, shoes off, feet fired and the paddock gates bolted!... Will he marry the girl? I should jolly well think so. He's probably up to his ears in love with her, but even if he loathed her name he would have to go through with it... And he'll espouse a dashed lot more than the buxom Miss Verona – all her uncles and her nephews and her cousins and her aunts for ever and ever. They say that when a man marries a Jewess he finds himself half-smothered under a great feather-bed of steamy consanguinity. Well, it will be the same with the Cortals, only the clan will be less sticky. Reggie will never again call his soul his own. I'm not sure that he'll want to, but anyhow he won't. They'll never let him alone. He used to be rather a solitary bird, but now he'll have his fill of relations, all as active as fleas. What does the Bible say? 'He shall receive an hundredfold houses, and brethren, and sisters, and mothers – with persecutions...' With persecutions, mark you. Reggie is for it all right."

As it happened I was so busy with arrears of cases that my life was cloistered during the last week of May and the first of June, and I thought no more of Reggie's fortunes. But on the seventh day of June I had a letter from him, enclosing the proof of a kind of prospectus and asking me what I thought of it.

I thought many things about it. It was a statement of the aims of the "Interpreter's House," which was to be circulated to a carefully selected list in England and America. In every sentence it bore the mark of Verona's fine Roman hand. No man could have written it. There was an indecency about its candour and its flat-footed clarity from which the most pachydermatous male would have recoiled.

In its way it was horribly well done. It was a kind of Stores List of the varieties of English charm and the easiest way to get hold of them. Merlin's Isle of Gramarye had at last got its auctioneer's catalogue. Not that it was written in the style of an estate-agent. It was uncommonly well written, full of good phrases and apposite quotations, and it carried a fine bookish flavour. But ye gods! it was terrible. Relentlessly it set down in black and white all the delicate, half-formed sentiments we cherish in our innermost hearts, and dare not talk about. It was so cursedly explicit that it brushed the bloom off whatever it touched. A June twilight became the glare of an arc lamp, the greenery of April the arsenical green of a chemist's shop. Evasive dreams were transformed into mercantile dogmas. It was a kind of simony, a trafficking in sacred things. The magic of England was "rationalised" with a vengeance... There could be no doubt about its effectiveness. I could see the shoddy culture of two continents seizing upon it joyously as a final statement of the "English proposition." It was a magnificent commercial prospectus for the "Interpreter's House." But I wondered how

Reggie felt about it – Reggie who had always had a maidenly shyness about his inner world.

It seemed to me that the time had come for a heart-to-heart talk with him. I resolved to be very careful, for I was dealing with perilous stuff. If he was in love with Verona I dared not speak my mind, and even if there was no love, there were deep obligations of gratitude.

He dined with me at the House on the evening of June eighth, and afterwards we talked in a corner of the terrace. His looks made me uneasy, for he seemed both listless and restless. He kept looking nervously about him, as if at any moment something hostile might attack him. He had the air of a smallish rabbit caught in a largish trap.

But it was a stoical rabbit, for to me he made no complaint. In a leaden voice he announced that he was the most fortunate of men. His business was flourishing, and in the autumn it was proposed to form a company... At last he had found a vocation in life. Yet there was as much conviction in his voice as in the babbling of a sleep-walker.

I asked him baldly when he was going to be married. In even tones he replied that nothing had as yet been settled. But the form of his answer implied that something would soon be settled. I forbore to enquire further, for his gaze was fixed glassily on the tower of Lambeth Palace.

Then of his own accord he asked me what I had thought of the prospectus. I hastily resolved that no good could come of candour. Reggie had made his bed and meant to lie on it, and it was not for me to put in extra thorns.

"Very well done," I said; "what the Germans call *appetitlich*. It should give you an excellent send-off."

"You didn't think it vulgar?"

"Not a bit," I lied. "Half-tones and broken lights won't do in business. You must be emphatic."

He nodded. "I agree with you. She wrote it, you know. Michael revised it, but in substance it was her work."

I said something silly about having detected the finer female touch. Then he rose to go – he had an appointment with an American at the Savoy. It had been the most hopeless evening, for I had never come near him. He seemed to be separated from me by a vast thicket, and I felt that if I laid an axe to the bushes they would scream like mandrakes.

When we said good-bye, I felt a sudden wave of liking and pity. I patted him on the shoulder. "I hope you're going to be very happy, old man," I said, but he made no answer.

As I went back to my rooms I suddenly thought with grim amusement of what had happened at Flambard a year before. That story, so far as Reggie was concerned, was over. Youth's infinite choice of roads had given place to a rigid groove, presided over by a relentless marmoreal blonde.

VII

But I was wrong. It may have been merely the sight of me as part of his old life, or it may have been my last words, but something that night brought Reggie to breaking-point. When he got home he rang up Tallis at Libanus, found that he was in London, ran him to ground at the Travellers', and arranged to meet him the following morning. I do not know why he turned to Tallis, except that it was at his house that he had first met Verona, and that he seemed to stand for him on the dividing-line between a world which he had loved and a world which he had come to hate and fear.

Tallis told me this part of the story. They lunched together, and talked afterwards beside the fireplace in the hall. He had not seen Reggie for nearly six months, and was shocked at the change in him. As he expressed it, Reggie's coat was all sulky and his body like a cab-horse.

According to Tallis, Reggie plunged at once into his tale, telling it with a kind of angry vehemence, rather dim about details, but desperately clear on the main points. He had lost everything he cared for in life, he said; he was involved in a juggernaut of a business, ground under a juggernaut of a family, and about to be tied up for life to a juggernaut of a girl. This last he only implied, for he spoke no disrespectful word of Verona.

"You haven't proposed to her?" Tallis asked.

Reggie said he hadn't, but that everybody expected him to, including, he feared, the lady herself. There was to be a Cortal family dinner the following night, and it had been gently but firmly hinted to him that that would be a fitting moment to announce the engagement.

"I gather that you're not in love with her?" said Tallis.

Reggie looked wooden. He was trying to live up to his code. "I admire her immensely," he stammered. "And I'm grateful to her – far more grateful than I can ever express – I owe her a tremendous lot... She has worked like a slave for me – given up most of her time – oh, she's a marvel! Unselfish, too... Nobody has ever taken such an interest in me..."

"I know, I know. But do you love her?"

Then, just as an ice jam cracks on a river, Reggie's decorum went with a rush.

"No, by God," he cried wildly. "I don't love her! And she doesn't love me. She has taken me up, and she'll stick to me till I'm in my grave, but she doesn't love me. She couldn't love anybody – not made that way. I'm only her business partner, the thing she needed to round off her life... Love her! O Lord, I'm nearer hating her. I'm in terror of her. She mesmerises me, like a stoat with a rabbit. She has twenty times my brains, and I've simply got to do as I'm told... And then there's her awful family. I'm lapped in them, suffocated by them. I loathe her infernal apes of brothers – they're so cursed gentlemanlike and efficient and patronising. Dash it all, man, there are times when I can scarcely keep from hitting their blinking faces."

He dragged a paper from his pocket, and flung it at Tallis.

"There's worse still. Look at that. Read it carefully and smack your lips over its succulent beastliness. That's the Cortal idea of what I'm going to give my life to. That's the prospectus of my business. The 'Interpreter's House,' by God! It has interpreted them to me all right. Do you grasp the perfect hell of it? I'm to spend my days with the things I thought I cared about, but the gloss is rubbed off every one of them. I'm to be a sort of Cook's guide to culture on a sound commercial basis. Damn it, I'd rather clean out drains in Chicago, for then I should know that there was a jolly world to which I might some day return. But it's just that jolly world that's been blasted for me."

He dropped his head on his hands and groaned.

"There's no way out except to cut my throat, and that wouldn't be playing the game. I suppose I must go through with it. I mustn't behave like a cad... Besides, I daren't. I simply haven't the nerve."

Tallis was smiling cryptically.

"Funny you should tell me this. For the same thing happened to me about a quarter of a century ago."

Reggie looked up quickly. "Gospel truth?" he asked.

"Gospel truth. She was an American – from Philadelphia – very pretty, and sweet, and sticky as barley sugar. She had a family, too, just like the Cortals, and she had a business mind. She took me up, and meant to run me, and at first I was fascinated. Then I saw that it would mean Gehenna – Gehenna for both of us."

"What did you do?" The question came like a pistol crack.

"I did the only thing. Ran away and hid myself. Very far away – to western Tibet. I thought at the time that I was behaving like a cad, but now I know that it would have been far more caddish to have gone on. Marriage by capture doesn't suit people like you and me."

Reggie stared.

"I am not going to Tibet," he said. He had forgotten all about Moe and Flambard, but something remained by way of an inhibition against the Orient.

"No need to. The world is wide. There's plenty of other places."

Tallis rose and rang a bell.

"I'm an abstemious man," he said; "but I always drink brandy in moments of crisis. This is a crisis for you, my lad, and I'm going to take charge of it. You must run away and hide, like a little boy. It's the only thing to do, and it's also the wisest and the most courageous thing. Cut the painter, burn the ship, hew down the bridge behind you."

There was light in Reggie's dull eyes.

"Where shall I run to?" he asked, and his voice had lost its flatness.

"Come with me," said Tallis. "I'm off tomorrow morning, and shall be away for the better part of a year. I have a bit of work to do before I can finish my book. I have shut up Libanus and sent my valuables to the bank. We go up to Liverpool tonight, so you will just have time to make your arrangements."

"I'm not going east," said Reggie, as the vague recollection rose again in him.

"No more am I. I am going west."

Tallis fetched a sheet of club notepaper on which he wrote with a fat gold pencil.

"We must proceed according to Cocker," he said. "No secret shuffling out of the country. This is an announcement of my departure which will appear in the press tomorrow, and I have added your name. It is your Declaration of Independence to all whom it may concern. Also you are going straight from here to see Verona and tell her. That will correspond to the tea chests in Boston Harbour. The train for Liverpool leaves at ten minutes past seven. We can dine on it."

"What shall I say to her?" Reggie faltered, but not as one without hope.

"That's your concern. You will find words if you really mean business. You are improving on my conduct, for I never made my adieux to the lady, but then Verona has done a good deal for you, and she is old Jim Jack's niece. After all, it's a kindness to her, for a girl with her brains can do better for herself than a chap like you. When you get home, you'll find that she has espoused some appalling magnate."

Reggie was on his feet, his lassitude gone, his shoulders squared. He spruced himself up with the help of an adjacent mirror, and his movements were brisk.

"Right," he said. "The seven-ten at Euston. I needn't take much luggage, for I can buy what I want in…" He stopped short. "New York is no good. I can't hide myself there. The Cortals know half the place, and those blighted brothers are always hopping over."

Tallis was paying for the brandy.

"You needn't worry about that," he said. "New York is only our jumping-off point. We are bound for farther south… Central America…a place called Yucatan."

V

SIR ROBERT GOODEVE

"A covert place
Where you might think to find a din
Of doubtful talk, and a live flame
Wandering, and many a shape whose name
Not itself knoweth, and old dew,
And your own footsteps meeting you,
And all things going as they came."

D G ROSSETTI, *The Portrait.*

V

Sir Robert Goodeve

I

For five months after that Whitsuntide at Flambard I saw and heard nothing of Goodeve. But I could not get him out of my mind, for of all the party he had struck me as the one to whom the experience meant the most, the one who had been the most tense and expectant. Whatever he had seen on the phantasmal *Times* page of a year ahead he would take with the utmost seriousness. I liked him so much that I was a little anxious about him. He was finer clay than the others.

My own attitude towards Moe's experiment varied during these months. Sometimes I was inclined to consider the whole thing the vagary of a genius gone mad. But there were moments when I remembered his brooding pits of eyes and the strange compulsion of his talk, and came again under his spell. I made an opportunity to see Landor – the man I had telephoned from Flambard before my first conversation with Moe – and tried to discover what substance a trained scientist might find in Moe's general theory. But Landor was not very helpful. The usual reaction had begun, and I gathered that at the moment the dead man had more critics than followers. Landor declared that he did not profess to understand him, but that the common view was that the speculations of his last years had been a sad declension from his earlier achievements in physics and mathematics. "It is the old story," he said. "Age means a breaking down of partition walls, and the imagination muddies the reason. Moe should have ended as a poet or a preacher. He had got a little beyond science." I tried to put limpingly Moe's theory of Time, and Landor wrinkled his brows. "I know that there are people working on that line," he said, "but I don't think they have made much of it. It's rather outside my beat. More psychology than physics."

This conversation did little to reassure me. So far as Goodeve was concerned, it was not the actual validity of Moe's doctrine that mattered, but his own reactions to the experience. And an incident in the last week of October rather shook the scepticism which I had been trying to cultivate. For I opened the newspaper one morning to learn that young Molsom had been appointed a Lord of Appeal straight from the Bar, a most unexpected choice. Yet *I* had expected it, for in my efforts to throw my mind a year forward under Moe's direction I had had a vision of the future House of Lords tribunal. The figure on the Woolsack had been blurred, but Molsom had been perfectly clear, with his big nose and his habit of folded arms.

In the beginning of November Sir Thomas Twiston died, and Goodeve, the prospective candidate, had to face a by-election. The Marton division of Dorset was reckoned one of the safest Tory seats in the land, but this contest had not the dullness of the usual political certainty. Goodeve was opposed, and though the opposition was futile, the election gave an opportunity for some interesting propaganda. It fell just after Geraldine had concluded his tour in the North, where he had made a feature of unemployment and his new emigration policy – a policy which, as I have already mentioned, was strongly disliked by many of his own party. Goodeve, who had always been an eager Imperialist, saw his chance. He expounded his leader's views with equal eloquence and far greater knowledge. The press reported him at length, for his speeches were excellent copy; he dealt wittily and faithfully with both Waldemar and the Liberals and the "big business" group in his own party. Before the contest, was over he had become a considerable personality in politics.

In fulfilment of an old promise I went down to speak for him on the eve of the poll. We had three joint meetings, and I was much impressed by his performance. Here was a new voice and a new mind, a man who could make platitudes seem novelties, and convince his hearers that the most startling novelties were platitudes. He looked vigorous and fit, and his gusto seemed to dispose of my former anxieties.

But at the hotel on the evening of the election day I realised that he had been trying himself high. His fine, dark face was too sharp for health, and his wholesome colour had gone. He was so tired that he could scarcely eat a mouthful of supper, but when I wanted him to go to bed he declared that it was no good, since he could not sleep. He kept me up till the small hours, but he did not talk much – not a word about the election and its chances. Next day he looked better, but I was glad when the declaration of the poll was over. He was in by an immense majority, nearly fourteen thousand, and there was the usual row in the streets and a tour of committee rooms. I had meant to get back to Town for luncheon, but something in his face made me change my plans. "Won't you spare me one night?" he begged. "Come back with me to Goodeve. I implore you, Leithen. You do me more good than anybody else on earth, and I need you to help me to recover my balance." I could not resist the appeal in his eyes, so I sent off a few telegrams, and in the late afternoon escaped with him from Marton.

It was a drive of about forty miles through a misty November twilight. He scarcely uttered a word, and I respected his mood and also kept silence. The man was clearly dog-tired. His house received us with blazing fires and the mellow shadows of the loveliest hall in England. He went straight upstairs, announcing that he would have a bath and lie down till dinner.

At dinner his manner was brisker. He seemed to feel the comfort of release from the sickening grind of an election, and I realised that the thing had been for him a heavy piece of collar work. Goodeve was not the man to enjoy the debauch of half-truths inevitable in platform speeches. I expected him to talk about politics, which at the time were in a considerable mess. I told him that he was entering Parliament at a dramatic moment with a reputation already made, and said the sort of encouraging things which the ordinary new member would have welcomed. But he did not seem much interested in the gossip which I retailed. When I speculated on Geraldine's next move he yawned.

He was far more inclined to talk about his house. I had never stayed at Goodeve before, and had fallen at once under the spell of its cloudy magnificence. I think I used that very phrase, for such was my main impression. It had an air of spaciousness far greater than its actual dimensions warranted, for all its perspectives seemed to end in shadows, to fade away into a world where our measurements no longer held... When I had first talked with him at Flambard he had been in revolt against the dominance of the old house which was always trying to drag him back into the past, and had spoken of resisting the pull of his ancestors. Now he seemed to welcome it. He had been making researches in its history, and was full of curious knowledge about his forbears. After dinner he had the long gallery on the first floor lit up, and we made a tour of inspection of the family portraits.

I was struck, I remember, by the enduring physical characteristics of his race. Most of his ancestors were dark men with long faces, and that odd delicacy about mouth and chin which one sees in the busts of Julius Caesar. Not a strong stock, perhaps, but a fine one. Goodeve himself, with his straight brows, had a more masterful air than the pictures, but when I looked at him again I thought I saw the same slight over-refinement, something too mobile in the lips, too anxious in the eyes. "Tremulous, impressional," Emerson says that the hero must be, and these were the qualities of the old Goodeves which leaped at once from their portraits. Many had been heroes – notably the Sir Robert who fell at Naseby and the Sir Geoffrey who died with Moore at Corunna – but it was a heroism for death rather than for life. I wondered how the race had managed to survive so long.

Oddly enough it was their deaths that seemed chiefly to interest Goodeve. He had all the details of them – this one had died in his bed at sixty-three, that in the hunting-field at forty, another in a drinking bout in the early twenties. They appeared for the most part to have been a short-lived race and tragically fated...

By and by this mortuary tale began to irritate me. I preferred to think of the cuirassed, periwigged or cravated gentlemen, the hooped and flounced ladies, as in the vigour of life in which the artist had drawn them. And then I saw that in Goodeve's face which set me wondering. On his own account he was trying to puzzle out some urgent thing – urgent for himself. He was digging into his family history and interrogating the painted faces on his walls to find an answer to some vital problem of his own.

What it might be I could not guess, but it disquieted me, and I lent an inattentive ear to his catalogue. And then I suddenly got enlightenment.

We had left the gallery and were making our way to the library through a chain of little drawing-rooms. All had been lit up, and all were full of pictures, mostly Italian, collected by various Goodeves during the Grand Tour. They were cheerful rooms, papered not panelled, with a pleasant Victorian complacency about them. But in the last the walls were dark oak, and above the fireplace was a picture which arrested me. Goodeve seemed to wish to hurry me on, but when he saw my interest he too halted.

It was a Spanish piece, painted I should think by someone who had come under El Greco's influence, and had also studied the Dutch school. I am no authority on art, but if it be its purpose to make an instant and profound impression on a beholder, then this was a masterpiece. It represented a hall in some great house, paved with black and white marble. There was a big fire burning in an antique fireplace, and the walls blazed with candles. But the hangings were a curious dusky crimson, so that in spite of the brilliant lighting the place was sombre, suggesting more a church than a dwelling. The upper walls and the corners were in deep shadow. On the floor some ten couples were dancing, an ordered dance in which there was no gaiety, and the dancers' faces were all set and white. Other people were sitting round the walls, rigidly composed as if they were curbing some strong passion. At the great doors at the far end men-at-arms stood on guard, so that none should pass. On every face, in every movement was fear – fear, and an awful expectation of something which was outside in the night. You felt that at any moment the composure might crack, that the faces would become contorted with terror and the air filled with shrieks.

The picture was lettered "La Peste," but I did not need the words to tell me the subject. It was a house in a city where the plague was raging. These people were trying to forget the horror. They had secluded themselves in a palace, set guards at the door, and tried to shut out the world. But they had failed, for the spectre rubbed shoulders with each. They might already have the poison in their blood, and in an hour be blue and swollen. One heard the rumble of the dead-cart on the outer cobbles making a dreadful bass to the fiddles.

I have never received a stronger impression from any picture. I think I must have cried out, for Goodeve came close to me.

"My God, what a thing!" I said. "The man who painted that was a devil!"

"He understood the meaning of fear," was the answer.

"Not honest human fear," I said. "That is the panic of hell."

Goodeve shook his head.

"Only fear. Everybody there has still a hope that they may escape. They are still only fearful and anxious. Panic will come when the first yellow pustules show on the skin. For panic you must have a certainty."

Something in his tone made me turn my eyes from the picture to his face. He had become like all his ancestors; the firm modern moulding had slackened into something puzzled and uncertain, as of a man groping in a dim world. And in his eyes and around his lips was the grey shadow of a creeping dread.

My mind flew back to Flambard. I knew now that on that June morning Goodeve had received some fateful message. I thought I could guess what the message had been.

II

We drifted to the library, and dropped into chairs on each side of the hearth. It was a chilly night, so the fire had been kept high, and the room was so arranged that the light was concentrated around where we sat, and the rest left in shadow. So I had a good view of Goodeve's face against a dusky background. He had lit a pipe, and was staring at the logs, his whole body relaxed like a tired man's. But I caught him casting furtive glances in my direction. He wanted to tell me something; perhaps he saw that I had guessed, and wanted me to ask a question, but I felt oddly embarrassed and waited.

He spoke first.

"Moe is dead," he said simply, and I nodded.

"It is a pity," he went on. "I should have liked another talk with him. Did you understand his theories?"

I shook my head.

"No more did I," he said. "I don't think I ever could. I have been reading Paston and Crevalli and all round the subject, but I can't get the hang of it. My mind hasn't been trained that way."

"Nor mine," I replied. "Nor, as far as I can gather, that of anybody living. Moe seems to have got into a world of his own where no one could keep up with him."

167

"It's a pity," he said again. "If one could have followed his reasoning and been able to judge for one's self its value, it would have made a difference...perhaps."

"I ought to tell you," I said, "that I've been making enquiries, and I find that our best people are not inclined to take Moe as gospel."

"So I gather. But I'm not sure that that helps. Even if his theories were all wrong, the fact would still remain that he could draw back the curtain a little. It may have been an illusion, of course, but we can't tell...yet."

He stared into the fire, and then said very gently, "You see – I got a glimpse inside."

"I know," I said.

"Yes," he went on, "and I believe you have guessed what I saw."

I nodded.

"Let me tell you everything. It's a comfort to me to be able to tell you... You're the only man I could ever confide in... You were there yourself and saw enough to take it seriously... I read, for about a quarter of a second, my own obituary. One takes in a good deal in a flash of time if the mind is expectant. It was a paragraph about two inches long far down on the right-hand side of *The Times* page opposite the leaders – the usual summary of what is given at length in the proper obituary pages. It regretted to announce the death of Sir Robert Goodeve, Baronet, of Goodeve, MP for the Marton division of Dorset. There was no doubt about the man it meant... Then it said something about a growing political reputation and a maiden speech which would not be soon forgotten. I have the exact words written down."

"Nothing more?"

"No...yes. There was another dead man in the paragraph, a Colonel Dugald Chatto, of Glasgow... That was all."

Goodeve knocked out his pipe and got to his feet. He stretched himself, as if his legs had cramped, and I remember thinking how fine a figure of a man he was as he stood tensely in the firelight. He was staring away from me into a dim corner of the room. He seemed to be endeavouring by a bodily effort to shake himself free of a burden.

I tried to help.

"I'm in the confidence of only one of the others," I said. "Reggie Daker. He read the announcement of his departure for Yucatan on a scientific expedition. Reggie knows nothing about science and hates foreign parts, and he declares that nothing will make him budge from England. He says that forewarned is forearmed, and that he is going to see that *The Times* next June is put in the cart. He has already forgotten all about the thing... There seems to me to be some sense in that point of view. If you know what's coming you can take steps to avoid it... For example, supposing you had given up your parliamentary candidature, you could have made *The Times* wrong on that point, so why shouldn't you be able to make it wrong on others?"

He turned and bent his strong dark brows on me.

"I thought of that. I can't quite explain why, but it seemed to me scarcely to be playing the game. Rather like funking. No. I'm not going to alter my plan of life out of fear. That would be giving in like a coward."

But there was none of the boisterousness of defiance in his voice. He spoke heavily, as if putting into words an inevitable but rather hopeless resolution.

"Look here, Goodeve," I said. "You and I are rational men of the world and we can't allow ourselves to be the sport of whimsies. There are two ways of looking at this Flambard business. It may have been pure illusion caused by the hypnotic powers of a tremendous personality like Moe, with no substance of reality behind it. It may have been only a kind of dream. If you dreamed you were being buried in Westminster Abbey next week you wouldn't pay the slightest attention."

"That is a possible view," he said. But I could see that it was not the view he took himself. Moe's influence upon him had been so profound, that, though he could not justify his faith on scientific grounds, he was a convinced believer.

I had a sudden idea.

"Listen to me. I can prove that it is illusion. Moe told us that our minds could get a larger field of observation, which would include part of the future. Yes, but the observing thing was still our mind, and that presupposes a living man. Therefore for a man to see the report of his death is a contradiction in terms."

He turned his unquiet eyes on me.

"Curious that you should say that, for I raised the very point with Moe. His answer was that the body of the observer might be dead, but that the mind did not die... I was bound to admit his argument, for, you see, I, too, believe in the immortality of the soul."

There was such complete conviction in his tone that I had to give up my point, though I was not convinced, even on Goodeve's hypothesis.

"Very well. The other view is that, by some unknown legerdemain, you actually saw what will be printed in *The Times* on the next tenth of June. But it may be a hoax or some journalistic blunder. False news of a man's death has often been published. You remember Billy Devereux seven years ago. Reggie Daker isn't going to Yucatan, and there's no more reason why you should be dead."

He smiled, and his voice was a little more cheerful. "I would point out," he said, "that there is a considerable difference between the cases. Going to Yucatan is a voluntary act which, requires the actor's co-operation, while dying is usually an involuntary affair."

"Never mind," I cried. "We are bound to believe in free will up to a point. It's the condition on which life is conducted. What you must try to do is to banish the whole thing from your mind. Defy that damned oracle. You've begun right by getting into Parliament. Go on and make the best maiden speech of the day. Fate will always yield if you stand up to it."

"Thank you, Leithen," he said. "I think that is sound advice. I'm ashamed to have let you see that the thing worried me. Nobody else in the world has the slightest notion... But you're an understanding fellow. If you're willing, you can be a wonderful stand-by to me, for I'm a lonely bird and apt to brood... I've another comfort, for there's that second man in the same case. I told you that I read the name of Colonel Dugald Chatto. I've made enquiries about him. He's a Glasgow wine merchant, who was a keen Territorial, and commanded a battalion in the War. Man about forty-seven, the hard, spare, scratch-man-at-golf type that never was ill in its life. Health is important, for *The Times* would have said 'killed,' if it had been death by accident. I've noticed that that's its custom."

"There's nothing much wrong with your health," I put in.

"No. I'm pretty fit."

Again he stretched his arms, as if pushing an incubus away from him. He looked down at me with an embarrassed smile. But the next moment his eyes were abstracted and back in the shadowy corners.

III

Goodeve took his seat in the House, and then for a fortnight sat stolidly on the back Opposition benches. Everybody was curious about him, and our younger people were prepared to take him to their hearts. They elected him straight off a member of a group of Left-wing Tories, who dined together once a week and showed signs of becoming a Fourth Party. But he seemed to be shy of company. He never went near the smoking-room, he never wrote letters in the library, one never saw him gossiping in the lobbies. He was polite and friendly, but as aloof as the planet Mars. There he sat among the shadows of the back benches, listening attentively to the debates, with a queer secret smile on his face. One might have thought that he was contemptuous of it all, but for his interested eyes. He was watching closely how the game was played, but at the same time a big part of his mind was sojourning in another country.

There was general interest in his maiden speech, and it was expected that it would come soon. You see, what was agitating the country at the moment was Geraldine's new crusade, and Goodeve had fought his election on that, and had indeed proved himself as good an exponent of the new Imperialism as his leader. Some of his sentences had already passed into the stock stuff of the press and the platform. He got the usual well-meant advice from the old hands. Members who did not know him would take him aside, and advise him to get the atmosphere of the place before he spoke. "It won't do," they told him, "to go off at half-cock. You've come here with a good deal of prestige, and you mustn't throw it away." Others thought that he should begin modestly and not wait for a full-dress occasion with red carpets down. "Slip into the debate quietly some dinner-hour," they counselled, "and try out your voice. The great thing is to get the ice broken. You'll have plenty of chances later for the bigger thing." Goodeve's smiling reticence, you see, made many people think that he would be nervous. I asked him about his plans, and he shook his head. "Haven't got any, I shall take my chance when it comes. I'm in no hurry." And then he added what I did not like. "It's a long time till the tenth of June."

I asked our Whips, and was told that he had never spoken to them about the best moment to lift up his voice. They seemed to find him an enigma. John Fortingall, who ran the dining group I have mentioned, confessed himself puzzled. "I thought we had got an absolute winner," he declared, "but now I'm not so sure. There's no doubt about the brains, and they tell me he can put the stuff across. Everybody who knows him says he's a good fellow too. But all I can say is, he's a darned bad mixer. He looks at you as if you were his oldest friend, and then shoves you gently away as if you were going to pinch his tie-pin. Too frosty a lad for my taste."

Goodeve told nobody about his plans, and he succeeded most successfully in surprising the House. He chose the most critical debate of the early session, which took place less than three weeks after he entered Parliament. It was a resolution of no confidence moved by Geraldine, and was meant to be a demonstration in force against the Government, and also a defiance to the stand-patters on our own side.

There was no hope of success, for Waldemar and the Liberals would vote against it, and we could not count on polling our full strength, but it was believed that it might drive a wedge into Labour and have considerable effect in the country. Goodeve must have had some private arrangement with the Speaker, but he said nothing to his Front Bench. The Leader of the Opposition was as much taken by surprise as anybody.

Geraldine moved the resolution in one of the best speeches I ever heard from him – conciliatory and persuasive, extraordinarily interesting, and salted with his engaging humour. He deliberately kept the key low, and attempted none of the flights of eloquence which had marked his campaign in the North. Mayot replied – the Prime Minister was to wind up the debate – and Mayot also was good. His line was the sagacious enthusiast, welcoming Geraldine's ideals, approving his general purpose, but damping down his ardours with wholesome common sense – the kind of speech which never fails of appeal to Englishmen. Then came Waldemar in a different mood. It was a first-class debating performance, and he searched out the joints in Geraldine's harness and probed them cunningly. He was giving no quarter, and there was vitriol on his sword's point. He concluded with a really fine defence of the traditional high-road of policy, and a warning against showy bypaths, superbly delivered and couched in pure, resounding, eighteenth-century prose. When he sat down there was nearly a minute of that whole-hearted applause which the House gives, irrespective of party, to a fine parliamentary achievement.

Then Goodeve was called, and not, as was expected, the ex-Foreign Secretary. He had a wonderful audience, for the House was packed, and keyed up, too, by Waldemar, but it was the kind of audience which should have made the knees of a novice give under him. There had been three speeches by old parliamentary hands, each excellent of its kind, and any maiden effort must be an anticlimax. But Goodeve seemed to be unconscious of the peril. He was sitting at the corner of the second bench above the gangway, and had been taking notes unconcernedly while the others were speaking. He had a few slips of paper in his hand, and that hand did not shake. He looked around his audience, and his eye was composed. He began to speak, and his voice was full and steady...

The House expects a new member to show a becoming modesty. A little diffidence, an occasional hesitation, are good tactics in a maiden speech, whether or not there be any reason for them. But there was no halting, no deprecatory air with Goodeve, and after the first minute nobody expected it. It would have been absurd, for this was clearly a master, every bit as much a master of the spoken word as Waldemar or Geraldine... I understood the reason for this composure. Goodeve knew that success was predestined.

He began quietly and a little dully, but the House was held by its interest in his first appearance and by his pleasant voice. First he dealt with Mayot, and his courtesy could not prevent his contempt from peeping out. Mayot and his kind, he said, were mongers of opinion, specialists in airy buildings, but incapable of laying one solid brick on another on solid earth – a view received with enthusiasm by Collinson and some of the Labour Left Wing. Mayot, who was very ingenious at digging out awkward sentences from past Tory speeches, had quoted something from Arthur Balfour. Goodeve retorted with a most apposite quotation from Canning: "It is singular to remark how ready some people are to admire in a great man the exception rather than the rule of his conduct. Such perverse worship is like the idolatry of barbarous nations, who can see the noonday splendour of the sun without emotion, but who, when he is in eclipse, come forward with hymns and cymbals to adore him."

But on the whole he dealt lightly with Mayot; it was when he turned to the more formidable Waldemar that he released his heavy batteries. He tore his speech to pieces with a fierce, but icy, gusto. There was no strained or rhetorical word, no excited gesture, no raising of the even, soothing voice, but every sentence was a lash flicking off its piece of skin. It was less an exposure of a speech than of a habit of mind and a school of thought. Waldemar, he said, was one of those to whom experience meant nothing, whose souls existed in a state of sacred torpidity prostrated before cold altars and departed gods. His appeal to common sense was only an appeal to the spiritual sluggishness which was England's besetting sin, and which in the present crisis was her deadliest peril. Waldemar's peroration had really moved the House, but Goodeve managed to strip the glamour from it and make it seem tinsel. He repeated some of the best sentences, and the connection in which he quoted them and the delicate irony of his tone made them comic. Members tittered, and the Liberal Front Bench had savage faces. It was one of the cleverest and cruellest feats I have ever seen performed in debate.

Then he turned on the "big business" section of his own party, who were hostile to Geraldine, and had begun to coquet with Waldemar. Here he fairly let himself go. He addressed the Speaker, but every now and then wheeled slowly round and looked the wrathful, high-coloured magnates in the face. The extraordinary thing was that they made no audible protest; the tension of the House was too great for that. In Mayot he had trounced the timid visionary, in Waldemar the arid dogmatist, and in these gentry he dealt with the strong, silent, practical man. He defined him, in Disraeli's words, as "one who practises the blunders of his predecessors." They were always talking about being consistent, about sticking to their principles, about taking a strong line. What were their principles? he asked urbanely. Not those of the Tory Party, which had always looked squarely at realities, and had never been hidebound in its methods. Was it not possible that they mistook stupidity for consistency, blind eyes for balanced minds? As for their vaunted strength, it was that of cast-iron and not of steel, and their courage was the timidity of men who lived in terror of being called weak. In the grim world we lived in there was no room for such fifth-form heroics.

All this was polished and deadly satire which delighted everyone but its victims. And then he suddenly changed his mood. After a warm expression of loyalty to Geraldine, he gave his own version of the road to a happier country. It was a dangerous thing for a man who had been making game of Waldemar's eloquence to be eloquent on his own account, but Goodeve attempted it, and he brilliantly succeeded. His voice fell to a quiet reflective note. He seemed to be soliloquising, like a weary man who, having been in the dust of the lists, now soothes himself with his secret dreams. The last part of his speech was almost poetry, and I do not think that in my long parliamentary experience I ever heard anything like it. Certainly nothing that so completely captured its hearers. Very gently he seemed to be opening windows beyond which lay a pleasant landscape.

He spoke for a few minutes under the hour, an extravagant measure for a maiden speech. There was very little applause, for members seemed to be spell-bound. I have never seen the House hushed for so long. Then an extraordinary thing happened. The Prime Minister thought it necessary to rise at once, but he had a poor audience. The House emptied, as if members felt it necessary to go elsewhere to get their bearings again and to talk over this portent.

Goodeve kept his place till Trant finished, and then he followed me out of the House. We went down to the terrace, which was empty, for it was a grey November afternoon with a slight drizzle. After a big oratorical effort, especially a triumphant effort, a man generally relaxes, and becomes cheerful and confidential. Not so Goodeve. He scarcely listened to my heartfelt congratulations. I remember how he leaned over the parapet, watching the upstream flow of the leaden tide, and spoke to the water and not to me.

"It is no credit to me," he said. "I was completely confident... You know why... That made me able to put out every ounce I had in me, for I knew it would be all right. If you were in for a race and knew positively that you would win, you would be bound to run better than you ever ran before."

I have a vivid recollection of that moment, for I felt somehow that it was immensely critical. Here was a man who by his first speech had turned politics topsy-turvy. Inside the Palace of Westminster every corridor was humming wth his name; in the newspaper offices journalists were writing columns of impressions, and editors preparing leaders on the subject; already London tea-tables would be toothing it, and that night it would be the chief topic at dinner. And here was the man responsible for it all as cold as a tombstone, negligent of the fame he had won, and thinking only of its relation to a few lines of type that would not be set up for half a year.

My problem was his psychology, not facts, but the way he looked at them, and I gave him what I considered sound advice. I told him that he had done a thing which was new in the history of Parliament. By one speech he had advanced to front-bench status. Party politics were all at sixes and sevens, and he had now the ear of the House as much as Trant and Geraldine. If he cared he could have a chief hand in the making of contemporary history. He *must* care, and for this reason – that it was the best way to falsify *The Times* paragraph. If he went on as he had begun, in six months anything that might happen to him would not get half a dozen lines but a column and half-inch headings. He had it in his own power to make that disquieting glimpse at Flambard an illusion... You see, I was treating the Flambard affair seriously. I had decided that that was the best plan, since it had so eaten into Goodeve's soul.

I remember that he sighed and nodded his head, as if he agreed with me. He refused an invitation to dine, and left without going back to the Chamber. Nor did he return for the division – an excited scene, for Geraldine's motion was only lost by seventeen votes, owing to many Labour members abstaining.

IV

Next week old Folliot asked me to luncheon. It was about the time when, under Mayot's influence, he was beginning to sidle back into politics. I had known him so long that I had acquired a kind of liking for him as a milestone – he made me feel the distance I had travelled, and I often found his tattle restful.

We lunched at his club in St James's Street. The old fellow had not changed his habits, for he still had his pint of champagne in a silver mug, and his eye was always lifting to note people whose acquaintance he liked to claim. But I found that what he wanted was not to impart the latest gossip but to question me. He was acutely interested in Goodeve, and wished to know everything about him.

"It is the sorrow of my life," he told me, "that I missed his speech. I had a card for the Distinguished Strangers' Gallery, as it happened, and I meant to go there for the opening of the debate. But I had some American friends lunching with me, and we stayed on talking and I gave up the idea. You heard it, of course? Did it sound as well as it read? I confess it seemed to me a most refreshing return to the grand manner. I remember Randolph Churchill…" Folliot strayed into reminiscences of past giants, but he always pulled himself up and came back to the point, for he seemed deeply curious about Goodeve. "His assurance now – astonishing in a young man, but I understand that it did not offend the House… Of course the speech must have been carefully prepared, and yet it had real debating qualities. That quip about Waldemar's reference to Mr G, for example – he could not have anticipated that Waldemar would give him such a chance... With the close, I confess, I was less impressed. Excellent English, but many people can speak good English. Ah, no doubt! Better to hear than to read. They tell me he has a most seductive voice."

I could tell him little, for I had only known Goodeve for six months, but I expanded in praise of the speech. Folliot cross-examined me closely about his manner. Was there a proper urbanity in his satire? Did he convince the House that he was in earnest? Was there no pedantry? – too many quotations, possibly? The House did not relish the academic. Above all, was there the accent of authority? Could he keep the field together as well as show it sport?

"He may be the man we have all been looking for," he said. "On paper he certainly fills the bill. Young enough, good-looking, well-born, rich, educated, fine War record, considerable business knowledge. He sounds almost too good to be true. My one doubt is whether he will stay the course. You see, I know something about the Goodeves. I knew his uncle, old Sir Adolphus."

I pricked up my ears. Folliot was beginning to interest me.

"A singular family, the Goodeves," he went on. "Always just about to disappear from the earth, and always saved by a miracle. This young man was the son of the parson, Adolphus' brother, who was cut off with a hundred pounds because he took up with the High Church lot, while his father was a crazy Evangelical. Adolphus avenged him, for he wasn't any sort of Christian at all. I remember the old man well. He was a militant Agnostic, a worshipper at the Huxley and Tyndall shrines – dear me, how all that has gone out today! He used to come to Town to address meetings in the Essex Hall, to which he invited a selection of the London clergy. They never went, but some of us young men used to go, and we were always rewarded. The old fellow had quite a Disraeli touch in vituperation. He was a shocking scarecrow to look at, though he had a fine high-nosed face. Not always washed and shaven, I fear. His clothes were a disgrace – his trousers were half-way up his legs, and his hat and coat were green with age. He never spent a penny he could avoid, always travelled third class and had only one club, because it did not charge for bread and cheese and beer, and so he could lunch free. He had a dread that he might die in beggary – scattered his money in youth, and then got scared and relapsed into a miser. He died worth a quarter of a million, but all the cash they found in the house was ninepence. Hence the comfortable fortune of your young friend. That was so like the Goodeves – they were always having notions – panics, you might call them – which perverted their lives."

Folliot had more to say about Sir Adolphus. He had been a distinguished marine biologist in his youth, and had made an expedition to the Great Barrier Reef and written a notable book about it. Then he had suddenly cut adrift from the whole business. Something gave him a distaste for it – the handling of an octopus, Folliot suggested, or too close an acquaintance with a man-eating shark. "Terribly high-strung people," said Folliot. "They didn't acquire dislikes, so much as horrors. People used to say that Adolphus' aversion to Christianity was due to his having been once engaged to Priscilla Aberley. She was very devout in those days, and was by way of saving his soul, so, when she jilted him for Aberley, Adolphus had no more use for souls in the parson's sense."

"He died only a year or two ago," I put in. "Did you see anything of him in his last days?"

Folliot smiled. "Not I. Nobody did, except the doctor. I understand that he wouldn't have this young man near the place. He shut himself up, and nursed his health as he nursed his money. He must have launched out at last, for he had a scientific valet to see that his rooms were kept at an even temperature, and he had a big consultant down from London if he had as much as a cold in his head... A little mad, perhaps. It looked as if he were in terror of death. Odd in a man who did not believe in any kind of after-life. I fancy that was one of the family traits."

"I can't agree," I said. "They were a most gallant race. I've poked a little way into the family history, and there was hardly a British war in which a Goodeve did not distinguish himself and get knocked on the head. Unlucky, if you like, but not a trace of the white feather."

Then Folliot said a thing which gave me some respect for his intelligence. "No doubt that is true. They could face death comfortably if it came to them in hot blood. But they could not wait for it with equanimity. They had spirit, if you like, but not fortitude."

I was so struck by this remark that I missed what Folliot said next. Apparently he was talking about a Goodeve woman, a great-aunt of my friend. She had been some sort of peeress, but I did not catch the title, and her Christian name had been Portia.

"Old Lady Manorwater knew her well, and used to speak much of her. She had been a raging beauty in her youth, and no better than she should be, people said. Lawrence painted her as Circe – they have the picture at Wirlesdon in the green drawing-room – you must remember it. When she married she ranged herself and gave no further occasion for scandal, but she was still the despair of other wives, for their husbands hung round her like flies round honey. The Duke of Wellington was said to write to her every day, and his brougham stopped at her door twice a week. Melbourne dangled about her skirts, and the young Disraeli wrote her infamous poetry... And then something snapped. She began to get crises of religious terror, and would have parsons to pray with her half the night. Gay as a bird in between, you understand, but when the cloud descended she was virtually a mad-woman. It heightened her beauty and made it more spiritual, for there was a haunted, other-world look in her face. There's a passage about her in one of Carlyle's letters. He met her somewhere, and wrote that he could not get her out of his head, for she had eyes like a stricken deer's. 'God pity the

181

man or woman' – I think these are his words – 'on whom the fear of Jehovah has fallen. They must break the world, or be themselves broken.' "

Folliot saw my interest and was flattered, for he omitted to fuss about the club port.

"Well, she broke," he continued. "She died…quite young. They called it a decline, but old Lady Manorwater said it was fear – naked fear. There was nothing the matter with her body… Yes, there were children. Rupert Trensham is her grandson, but the Trensham stock is prosaic enough to steady the Goodeve blood."

I had to hurry back to chambers, and left Folliot ordering a liqueur.

"A queer race," were his parting words. "That is why I wonder if this young man will last the course. They have spirit without fortitude."

My appreciation of that phrase had pleased the old fellow. I knew that for the next fortnight he would he repeating it all over London.

V

During the next three months I had the miserable job of looking on at what was nothing less than a parliamentary tragedy. For I watched Goodeve labouring to follow my advice and dismally failing.

He began with every chance. The impression made by his maiden speech was a living memory; he was usually called by the Speaker when he got up, and the House filled when the word went round that he was on his feet. Geraldine's new policy was still the chief issue, and, after its author, Goodeve was its chief exponent. Moreover, he had established a reputation for wit, and for dealing faithfully with opponents, and the House loves a gladiatorial show.

Having started with fireworks, he attempted in the orthodox way to get a name for solid sense and practical knowledge. His next effort, a week later, was on some supplementary estimates, a rather long and quite prosaic analysis of a batch of figures. I heard much of it, and was on the whole disappointed. It was all too laboured; he did not make his points cleanly enough; indeed, it was just the kind of thing which your city man fires off once every session to a small and inattentive House. It had none of the art of his first speech and, though he got a good press, it had no real effect upon the debate.

Then he took to intervening briefly in every kind of discussion. He was always more or less relevant, but what he said was generally platitudinous. On the occasions I heard him I missed any note of distinction. He was the ordinary, fairly intelligent member putting up ordinary, fairly intelligent debating points. Our Whips loved him, for he was always ready to keep a debate going when called upon, and I think members approved his modesty in not reserving himself for full-dress occasions. But I could not disguise from myself the fact that his reputation was declining. He, who had got well ahead of other people, had now decorously fallen back into the ranks.

All this time he mixed little with his fellows. He only once attended a dinner of his group, and then scarcely uttered a word. Sally Flambard attempted in vain to get him to her political luncheons. So far as I knew, he never talked politics with anybody. But he rarely missed a division, and would sit solidly to the close of the dreariest debate. He had taken his seat near the end of the third bench below the gangway, so I had no chance of watching his face. But one evening I made an opportunity by going up into the opposite gallery. He sat very still and composed, I remember, with his eyes narrowed and his head a little bent forward. But the impression I got was of a terrific effort at self-restraint. He was schooling himself to something which he hated and dreaded, bracing himself to an effort on which fateful things depended, and the schooling had brought his nerves to cracking-point.

I did not see him during the Christmas vacation. Then in February came the crisis which I have already recorded, when the nation suddenly woke up to the meaning of the unemployment figures, and Chuff began his extra-mural campaign, and parties split themselves up into Activists and Passivists. You would have said that it was the ideal occasion for Goodeve to take the lead. It was the situation which his maiden speech had forecast and it was the spirit of that maiden speech which was needed. Waldemar and Mayot were the leading Passivists, and, Heaven knows, they gave openings enough for a critic. Judging by his early form, Goodeve could have turned them inside out and made them the laughing-stock of the country, and he could have made magnificent play with the Prime Minister's shuffling. He could have toned down Collinson's violence, and steadied some of the younger Tories who were beginning to talk wildly. Above all, he could have produced an Activist policy based on common sense, which was the crying need. Geraldine could not do it; he was always the parliamentarian rather than the statesman.

Goodeve tried and most comprehensively failed. He simply could not hold the House – could hold it far less than Lanyard, who had a voice like a pea-hen, or John Fortingall, who stuttered and hesitated and rarely got a verb into his sentences. At his first appearance he had shown an amazing gift of catching the atmosphere of the assembly and gripping its attention in a vice. His air had had authority in it, his voice had been compelling, his confidence had impressed without offending. But now...great God! he seemed a different man. I heard him try to tackle Mayot, but Mayot, who had looked nervous when he rose, beamed happily as he continued and laughed aloud when he sat down. There was no grip in him, no word spoken out of strong belief, no blow launched with the weight of the body behind it. He seemed to be repeating – hesitatingly – a lesson which he had imperfectly learned by heart. His personality, once so clean-cut and potent, had dissolved into a vapour.

I missed none of his speeches, and with each my heart grew heavier. For I realised the cause of his fiasco... Goodeve was a haunted man, haunted by a dreadful foreknowledge of fate. In his maiden speech fate had been on his side, since he had a definite assurance that he must succeed. But now he was fighting against fate. The same source, which gave him the certainty of his initial triumph, had denied him the hope of further success. As I had advised, he was striving now to coerce fate, to alter what he believed to be his destiny, to stultify what had been decreed... He could not do it. That very knowledge which had once given him confidence was now keeping it from him. He had no real hope. He was battling against what he believed to be foreordained. How could a man succeed when he understood in his heart that the Eternal Powers had predestined failure?

Yet most gallantly he persevered, for it was a matter of life and death. I alone knew the tragedy of it. To other people he was only a politician who was not living up to his promise, the "Single-speech Hamilton" of our day. But behind the epigrams which did not sting, the appeals which rang feebly, the arguments which lacked bite, the perorations which did not glow, I saw a condemned man struggling desperately for a reprieve.

His last speech was on the Ministry of Labour estimates, when John Fortingall's motion nearly brought the Government down. He rose late in the debate, when the House was packed and the air was electric, since a close division was certain. Waldemar had made one of his sagacious, polysyllabic, old-world orations, and Collinson from the Labour benches had replied with a fiery appeal to the House to give up ancestor-worship and face realities. For one moment I thought that Goodeve was going to come off at last. He began briskly, almost with spirit, and he looked the Treasury bench squarely in the face. His voice, too, had a better ring in it. Clearly he had braced himself for a great effort… Then he got into a mesh of figures, and the attention of members slackened. He managed them badly, losing his way in his notes, and, when one item was questioned, he gave a lame explanation. He never finished that section of his case, for he seemed to feel that he was losing the House, so he hurried on to what he must have prepared most carefully, a final appeal somewhat on the lines of his maiden speech. But ah! the difference! To be eloquent and moving one must have either complete self-confidence or complete forgetfulness of self, and Goodeve had neither. He seemed once again to be repeating a lesson badly learned; his voice broke in a rotund sentence so that it sounded falsetto; in an appeal which should have rung like a trumpet he forgot his piece, and it ended limply. Never have I listened to anything more painful. Members grew restless and began to talk. Goodeve's voice became shrill, he dropped it to a whisper, and then raised it to an unmeaning shout… He paused – and someone tittered… He sat down.

When Trant rose an hour later to wind up the debate Goodeve hurried from the House. To the best of my belief he never entered it again.

VI

Towards the end of March I had to speak in Glasgow, and since my meeting was in the afternoon I travelled up by the night train. I was breakfasting in the hotel, when to my surprise I saw Goodeve at an adjacent table. Somehow Glasgow was not the kind of place where one expected to find him.

He joined me, and I had a good look at him. The man was lamentably thin, but at first sight I thought that he looked well. His dusky complexion was a very fair imitation of sunburn, and that and his lean cheeks suggested a man in hard training. But the next moment I revised my view. He moved listlessly and wearily, and his eyes were sick. It was some fever of spirit, not health, that gave him his robust colouring.

186

I had to hurry off to do some business, so I suggested that we should lunch together. He agreed, but mentioned that he had invited a man to luncheon – that very Colonel Dugald Chatto whose name he had read in the same obituary paragraph as his own. I said that I should like to meet him, and asked how Goodeve had managed to achieve the acquaintance. Quite simply, he said. He had got a friend to take him to golf at Prestwick, where Colonel Chatto played regularly, had been introduced to him in the club-house, and had on subsequent occasions played several rounds with him... "Not a bad fellow," he said, and then, when he saw my wondering eyes, he laughed. "I must keep close to him, for, you see, we are more intimately linked than any other two people in the world. We are like the pairs tied up by Carrier in his *noyades* in the Loire – you remember, in the French Revolution. We sink or swim together."

You could not have found a starker opposite to Goodeve than Chatto if you had ransacked the globe. He was a little stocky man, with a scraggy neck, sandy hair and a high-coloured face, who looked as if he took a good deal of both exercise and whisky. He said he was pleased to meet me, and he thumped Goodeve on the back. He was a cheerful soul.

He ate a hearty luncheon and he was full of chat in the juiciest of accents. He had grievances against the War Office because of their treatment of the Territorial division in which he had served, and he had some scathing things to say about politicians. His sympathies were with the Right Wing of our party, which Goodeve disliked. "I'm not blaming you, Sir Edward," he told me. "You're a lawyer, and mostly talk sense, if you don't mind my saying so. But Goodeve here used to splash about something awful. I remember reading his speeches, and wishing I could get five minutes with him in a quiet place. I tell you, I've done a good job for the country in keeping him out of Parliament, for he hasn't been near it since him and me foregathered. I'm making quite a decent golfer of him, too. A wee bit weak in his short game still, but that'll improve."

187

He was a vulgar, jolly little man with nothing in his head, and no conversation except war reminiscences, golf shop, and a fund of rather broad Scots stories. Also he was a bit of an angler, the kind that enters for competitions on Loch Leven. When I listened to him I wondered how the fastidious Goodeve could endure him for half an hour. But Goodeve did more than endure him, for a real friendship seemed to have sprung up between them. There was interest, almost affection, in his eyes. Chatto, no doubt, thought it a tribute to his charms, and being a simple soul, he returned it. He did not know of the uncanny chain which linked the two incompatibles. I can imagine, if Goodeve had told him, the stalwart incredulity with which he would have received the confession.

The hotel boasted some old brandy which Chatto insisted on our sampling. "Supplied by my own firm, gentlemen, long before I was born." After that he took to calling Goodeve "Bob." "Bob here is coming with me to Macrihanish, and we're going to make a week of it."

"Don't forget that you're coming to me for the Mayfly," Goodeve reminded him.

"Not likely I'll forget. That'll be a new kind of ploy for me. I'm not sure I'll be much good at it, but I'm young enough to learn… Man, I get younger every day. I got a new lease of life out of that bloody war. Talk about shellshock! I'm the opposite! I'm shell-stimulated, if you see what I mean."

He expanded in recollections, comments, anticipations, variegated by high-flavoured anecdotes. He had become perhaps a little drunk. One could not help liking the fellow, and I began to feel grateful to him when I saw how Goodeve seemed to absorb confidence from his company. The man was so vital and vigorous that the other drew comfort from the sight of him. Almost all the sickness went out of Goodeve's eyes. His comrade in the *noyades* was not likely to drown, and his buoyancy might sustain them both.

Goodeve saw me off by the night train. I said something complimentary about Chatto.

"There's more in him than you realise at first," he said, "and he's the kindliest little chap alive. What does it matter that he doesn't talk our talk? I'm sick of all that old world of mine."

I said something about Chatto's health.

"Pretty nearly perfect. Now and then he does himself a little too well, as at luncheon today, but that was the excitement of meeting a swell like you. Usually he is very careful. I've made enquiries among his friends, and have got to know his doctor. The doctor says he has a constitution of steel and teak."

"And you yourself?" I asked. "You're a little fine-drawn, aren't you?"

For a moment there was alarm in his eyes.

"Not a bit of it. I'm very well. I've been vetted by the same doctor. He gave me the cleanest bill of health, but advised me not to worry. That's why I have cut out Parliament and come up here. Being with Chatto takes me out of myself. He's as good for me as oxygen."

When I asked about his plans he said he had none. He meant to be a good deal in the North, and see as much of Chatto as possible. Chatto was a bachelor with a country-house in Dumbartonshire, and Goodeve was in treaty for a shooting near-by. I could see the motive of that: it was vital for him to pretend to himself that the coming tenth of June meant nothing, and to arrange for shooting grouse two months later.

I entered my sleeping-berth fairly well satisfied. It was right that Goodeve should keep in close touch with the man whom destiny had joined to him, and it was the mercy of Providence that this man should be an embodiment of careless, exuberant life.

VII

May was of course occupied with the General Election, and for the better part of it I had no time to think of anything beyond the small change of political controversy. I saw that Goodeve was not standing again for the Marton division, and I wondered casually if the florid Chatto had spent the May-fly season on the limpid and intricate waters which I knew so well. I pigeonholed a resolution to hunt up Goodeve as soon as I got a moment to turn round.

Oddly enough, the first news I got of him was from Chatto, whom I met at a Scottish junction.

"Ugh, ay!" said that worthy. "I've been sojourning in the stately homes of England. Did you ever see such a place as yon? I hadn't a notion that Bob was such a big man in his own countryside? Ay, I caught some trout, but I worked hard for them. Yon's too expert a job for me, but, by God, Bob's the fine hand at it."

I asked him about Goodeve's health and whereabouts. "He's in London," was the answer. "I had a line from him yesterday. He was thinking of going on a wee cruise in a week or two. One of those yachting trips that the big steamship companies run – to Norway or some place like that. His health, you say? 'Deed, I don't quite know how to answer that. He wants toning up, I think. Him and me had a week at Macrihanish and, instead of coming on, his game went back every day. There were times when he seemed to have no pith in him. Down at Goodeve he was much the same. There's not much exertion in dry-fly fishing, but every now and then he would lie on his back and appear as tired as if he had been wrestling with a sixteen-foot salmon rod on the Awe. And yet he looks as healthy as a deep-sea sailor. As I say, he wants toning up, and maybe the sea-air is the thing for him."

The consequence of this talk was that I wired to Goodeve, and found that he was still in London on some matter of business. Next day – I think it was May thirty-first – we dined together at his club. This time I was genuinely scared by his looks, for in the past five or six weeks he had gone rapidly downhill. His colour was still high, but now it was definitely unwholesome, and his thinness had become emaciation. His clothes hung on him loosely and there were ugly hollows at his temples. Also – and this was what alarmed me – his eyes had the gaunt, hungry, foreboding look that I remembered in Moe's.

Of course I said nothing about his health, but his first enquiry was about Chatto's, when he heard that I had seen him. I told him that I had never seen such an example of bodily well-being, and he murmured something which sounded like "Thank God!"

It was no good beating about the bush, for the time for any pretence between us had long passed.

"In another fortnight," I said, "you will be rid of this nightmare. Now, what is the best way of putting in the time? I'm thinking of your comfort, for, as you know, I don't believe there is the slightest substance in all that nonsense. But it is real to you, and we must make our book for that."

"I agree," he said. "I thought of going for a cruise in the North Sea. The boat's called the *Runeberg*, I think – a Norwegian steamer chartered by a British firm. I fancy it's the kind of thing for me, for these cruises are always crowded – a sort of floating Blackpool. There's certain to be nobody I know on board, and the discomfort of a rackety company will keep me from brooding. If we get bad weather, so much the better, for I'm a rotten sailor. I've booked my cabin, and we sail from Leith on the sixth."

I told him that I warmly approved. "That's the common sense of the thing," I said. "You must bluff your confounded premonitions. On June tenth you'll be sitting on deck inside the Skerrygard, forgetting that there's such a thing as a newspaper. What's Chatto doing?"

"Going on as usual. Business four days a week and golf the rest. He has no foreboding to worry him. I get frequent news of his health, you know. I have a friend in a Glasgow lawyer's office, who knows both him and his doctor, and he sends me reports. I wonder what he thinks of it all. A David and Jonathan friendship,

I hope; but these Glasgow lawyers never let you see what is inside their mind."

On the whole I was better pleased with the situation. Goodeve was facing it bravely and philosophically, and Chatto was a sheet-anchor. In a fortnight it would be all over, and he could laugh at his tremors. He was due back in Town from the cruise on the twentieth, and we arranged to dine together. I could see that he was playing up well to his plan, and filling up his time with engagements beyond the tenth.

I asked him what he proposed to do before he sailed. There was a weekend with Chatto, he said, and then he must go back to Goodeve for a day or two on estate business. I had to return to the House for a division, and, being suddenly struck afresh by Goodeve's air of fragility, I urged him, as we parted, to go straight to bed.

He shook his head. "I'm going for a long walk," he said. "I walk half the night, for I sleep badly. My only chance is to tire out my body."

"You can't stand much more of that," I told him. "What does your doctor say?"

"I don't know. It isn't a case for doctors. I'm fighting, you see, and it's taking a lot out of me. The fight is not with the arm of flesh, but the flesh must pay."

"You're as certain to win as that the sun will rise tomorrow." These were my last words to him, and I put my hand on his shoulder. He started at the touch, but his eyes looked me steadily in the face. God knows what was in them – suffering in the extreme, fear to the uttermost, courage, too, of the starkest. But one thing I realised – they were like Moe's eyes; and I left the club with a pain at my heart.

VIII

I never saw Goodeve again. But the following are the facts which I learned afterwards.

He went to Prestwick with Chatto and played vile golf. Chatto, who was on the top of his game and in high spirits, lost his temper with his pupil, and then began in his kindly way to fuss about his health. He asked a doctor friend in the club-house to have a look at him, but Goodeve refused his attentions, declaring that he was perfectly fit. Then, after arranging to lunch with Chatto in Glasgow on the sixth before sailing from Leith, Goodeve went south.

It was miserable weather in that first week of June, wet and raw, with a searching east wind. Chatto went to Loch Leven to fish, and got soaked to the skin. He came home with a feverish cold which developed into pleurisy, and on the fifth was taken into a nursing-home. Early on the sixth he developed pneumonia, and before noon on that day Goodeve's Glasgow lawyer friend had sent him this news.

Goodeve should have been in Glasgow that morning, since he was to sail in the *Runeberg* in the late afternoon. But he had already cancelled his passage – I think on the fifth. Why he did that I do not know. It could have had nothing to do with Chatto's illness, of which he had not yet heard. He may have felt that a sea-voyage was giving an unnecessary hostage to destiny. Or he may have felt that his own bodily strength was unequal to the effort. Or some overpowering sense of fatality may have come down like a shutter on his mind. I do not know, and I shall never know.

What is clear is that at Goodeve before the sixth his health had gravely worsened. He could not lie in bed, and he refused to have a doctor, so he sat in a dressing-gown in his shadowy library, or pottered weakly about the ground-floor rooms. His old butler grew very anxious, for his meals were left almost untasted. Several times he tried to rally his spirits, and he drank a little champagne, and once he had up a bottle of the famous port. He had a book always with him, the collected works of Sir Thomas Browne, but according to the butler, it was generally lying unread on his knee.

When he got the telegram about Chatto's illness, his valet told me, he read it several times, let it drop on the floor, and sat for a minute or two looking fixedly before him. Then he seemed to make an effort to pull himself together. He ordered fires to be lit in the long gallery upstairs, and said that henceforth that should be his sitting-room.

For three days Goodeve lived in that cloudy chamber under the portraits of his ancestors with their tremulous, anxious eyes. There was a little powdering-closet next door, where he had a bed made up. Fires were kept blazing night and day on all the four hearths, for he seemed to feel the cold. I believe that he had made up his mind that Chatto must die, and that he must follow. He had several bulletins daily from Glasgow, and, said his valet, seemed scarcely to glance at them. But on the ninth he asked eagerly for telegrams, as if he expected one of moment. He was noticeably frailer, the servants told me, and he seemed sunk in a deep lethargy, and sat very still with his eyes on the fire. Several times he walked the length of the gallery, gazing at the portraits.

About six o'clock on the evening of the ninth the telegram came announcing Chatto's death. Goodeve behaved as if he had expected it, and there came a flicker of life into his face. He sent for champagne and drank a little, lifting up his glass as if he were giving a toast. He told his valet that he would not require him again, but would put himself to bed. The last the man saw of him he was smiling, and his lips were moving...

In the morning he was found dead in his chair. The autopsy that followed resulted in a verdict of death from heart failure. I alone knew that the failure had come about by the slow relentless sapping of fear.

There was wild weather in the North Sea on the eighth, and in the darkness before dawn on the ninth the *Runeberg* was driven on to a reef and sank with all on board. As it chanced, Goodeve's name was still on its list of passengers, and it was because of the news of the shipwreck that *The Times* published his obituary on the tenth. Next day it issued the necessary correction, and an extended obituary which recorded that his death had really taken place at his country house.

VI

CAPTAIN CHARLES OTTERY

"And because time in it selfe…can
receive no alteration, the hallowing
must consist in the shape or countenance
which we put upon the affaires that are
incident in these dayes."

RICHARD HOOKER, *Ecclesiastical Polity.*

VI

Captain Charles Ottery

I

The announcement on the first page of *The Times*, which Charles Ottery read at Flambard, and every letter of which was printed on his mind, ran thus:

"OTTERY – Suddenly in London on the 9th inst., Captain Charles Ottery, late Scots Fusiliers, of Marlcote, Glos., at the age of 36."

It fitted his case precisely. The regiment was right (the dropping of the "Royal" before its title was a familiar journalistic omission), Marlcote was his family place, and in June of the following year he would have just passed his thirty-sixth birthday.

I had known Charles since he was a schoolboy, for he was my nephew's friend, and many a half-sovereign I had tipped him in those days. He was the only child of a fine old Crimean veteran, and had gone straight from school into the family regiment, for a succession of Otterys had served in the Royal Scots Fusiliers, though they had not a drop of Scots blood. They came originally, I believe, from Devonshire, but had been settled for a couple of centuries in the Severn valley. Charles was a delightful boy, with old-fashioned manners, for he had been strictly brought up. He always called his father "sir," I remember, and rose when he entered the room. He had a rather sullen, freckled face, tawny hair which curled crisply, and pale-blue eyes which could kindle into a dancing madness, or freeze into a curious mature solemnity. What impressed one about him as a boy was the feeling he gave of latent power. He never seemed to put all of himself into anything – there was an impression always of heavy reserves waiting to be called up. He was the average successful schoolboy, not specially brilliant at anything except at court-tennis, but generally liked and greatly respected. No one ever took liberties with Master Charles, for the sheath of pleasant manners was felt to cover a particularly stiff bone.

The War broke out when he had been a soldier for six months, and Charles went to France in September 1914. As his friends expected, he made an admirable regimental officer – one of the plain fighting men who were never sick or sorry during four gruelling years. Being a regular, he had no sensational advancement; he got his company during the Somme, and later had one or two staff jobs, from which he always managed to wangle a speedy return to his battalion. He was happy, because he was young and healthy and competent, and loved his men. After the Armistice he had the better part of a year in Ireland, a miserable time which tried him far more sorely in mind and body than his four years in France. Then his father died, and as soon as the Scots Fusiliers had finished their Irish tour Charles left the Service.

He inherited a large and unlucrative landed estate; he was devoted to Marlcote, and he had to find some means of earning money if he wanted to retain it. Through the influence of an uncle he was taken into a London firm of merchant-bankers, and in his quiet resolute way set himself to learn his job. He proved to have a genuine talent for business. His mind was not quick, but it was powerful, and he used to burrow his way like a mole to the bottom of a question. Also there was something about his stability and force of character which made men instinctively trust him, and he earned that reputation for judgement the price of which is above rubies. No one called him clever, but everyone believed him to be wise. In three years he was a junior partner in his firm, and after that his advance was rapid. He became a director of the Bank of England, the youngest man, I believe, except Goschen, who ever entered the Bank Parlour; he sat on more than one Government Commission, and he was believed to be often consulted by the Treasury. He figured also in the public eye as an athlete, for he played his favourite court-tennis regularly, and had been twice runner-up for the amateur championship.

Then into his orderly life, like a warm spring wind upon a snowfield, came Pamela Brune. Pamela was my god-daughter, and I had watched with amazement her pass from a plain, solemn child to a leggy girl and then to the prettiest debutante of her year. Almost in a moment, it seemed to me, the lines of her body changed from angularity to grace, the contours of her small face were moulded into exquisiteness, and her thin little neck became a fit setting for her lovely head. She was tall for a woman, nearly as tall as Charles, but so perfectly proportioned that her height did not take the eye; exquisiteness was the dominant impression, and a kind of swift airy vigour. In her colouring she had taken after her father, and I can best describe it as a delicate ivory lit up, as it were, from within, and nobly framed by her dusky hair. Her eyes were grey, with blue lights in them. Beyond doubt a beauty, and of a rare type. The transformation in her manner was not less striking. She had been a shy child, rather silent and reflective, a good companion on a long walk, when she would expound to me her highly original fancies, but apt at most times to escape notice. Now she was so brilliant to look at that such escape was not for her, and she had developed a manner which was at once defiant and defensive. Young men were a little afraid of her, her eyes were so compelling, taking in much and revealing little, and her deep voice had a disquieting candour.

Charles fell headlong in love, and I could see from the start that the affair would not go smoothly. To begin with, she was very young – scarcely nineteen – and was like a bird preening her wings for flight, whereas Charles was thirty-five and fixed solidly on his perch. He was a little set in his ways and cocksure in his opinions, while she had the sceptical and critical innocence of youth. They became friends at once, but their friendship seemed slow to ripen into anything deeper. Pamela had nothing of the flirt in her, and though young men swarmed round her, there was no other suitor to give Charles heart-disease. The trouble was that he got no farther forward. One reason, perhaps, was that he was far too eligible. The girl had a notion that everyone desired the match, and that her parents counted on it, so naturally she revolted. Another thing – she was quicker-witted than Charles, and had a dozen interests to his one, so that his circumscription was apt to show up poorly in contrast. This was bad for him, for it cast him into a kind of irritable despair, and bad for Pamela, since it made her more critical. When he was schoolmasterish, the pupil put him to shame; when his mood was humble, hers was arrogant.

So during the month before the Flambard party the course of true love did not run smooth. The effect of a grand passion on Charles's tough solidity was what might have been looked for. His nature was not elastic, and instead of expanding under heat was in danger of warping. He was so desperately in love that all his foundations were upset. He could not fit his passion into his scheme of life, so his scheme of life went by the board. He was miserably conscious of being in a world which he did not understand, of dealing with imponderable things over which he had no mastery. A hasty word, a cold glance from Pamela would thrust this man, who had always prided himself upon his balance, into a fever of indecision...

And just before Whitsuntide they had had something like a quarrel. He had been magisterial and she had been pert – no, "pert" is not the word – rather disdainful in a silken way, airily detached and infinitely distant. She had not sulked – that would have been far easier for Charles: she had simply set him back

firmly among the ranks of her acquaintances. So he had gone to
Flambard in a wretched state of mind, and her treatment of him
there had been like an acid to his wounds. He found himself in
a condition which he had never dreamed of – cut off from the
common-sense world which he understood, and condemned to
flounder among emotions and problems as evasive as dreams and
yet with a terrible potency of torture. Moe was right: Charles
Ottery was profoundly unhappy.

II

He had entered upon the experiment at Flambard with a vague
hope that he might learn something about the future which
would ease his mind. What he did learn was that in a year's time
he would be dead.

His first reaction was anger. For four years he had faced the
daily possibility, even the likelihood, of death. Now, if during
those years anyone had prophesied his certain death at a certain
time, he would have assaulted the prophet. That kind of thing
was a breach of the unwritten rules of the game: one had to
pretend to one's self and to the world that one would continue
to live: it was the assumption which alone made war endurable.
Therefore Charles Ottery's first feeling was wrathful and contemptuous. The Professor was dead; otherwise he would have
had something to say to him.

This mood lasted perhaps two days – no longer. Gradually it
dawned on his mind that this was a revelation altogether outside
the control of the human will. He had believed completely in
Moe, and he had seen *The Times* announcement with a blinding
clarity which precluded the idea of a mistake. Pamela had shaken
him out of his old world, and now he had fallen into a far
stranger one, altogether beyond the kindly uses of humanity. He
tried to be sceptical, but he had never had much gift for
scepticism. Critical in any serious sense he could not be, for he
had not the apparatus for criticism. Anger was succeeded by a

fear which was almost panic. Charles was a notably brave man, and his courage had been well disciplined and tested. He had always been perfectly willing to run risks, and, if need be, to face death with his eyes open. But this was different – this undefined but certain fate towards which he must walk for the next twelve months. He discovered that he passionately wanted to live. Pamela had dropped out of his thoughts, for she was now utterly beyond him – a doomed man could not be a lover – but his passion for her had enriched and deepened the world for him and therefore increased his love of life.

The first panic passed, and Charles forced himself into a kind of stoicism. Not scepticism, for he could not disbelieve, but a resolution to face up to whatever was in store. He felt hideously lonely, for not only was he too proud to confide in anyone, but he could think of no mortal man who had ever been in a like predicament. If he could have discovered a parallel case, past or present, he would have been comforted. So since there was no one to whom he could unburden his soul, he started to keep a diary... I was not at this time in his confidence, but I have had the use of that diary in telling this story. In it he put down notes of his daily doings and of his state of mind, together with any thoughts that seemed to him cheering or otherwise. It is a scrappy and often confused record, but very illuminating, for he was honest with himself.

His first duty was to keep a stout face to the world, and therefore he must try to forget *The Times* paragraph in violent preoccupations. He could not face the society of his fellows, so he went little into the City, but he strove to crowd his life with intense activities. He practised his court-tennis for several hours each day, played a good deal of golf, and took to keeping a six-tonner on Southampton Water and making weekend expeditions along the coast. From the diary it appeared that this last pursuit was the best aid to forgetfulness, so long as the weather was bad. In a difficult wind he had to concentrate all his faculties on managing the boat, but when there was no such need, he found the deck of his little yacht too conducive to painful meditation.

Presently he realised that these anodynes were no manner of good. Each spell of freedom from thought was succeeded by a longer spell of intense brooding. He had found no philosophy to comfort him, and no super-induced oblivion lasted long. So he decided that he must seek a different kind of life. He had an idea that if he went into the wilds he might draw courage from the primeval Nature which was all uncertainties and hazards. So in August he set off for Newfoundland alone, to hunt the migratory caribou.

Purposely he gave himself a rough trip. He went up-country to the Terra Nova district, and then with two guides penetrated far into the marshes and barrens of the interior. He limited his equipment to the bare necessaries, and courted every kind of fatigue. He must have taken a good many risks in his river journey, for I heard from a man who followed his tracks for the brief second season in October that his guides had sworn never again to accompany such a madman. You see, he knew for certain that nothing could kill him for many months. The diary, written up at night in his chilly camps, told the story fully. He got with ease the number of stags permitted by his licence – all of them good beasts – for, since he did not care a straw whether he killed or not, he found that he could not miss. But the interesting things were his thoughts, as they came to him while watching in the dusk by a half-frozen pond, or lying awake in his sleeping-bag looking at the cold stars.

He had begun to reflect on the implications of death, a subject to which he had never given much heed before. His religion was of the ordinary public-school brand, the fundamentals of Christianity accepted without much comprehension. There was an after-world, of course, about which a man did not greatly trouble himself: the important thing, the purpose of religion, was to have a decent code of conduct in the present one. But now the latter did not mean much to him, since his present life would soon be over... There were pages of the diary filled with odd amateurish speculations about God and Eternity, and once or twice there was even a kind of prayer. But somewhere in the barrens Charles seems to have decided that he had better let metaphysics alone. What concerned him was how to pass the next eight months without disgracing his manhood. He noted cases of people he had known who, when their death sentence was pronounced by their doctor, had lived out the remainder of their days with a stiff lip, even with cheerfulness.

The conclusion of this part of the diary, written before he sailed for home, seems to have been that all was lost but honour. He was like a man on a sinking ship, and owed it to himself to go down with fortitude. There were no entries during the voyage from St John's, so the presumption is that this resolve gave him a certain peace.

That peace did not survive his return to England. He went back to the City, where he was badly needed, for the bottom was falling out of business. But he seemed unable to concentrate on his work. The sight of his familiar surroundings, his desks, his clerks, the business talks which assumed the continuity of life, the necessity of making plans which would not mature before the following June, put him into a fever of disquiet. I think that he had perhaps overtired himself in Newfoundland, and was physically rather unstrung; anyhow, on the plea of health, he again began to absent himself from his work. He felt that he must discover an anodyne to thought, or go mad.

The anodyne he tried was the worst conceivable. Charles had never led the life of pleasure, and had no relish for it; so now, when he attempted it, it was like brandy to a teetotaller. He belonged to Dillon's, and took to frequenting that club, and playing cards for high stakes. Now, it is a dangerous thing to gamble if you have the mania for it in your blood, but it is more dangerous if your object is to blanket your mind. He won a good deal of money and lost a good deal, and he played with a cold intensity which rather scared his partners... Also he, who had always been abstemious, took to doing himself too well. I met him one night in St James's Street, and got the impression that the sober Charles was rather drunk... Then there was hunting. He had not had time for years to do much of that, but now he kept horses at Birkham, and went out twice a week. He behaved as he had behaved in the Terra Nova rapids, and took wild risks because he believed that nothing could harm him. For a couple of months he rode so hard that he made himself a nuisance in the field... Then his confidence suddenly deserted him.

It occurred to him that any day he might have a smash, and linger bed-ridden till the following June. So he got rid of his hunters and fled from Birkham.

The result of all this was that before Christmas he had begun to get for himself a doubtful name. At first no one believed that this decorous young man could run amok, but nobody's repute is iron-clad, and presently too many people were ready to surmise the worst. City men reported that he rarely showed up at his office, and was useless when he did. Hunting men had tales to tell of strange manners in the field and an insane foolhardiness. My nephew, who was one of his oldest friends, and belonged to Dillon's, would say nothing at first when I asked him about the stories, but in the end he admitted reluctantly that they were true. "Charles has got mixed up with a poor lot," he said. "Drunken swine like L—, and half-witted boys like little E— and fine old-fashioned crooks like B—. He hardly recognises me when we meet in the club, for he knows I don't like his bunch. In the evening he's apt to be tight after ten o'clock.

"God knows what's done it!" said my nephew dismally. "Looks as if he weren't able to take his corn. Too big a success too soon, you know. Well, he won't be a success long... I put it down to a virtuous youth. If you don't blow off steam under twenty-five, you're apt to have a blow up later and scald yourself... No, I don't think it is unrequited affection. I've heard that yarn, but I don't believe it. I saw Lady Pam at a dinner last week, and she had a face like a death's head. She's going the pace a bit herself, but she's not enjoying it. Whoever is behaving badly, it ain't her. My notion is that Charles hasn't given the girl a thought for months. Don't ask me for an explanation. Something has snapped in him, the way a racehorse goes suddenly wrong."

I confess that at the time I was more anxious about my god-daughter than about Charles. I knew him fairly well and liked him, but Pamela was very near my heart. I could not blame him, for it was she who had hitherto caused the trouble, but now it was very clear that things were not well with her... She had refused to pay her usual Scots visits, and had gone off with the Junipers to their place on the Riviera. The Juniper girl had only been an acquaintance, but she suddenly blossomed into a bosom friend. Now, the Junipers were not too well regarded by old-fashioned people. Tom and Mollie Nantley hated the business, but they had always made it a rule never to interfere with their daughters, and certainly up to now Pamela had deserved their confidence. It must have been gall and wormwood to them to see the papers full of pictures of the Juniper doings, with Pamela bathing and playing tennis and basking on the sands in the most raffish society... After that she went on a cruise to the Red Sea with some Americans called Baffin. The Nantleys knew very little about the Baffins, so they hoped for the best; but from what I learned afterwards the company on the yacht was pretty mixed – a journalistic peer, two or three financiers, and a selection of amorous and alcoholic youth.

Pamela returned to England before the end of November. The family always stayed on at Wirlesdon till well into the new year, but she insisted on taking up her quarters in London. She acted in several entertainments got up for charity, and became the darling of the illustrated press. I saw her once in December, at a dinner given for a ball, and was glad that Mollie Nantley was not present. The adorable child that I had known had not altogether gone, but it was overlaid with tragic affectations. She had ruined her perfect colouring with cosmetics, and her manner had acquired the shrill vulgarity which was then the fashion. She was as charming to me as ever, but in her air there was a curious defiance. Her face had been made up to look pert, but in repose it was tragic. I realised that it was all a desperate bravado to conceal suffering.

III

Lamancha had a Christmas party at his house in Devonshire, and I went there on the twenty-seventh. After tea my hostess took me aside.

"We've made an awful *gaffe*," she said. "Charles Ottery is here, and I find to my horror that Pamela Brune is coming tomorrow. I can't very well put her off, but you know that things have not been going well with her and Charles, and their being together may be very painful for both of them."

I asked if Charles knew that Pamela was coming.

"I told him this morning, but he didn't seem interested. I hoped he would discover that he had an engagement elsewhere, but not a bit of it – he only looked blank and turned away. What on earth has happened to him, Ned? He is rather quarrelsome, when he isn't simply deadly dull, and he has such queer moping moods. There is something on his mind, and I don't believe that it's Pamela."

"Couldn't you let her know he is here?" I asked.

"I wired to Mollie Nantley, but the only reply I got was about Pamela's train. She is evidently coming with her eyes open."

Pamela duly arrived during the following afternoon, when we were out shooting Lamancha's hedgerow pheasants. I did not see her till dinner, and I had to go off at dawn next morning to London for an unexpected consultation. But that evening I had a very dear and most disquieting impression of her and Charles. Her manner was shrill and rather silly; she seemed to be acting a part which was utterly unsuited to her kind of beauty and to her character as I had known it. The house-party was not exciting, only pleasant and friendly, and she succeeded in making us all uncomfortable. I did not see her first meeting with Charles, but that evening she never looked at him, nor he at her. He drank rather too much wine at dinner, and afterwards played bezique owlishly in the smoking-room. I had tried to get a word with him, but he shunned me like the plague.

What happened after I left I learned from the diary. Behind the mask he had been deeply miserable, for the sight of the girl had brought back his old happier world. He realised that far down below all his anxieties lay his love for her – that indeed this love was subconsciously the cause of his frantic clutch on life. He had tried stoicism and had failed; he had tried drugging himself by excitement into forgetfulness and had failed not less dismally. Pamela's presence seemed to recall him to his self-respect. He did not notice any change in her – his eyes had been too long looking inward to be very observant: he only knew that the woman who had once lit up his life was now for ever beyond him – worse still, that he had dropped to a level from which he could not look at her without shame. He fell into a mood of bitter abasement, which was far healthier than his previous desperation, for he was thinking now less of the death which was in store for him than of the code of honourable living to which he had been false.

That night he slept scarcely a wink, and next morning he did not show up at breakfast. He told the servant who called him that he was going for a long walk, and slipped out of the house before anybody was down. He felt that he had to be alone to wrestle with his soul.

The diary told something of his misery that day on the high Devon moors. The weather was quiet and tonic with a touch of frost, and he walked blindly over the uplands. Charles was too stiff-backed a fellow to indulge in self-pity, but his type is apt to be a prey to self-contempt. He can have seen nothing of the bright landscape, for he was enveloped in a great darkness –

regrets, remorse, a world of wrath with the horror of a deeper shade looming before him. He struggled to regain the captaincy of his soul, but he had no longer the impulse to strive, since he seemed to himself to have already foresworn his standards. There was nothing before him but a dreadful, hopeless passivity, what the Bible calls an "awful looking-for of judgement." The hours of spiritual torment and rapid movement wore down his strength, and in the afternoon he found that he was very weary. So he walked slowly homeward, having dulled his bodily and mental senses but won no comfort.

In the dusk, at the head of one of the grassy rides in the home woods, as the fates ordained it, he met Pamela. She, unhappy also, had fled from the house for a little air and solitude. Both were so full of their own thoughts that they might have passed without recognition had they not encountered each other at a gate. Charles opened it, and held it wide for the stranger to pass, and it was the speaking of his name that enlightened him as to the personality of the stranger.

"Good evening, Captain Ottery," Pamela said.

He started and stared at her. Something in his appearance held her eyes, for a man does not go through hell without showing it. In those eyes there must have been wonder; there must have been pity too. He saw it, dulled though his senses were, and perhaps he saw also some trace of that suffering which I had noticed in London, for the girl was surprised and had no time to don her mask.

"Pamela!" he cried, and then his strength seemed to go from him, and he leaned heavily on the gate, so that his shoulder touched hers.

She drew back. "You are ill?"

He recovered himself. "No, not ill," he said. He could say no more, for when a man has been wrestling all day with truth he cannot easily lie.

She put a hand on his arm. "But you look so ill and strange."

And then some of the old tenderness must have come into her eyes and voice. "Oh, Charles," she cried, "what has happened to us?"

It was the word "us" that broke him down, for it told him that she too was at odds with life. He had a sudden flash of illumination. He saw that what he had once longed for was true, that her heart was his, and the realisation that not only life but love was lost to him was the last drop in his cup. He stood holding the gate, shaking like a reed, with eyes which, even in the half-light, seemed to be devoured with pain.

"You must have thought me a cad," he stammered. "I love you – I loved you beyond the world, but I dared not come near you... I am a dying man... I will soon be dead."

His strength came back to him. He had a purpose now. He had found the only mortal in whom he could confide – must confide.

As they walked down the ride in the winter gloaming, with the happy lights of the house in the valley beneath them, he told her all, and as he spoke it seemed to him that he was cleansing his soul. She made no comment – did not utter a single word.

At the gate of the terrace gardens he stopped. His manner was normal again, and his voice was quiet, almost matter-of-fact.

"Thank you for listening to me, Pamela," he said. "It has been a great comfort to me to tell you this... It is the end for both of us. You see that, don't you?... We must never meet again. Good-bye, my dear."

He took her hand, and the touch of it shivered his enforced composure. "I love you... I love you," he moaned...

She snatched her hand away.

"This is perfect nonsense," she said. "I won't..." and then fled down an alley, as she had once fled from me at Flambard.

Charles had some food in his room, and went to bed, where he slept for the first time for weeks. He had been through the extremes of hell, and nothing worse could await him. The thought gave him a miserable peace. He wrote a line to his hostess, and left for London by the early train.

IV

He was sitting next afternoon in his rooms in Mount Street when a lady was announced, and Pamela marched in on the heels of his servant. The room was in dusk, and it was her voice that revealed her to him.

"Turn on the light, Crocker," she said briskly, "and bring tea for two. As quick as possible, please, for I'm famishing."

I can picture her, for I know Pamela's ways, plucking off her hat and tossing it on to a table, shaking up the cushions on the big sofa, and settling herself in a corner of it – Pamela no longer the affected miss of recent months, but the child of April and an April wind, with the freshness of a spring morning about her.

They had tea, for which the anxious Crocker provided muffins, rejoicing to see once again in the flat people feeding like Christians. Pamela chattered happily, chiefly gossip about Wirlesdon, while Charles pulled himself out of his lethargy and strove to rise to her mood. He even went to his bedroom, changed his collar and brushed his hair. When Crocker had cleared away the tea, she made him light his pipe. "You know you are never really happy with anything else," she said; and he obeyed, not having smoked a pipe since Newfoundland.

"Now," she said at last, when she had poked the fire into a blaze, "I want you to repeat very carefully all that rubbish you told me yesterday."

He obeyed – told the story slowly and dispassionately, without the emotion of the previous day. She listened carefully, and wrote down from his dictation the exact words he had read in *The Times*. She knitted her brows over them. "Pretty accurate, aren't they?" she asked. "Not much chance of mistaken identity."

"None," he said. "There are very few Otterys in the world, and every detail about me is correct."

"And you believe in it?"

"I must."

"I mean to say, you believe that you really saw that thing in *The Times*? You didn't dream it afterwards?"

"I saw it as clearly as I am seeing you."

"I wondered what tricks that old Professor man was up to at Flambard, but I had no notion it was anything as serious as this. What do you suppose the others saw? Uncle Ned is sure to know – I'll ask him."

"He saw nothing himself – he told me so. Lady Flambard fainted, and he was looking after her."

"She saw nothing either, then? I'm sorry, for I can't ask any of the men. I don't know Mr Tavanger or Mr Mayot or Sir Robert Goodeve, and Reggie Daker is too much of a donkey to count. It would be too delicate a subject to be inquisitive about with strangers... You really are convinced that the Professor had got hold of some method of showing you the future?"

"Convinced beyond any possibility of doubt," said Charles dismally.

"Good. That settles one thing... Now for the next point. The fact that you saw that stuff is no reason why it should happen. Supposing you had dreamed it, would you have allowed a dream, however vivid, to wreck your life?"

"But, Pamela dear, the case is quite different. Moe showed us what he called 'objective reality.' A dream would have been my own concern, but this came from outside, quite independent of any effort of mine. It was the result of a scientific experiment."

"But the science may have been all cock-eyed. Most science is – at any rate, it changes a good deal faster than Paris fashions."

"You wouldn't have said that if you had been under his influence. He didn't want me to die – he didn't make *The Times* paragraph take that form – he only lifted the curtain an inch so that I could see what had actually happened a year ahead. How can I disbelieve what science brought to me out of space, without any preparation or motive? The whole thing was as

212

mathematical and impersonal as an eclipse of the moon in an almanack."

"All right! Let's leave it at that. Assume that *The Times* is going to print the paragraph. The answer is that *The Times* is going to be badly diddled. Somebody will make a bloomer."

Charles shook his head. "I've tried to think that, but well – you know, that kind of mistake isn't made."

"Oh, isn't it? The papers announced Dollie's engagement to three different men – exact as you please – names and dates complete."

"But why should it make a blunder in this one case out of millions? Isn't it more reasonable to think that there is a moral certainty of its being right?"

Pamela was not succeeding with her arguments. They sounded thin to her own ears, in spite of her solid conviction at the back of them. She sat up, an alert, masterful figure, youth girt for command. She had another appeal than logic.

"Charles," she said solemnly, "this is a horrible business for you, and you've got to pull yourself together. You must defy it. Make up your mind that you're not going to give it another thought. Get back to your work, and resolve that you don't care a lop-eared damn for Moe or science or anything else. Lose your temper with fate and frighten the blasted hussy." Tom Nantley had a turn for robust speech in the hunting-field, and his daughter remembered some of it.

Charles shook his head miserably.

"I've tried," he said, "but I can't. I simply haven't the manhood... I know it's the right way, but my mind is poisoned already. I've got a germ in it that fevers me... Besides, it isn't sense. You can't stop what is to be by saying that it won't be."

"Yes, you can," said the girl firmly. "That's the meaning of Free Will."

Charles dropped his head into his hands. The sight of Pamela thus restored to him was more than he could bear.

Then she had an inspiration.

"Do you remember the portrait in the dining-room at Wirlesdon of old Sir Somebody-Ap-Something – Mamma's Welsh ancestor? You know the story about him? He was on the side of Henry Tudor, and raised his men to march to Bosworth. But every witch and warlock in Carmarthen got on to their hindlegs and prophesied – said they saw him in a bloody shroud, and heard banshees wailing for him, and how Merlin had said that when the Ap-Something red and gold crossed Severn to join the Tudor green and white it would be the end of the race – all manner of cheery omens. Everybody in the place believed them, including his lady wife, who wept buckets and clung to his knees. What did the old sportsman do? Told all the warlocks to go to the devil, and marched gaily eastward, leaving his wife sewing his shroud and preparing the family vault."

'What happened?" Charles had lifted his head.

"Happened? He turned the day at Bosworth, set the Tudor on the throne, got the Garter for his services – you see it in the portrait – and about half South Wales. He and his men came merrily home, and he lived till he was ninety-three. There's an example for you!"

Pamela warmed to her argument.

"That sort of thing happened all the time in the old days. Whenever anybody had a down on you he got a local soothsayer to prophesy death and disaster in case you might believe it and lose your nerve. And if you had been having a row with the Church, some priest or bishop had an unpleasant vision about you. What was the result? Timid people took to their beds and died of fright, which was what the soothsayers wanted. Bold men like my ancestor paid not the slightest attention, and nothing happened – except that, when they got a chance, they outed the priest and hanged the soothsayer."

Charles was listening keenly.

"But the soothsayers were often right," he objected.

"They were just as often wrong. The point is, that there were men brave enough to defy them – as you are going to do."

214

"But the cases aren't the same," he protested. "That was ordinary vulgar magic, with a personal grudge behind it. I'm up against the last word in impersonal science."

"My dear Charles," she said sweetly, "you've let your brains go to seed. I never knew you miss a point before. Magic and astrology and that kind of thing were all the science the Middle Ages had, and they believed in them just as firmly as you believe in Moe. The point is that, in spite of their belief, there were people bold enough to defy it – and to win, as you are going to do. A thousand years hence the world may think of Moe and Einstein and all those pundits as babyish as we think the old necromancers. Beliefs change, but courage is always the same. Courage is the line for you, my dear."

At last she had moved him. There was a light in his eyes as he looked at her, perplexed and broken, but still a light.

"You think..." he began, but she broke in...

"I think that you're face to face with a crisis, Charles dear. Fate has played you an ugly trick, but you're man enough to beat it. It's like the thing in the Bible about Jacob wrestling with the angel. You've got to wrestle with it, and if you wrestle hard enough it may bless you."

Her voice had lost its briskness, and had become soft and wooing. She jumped up from the sofa and came round behind his chair, as if she did not want him to see her face.

"I refuse to give another thought to the silly thing," she said. "We are going to behave as if Moe had never been born." Her hand was caressing his hair.

"But *you* are not condemned to death," he said.

"Oh, am I not?" she cried. "It's frightfully important for me. On June tenth of next year I shall be starting on my honeymoon."

That fetched him out of his chair.

He gazed blindly at her as she stood with her cheeks flushed and her eyes a little dim. For a full minute he strove for words and none came.

215

"Have you nothing to say?" she whispered. "Do you realise, sir, that I am asking you to marry me?"

V

It was now that I entered the story. Mollie Nantley came to Town and summoned me to a family conclave. She and Tom were in a mood between delight and anxiety.

"You got my wire?" she asked. "The announcement will be in the papers tomorrow. But they are not to be married till June. Too long to wait – I don't like these long engagements."

"You are pleased?" I asked.

"Tremendously – in a way. But we don't quite know what to think. They never saw each other for six months, and then it all came with a rush. Pam has been rather odd lately, you know, and Tom and I have been very worried. We saw that she was unhappy, and we thought that it might be about Charles. And Charles's behaviour has been something more than odd – so odd that Tom was in two minds about consenting to the engagement. You know how fond we were of him and how we believed in him, but his conduct before Christmas was rather shattering. You are too busy to hear gossip, but I can assure you that Charles has been the most talked-of man in London. Not pleasant gossip either."

"But the explanation seems quite simple," I said. "Two estranged lovers, both proud and both miserable and therefore rather desperate. Chance brings them together, misunderstandings disappear, and true love comes into its own."

Mollie bent her brows.

"It's not as simple as that. If that had been the way of things they ought to be riotously happy. But they're not – not in the least. Pam is as white as a sheet, and looks more like a widow than a bride. She's very sweet and good – very different from before Christmas, when she was horribly tiresome – but you never saw such careworn eyes. She has something heavy on her mind... And as for Charles! He is very good too and goes steadily to the City again, but he's not my notion of the happy lover. Tom and I are at our wits' end. I do wish you would have a talk with Pamela. She won't tell me anything – I really don't dare to ask – but you and she have always been friends, and if there is any trouble you might help her."

So Pamela came to tea with me, and the first sight of her told me that Mollie was right. In a week or two some alchemy had changed her utterly. Not a trace now of that hard, mirthless glitter which had scared me at the Lamanchas'. Her face was pale, her air quiet and composed, but there was in her eyes what I had seen in Charles Ottery's, an intense, anxious preoccupation.

She told me everything without pressing. She could not tell her parents, she said, for they would not understand, and, if they did, their sympathy would make things worse. But she longed for someone to confide in, and had decided on me.

I saw that it would be foolish to make light of the trouble. Indeed, I had no inclination that way, for I had seen the tortures that Goodeve was undergoing. She told me what she had said to Charles, and the line they were taking. I remember wondering if the man had the grit to go through with it; when I looked at Pamela's clear eyes I had no doubt about the woman.

"He has gone back to his business and has forced himself to slave at it. He is crowding up his days with work. And he is keeping himself in hard training... You see, he has tried the other dopes and found them no good... But he has to fight every step of the road. Oh, Uncle Ned, I could howl with misery sometimes when I see him all drawn at the lips and hollow about the eyes. He doesn't sleep well, you see. But he is fighting, and not yielding one inch."

And then she quoted to me her saying about Jacob wrestling with the angel. "If we keep on grappling with the brute, it *must* bless us."

"I have to hold his hand all the time," she went on. "That's his hope of salvation. He is feeding on my complete

217

confidence... Oh no, it's not easy, but it's easier than his job. I've to pretend to be perfectly certain that we'll be married next June tenth, and to be always talking about where we shall go for our honeymoon, and where we shall live in Town, and how we shall do up Marlcote."

She smiled wanly.

"I chatter about hotels and upholsterers and house-agents when I want to be praying... But I think I understand my part. I have a considerable patch of hell to plough, but it's nothing like as hot as Charles's... No, you can't help, Uncle Ned, dear. We have to go through with this thing ourselves – we two – nobody else. Charles must never know that I have told you, for if he thought that anyone else knew it would add shyness to his trouble... But it's a comfort to me to feel that you know. If anything happens...if we fail... I want you to realise that we went down fighting."

She kissed me and ran away, and I sat thinking a long time in my chair. She was right: no one could help these two through this purgatory. My heart ached for this child not out of her teens who was trying to lift her lover through the Slough of Despond by her sheer courage. I do not think that I have ever in my life so deeply admired a fellow-mortal. Pamela was the very genius of fortitude, courage winged and inspired and divinely lit... I told myself that such a spirit could not fail if there was a God in Heaven.

I can only guess at what Charles suffered in the first months of the year. The diary revealed something, but not much, for the entries were scrappy: you see, he was not fighting the battle alone, as he had done in the autumn; he had Pamela for his guide and confessor.

He stuck like a leech to his work, and from all accounts did it well. My nephew said that old Charles had "taken a pull on himself, but had become a cheerless bird." People in the City, when I asked about him, were cordial enough. He had been put on a new economic commission at which he was working hard.

One man said that his examination of a high Treasury official was one of the most searching things he had ever heard. Our financial affairs at that time were in a considerable mess, and Charles was bending all his powers to straightening them out.

It was much to have got his brain functioning again. But of course it did not mean the recovery of his old interests. He had only one interest – how to keep his head up till June, and one absorbing desire – to be with Pamela. The girl gave him more than the sustenance of her confidence; there were hours when the love of her so filled his mind that it drove out the gnawing pain, and that meant hours of rest. As sleep restores the body, so these spells of an almost happy absorption restored his spirit.

But he had patches of utter blackness, as the diary showed. He held himself firm to his resolution by a constant effort of will. He could not despair when Pamela kept her courage... But he would waver at moments, and only recover himself out of shame. There were times, too, when he bitterly reproached himself. He had brought an innocent child into his tortured world, and made her share in the tortures. Another life besides his own would be ruined. Out of such fits of self-contempt he had to be dragged painfully by Pamela's affection. She had to convince him anew that she preferred Tophet in his company to Paradise alone.

In March Pamela told me that she had offered to marry him at once, and that he had refused. He was on his probation, he said, and marriage was to be the reward of victory. Also, if he was to be in the grave on June tenth, he did not want Pamela to be a widow. The girl argued, she told me, that immediate marriage would be an extra defiance to Fate, and a proof of their confidence, but Charles was adamant. I dare say he was right: he had to settle such a question with his own soul.

I met him occasionally during those months. Never in ordinary society: by a right instinct Pamela and he decided that they could not go about together and be congratulated – that would make too heavy demands on their powers of camouflage. But I ran across him several times in the street; and

I sat next to him at a luncheon given by the Prime Minister to the American Debt Commission. Knowing the story, I looked for changes in him, and I noted several things which were probably hidden from other people. He had begun to speak rather slowly, as if he had difficulty in finding the correct words. He did not look an interlocutor in the face, but fixed his eyes, while he spoke, steadily on the tablecloth. Also, though his colour was healthy, his skin seemed to be drawn too tight around his lips and chin, reminding me of a certain Army Commander during the bad time in '18.

I asked about Pamela.

"Yes, she's in Town," he said. "The Nantleys have been up since January. She has caught a beastly cold, and I made her promise to stay indoors in this bitter weather."

Two days later I picked up an evening paper and read a paragraph which sent me post-haste to the telephone. It announced that Lady Pamela Brune was ill with pneumonia, and that anxiety was felt about her condition.

VI

The diary told the tale of the next three weeks. Charles had to return to his diary, for he had no other confidant. And a stranger story I have never read.

From the first he was certain that Pamela would die. He was quite clear about this, and he had also become assured of his own end. Their love was to be blotted out by the cold hand of death. For a day or two he was in a stupor of utter hopelessness, waiting on fate like a condemned man who hears the gallows being hammered together and sees the clock moving towards the appointed hour.

Some of the entries were clear enough. He thought that Pamela would die at once while he himself must wait until June, and there were distraught queries as to how he could endure the interval. His appointed hour could not be anticipated, and a world without Pamela was a horror which came near to unhinging his mind. His writing tailed away into blots and dashes. In his agony he seemed several times to have driven his pen through the paper...

Then suddenly the mist cleared. The diary was nothing but jottings and confused reflections, so the sequence of his moods could not be exactly traced, but it was plain that something tremendous had happened...

It seemed to have come suddenly late at night, for he noted the hour – one thirty – and that he had been walking the Embankment since eight. Hitherto he had had a dual consciousness, seeing Pamela and himself as sufferers under the same doom, and enduring a double torture. Love and fear for both the girl and himself had brought his mind almost to a delirium, but now there descended upon it a great clarity.

The emotion remained, but now the object was single, for his own death dropped out of the picture. It became suddenly too small a thing to waste a thought on. There were entries like this: "I have torn up the almanack on which I had been marking off the days till June tenth... I have been an accursed coward, God forgive me... Pamela is dying, and I have been thinking of my own wretched, rotten life."

He went on steadily with his work, because he thought she would have wished him to, but he never moved far from a telephone. Meanwhile, the poor child was fighting a very desperate battle. I went round to South Audley Street as often as I could, and a white-faced Mollie gave me the last bulletins. There was one night when it seemed certain that Pamela could not see the morning, but morning came and the thread of life still held. She was delirious, talking about Charles mostly, and the mountain inn in the Tyrol where they were going for their honeymoon. Thank God, Charles was not there to listen to that!

He did not go near the house, which I thought was wise, but the diary revealed that he spent the midnight hours striding about Mayfair. He was waiting for her death, waiting for Mollie's summons to look for the last time upon what was so dear...

He was no longer in torment. Indeed, he was calm now, if you can call that calm which is the uttermost despair. His life was bereft of every shadow of value, every spark of colour, and he was living in a bleak desert, looking with aching eyes and a breaking heart at a beautiful star setting below the sky-line, a star which was the only light in the encroaching gloom to lead him home. That very metaphor was in the diary. He probably got it out of some hymn, and I never in my life knew Charles use a metaphor before.

And then there came another change – it is plain in the diary – but this time it was a wholesale revolution, by which the whole man was moved to a different plane...

His own predestined death had been put aside as too trivial for a thought, but now suddenly Death itself came to have no meaning. The ancient shadow disappeared in the great brightness of his love.

Every man has some metaphysics and poetry in his soul, but people like Charles lack the gift of expression. The diary had only broken sentences, but they were more poignant than any eloquence. If he had cared about the poets he might have found some one of them to give him apt words; as it was, he could only stumble along among clumsy phrases. But there was no doubt about his meaning. He had discovered for himself the immortality of love. The angel with whom he had grappled had at last blessed him.

He had somehow in his agony climbed to a high place from which he had a wide prospect. He saw all things in a new perspective. Death was only a stumble in the race, a brief halt in an immortal pilgrimage. He and Pamela had won something which could never be taken away... This man of prose and affairs became a mystic. One side of him went about his daily round, and waited hungrily for telephone calls, but the other was in a quiet country where Pamela's happy spirit moved in eternal vigour and youth. He had no hope in the lesser sense, for that is a mundane thing; but he had won peace, the kind that the world does not give…

Hope, the lesser hope, was to follow. There came a day when the news from South Audley Street improved, and then there was a quick uprush of vitality in the patient. One morning early in May Mollie telephoned to me that Pamela was out of danger. I went straightway to the City and found Charles in his office, busy as if nothing had happened.

I remember that he seemed to me almost indecently composed. But when he spoke he no longer kept his eyes down, but looked me straight in the face, and there was something in those eyes of his which made me want to shout. It was more than peace – it was a radiant serenity. Charles had come out of the Valley of the Shadow to the Delectable Mountains. Nothing in Heaven or earth could harm him now. I had the conviction that if he had been a poet he could have written something that would have solemnised mankind. As it was, he only squeezed my hand.

VII

I went down to Wirlesdon for the wedding, which was to be in the village church. Charles had gone for an early morning swim in the lake, and I met him coming up with his hair damp and a towel over his shoulder. I had motored from London and had *The Times* in my hand, but he never glanced at it. Half an hour later I saw him at breakfast, but he had not raided the pile of newspapers on the side-table.

It was a gorgeous June morning, and presently I found Pamela in the garden, busy among the midsummer flowers – a taller and paler Pamela, with the wonderful pure complexion of one who has been down into the shades.

"It's all there," she whispered to me, so that her sister Dollie should not hear. "Exactly as he saw it... We shall have a lot of questions to answer today... I showed it to Charles, but he scarcely glanced at it. It doesn't interest him. I believe he has forgotten all about it."

"A queer business, wasn't it?" Charles told me in the autumn. "Oh yes, it was all explained. There was an old boy of my name, a sort of third cousin of my great-grandfather. I had never heard of him. He had been in the Scots Guards, and had retired as a captain about fifty years ago. Well, he died in a London hotel on June ninth. He was a bachelor, and had no near relations, so his servant sent the notice of his death to *The Times*. The man's handwriting was not very clear, and the newspaper people read the age as thirty-six instead of eighty-six... Also, the old chap always spoke of his regiment as the Scots Fusilier Guards, and the servant, not being well up in military history, confused it with the Scots Fusiliers... He lived in a villa at Cheltenham, which he had christened Marlcote, after the family place."

JOHN BUCHAN

THE COURTS OF THE MORNING

South America is the setting for this adventure from the author of *The Thirty-nine Steps*. When Archie and Janet Roylance decide to travel to the Gran Seco to see its copper mines they find themselves caught up in dreadful danger; rebels have seized the city. Janet is taken hostage in the middle of the night and it is up to the dashing Don Luis de Marzaniga to aid her rescue.

GREENMANTLE

Sequel to *The Thirty-nine Steps*, this classic adventure is set in war-torn Europe. Richard Hannay, South African mining engineer and hero, is sent on a top-secret mission across German-occupied Europe. The result could alter the outcome of World War I. Other well-known characters make a reappearance here: Sandy, Blenkiron and Peter Pienaar.

John Buchan

Grey Weather

Grey Weather is the first collection of sketches from John Buchan, author of *The Thirty-nine Steps*. The subtitle, *Moorland Tales of My Own People*, sets the theme of these fourteen stories. Shepherds, farmers, herdsmen and poachers are Buchan's subjects and his love for the hills and the lochs shines through.

The Long Traverse

This enchanting adventure tells the story of Donald, a boy spending his summer holidays in the Canadian countryside. John Buchan knew that some Indians were said to have the power of projecting happenings of long ago onto a piece of calm water.

In this tale he chooses Negog, the Native American Indian, as Donald's companion and guide. Negog conjures up a strange mist from a magic fire and brings to life visions from the past. Through these boyish adventures peopled with Vikings, gold prospectors, Indians and Eskimos, Donald learns more about history than school has taught him.

JOHN BUCHAN

SICK HEART RIVER

Lawyer and MP Sir Edward Leithen is given a year to live. Fearing he will die unfulfilled, he devotes his last months to seeking out and restoring to health Galliard, a young Canadian banker. Galliard is in remotest Canada searching for the River of the Sick Heart. Braving an Arctic winter, Leithen finds the banker. Leithen's health returns, but only one of the men will return to civilization.

THE THIRTY-NINE STEPS

John Buchan's most famous and dramatic novel presents spy-catcher Richard Hannay. Hannay is in London when he suddenly finds himself caught up in a dangerous situation and the main suspect for a murder committed in his own flat. He is forced to go on the run to his native Scotland.